THE DUKE AND THE SPITFIRE

JESSIE CLEVER

SOMEDAY LADY PUBLISHING, LLC.

THE DUKE AND THE SPITFIRE

Published by Someday Lady Publishing, LLC

Copyright © 2021 by Jessica McQuaid

ISBN-13: 978-1-7362903-6-1

Cover Design by The Killion Group

Edited by Judy Roth

For secret loves.

Is there anything more wonderful and more heart wrenching?

CHAPTER 1

*J*ohanna Darby didn't know when it was she fell in love.

This was likely because she was eight at the time, and had she been questioned directly about her feelings for him, she would have informed the inquisitor that Benedict Carver was singularly annoying.

He was still annoying. She knew this because only Benedict Carver would show up, newly widowed and titled, at the exact moment she had determined she must let her love for him go if she had any hope of happiness in her life, to say nothing of her sister Viv's quest to see all the Darby sisters married.

The man was a damned nuisance.

He was like a magnet, drawing her eyes to him through the crowd of her ball as if he weren't one of a hundred people crammed into the ballroom. It was as if it was only the two of them standing there with no one between them. No orchestra, no marrying mamas, no lecherous old bachelors.

Just them.

They were young again, racing their horses across the

fields of Yorkshire, the sun warm on their shoulders, the wind pulling her hair from its pins, her bonnet long forgotten as it bounced against her back, and Ben's laugh as she pulled ahead. Ben had the best laugh. That she would never forget.

He wore all black as mourning would have dictated, and he stood to the periphery of the ballroom, a glass of something in his hand. His eyes were hooded. She could see that even from where she stood, and her heart clenched at the sight, her mind conjuring all of the terrible things that might have caused such guardedness.

"And that was exactly what I said to my tailor. I said I can't possibly be seen in peach again this year. We all know the correct palette is far more muted."

Johanna blinked, forcibly moving her eyes from Ben to the man who stood beside her with whom she was supposed to be conversing.

Lord Blevens was best described as a sock that had seen far too many washes. He was willowy and tall and robbed of all color as he abhorred daylight and exercise. He made up for his paleness with a jarring rainbow of clothing.

He smiled at her now, showing immense canine teeth, as if he expected a reply from her.

"Yes, I see," she muttered, hoping that was the correct thing to say.

His smile got wider if that were possible, and she wondered if he were secretly a wolf in disguise. She took a small step back.

"I'm sure your modiste is far more skilled at deciphering the current trends than my tailor. Perhaps I should seek a new one."

She nodded, her eyes drifting past the viscount to where she'd last seen Ben, but he had disappeared.

Disappointment swamped her, and she clasped her hands

together in front of her, worrying them so, she feared for the delicate silk of her gloves. Her dance card bounced against her wrist, and she was reminded of how pitifully empty it was. Her sister Louisa had already come over to her once to remind her of the point of the evening, and Johanna had tried to accept more offers of dancing. But it was entirely too difficult when one's heart was not in the matter.

But that was also how she had become trapped in conversation with a sock of a man.

"Do you find the latest fashions from Paris to your liking, Lady Johanna? I find I'm more inclined to the Italian school, but you know how difficult it can be to convince people of its merits."

"Em, yes, quite so."

Where had Ben gone?

He was probably seeking out her brother, Andrew, in the card rooms. Andrew and Ben had practically grown up together after all. Of course Ben should seek his company. She probably wasn't an inkling in his mind as she was just the little sister of his best friend who had relentlessly tagged after them.

Her chest squeezed.

Come on, Jo. It's been five years. You should be stronger than this.

It wasn't as though she imagined he had thought of her in the five years he was in America. He had been married, of course. He should have been thinking of Minerva, his wife.

Her chest squeezed again, harder this time, and she pressed a hand there as if she could stop the pain.

She had gone to his wedding. All the Darbys were expected to attend, and it would have looked odd had she not been there.

It was the singularly most awful day of her life.

Lady Minerva Wallington had been beautiful, even more

so as the captivating bride to the son of a duke. With her raven locks and voluptuous curves, her effervescent smile and polished wit, Johanna couldn't imagine Ben would be disappointed in his marriage.

Johanna also couldn't help but compare herself to Ben's bride. It was almost impossible not to really. While Johanna was not plain by any stretch of the word, she was neither gorgeous the way Minerva had been. Johanna had never given a care to her looks before she'd seen Lady Wallington on her wedding day.

She felt a pang of regret at the loss of innocence but forced a smile as Lord Blevens picked up the topic of patterned waistcoats.

"So you can see why a pattern is far superior to a simple silk."

"Mmm, yes," Johanna muttered, her eyes scanning in the other direction.

Lord Blevens's smile reached atmospheric proportions.

"Do you know I think everyone is wrong about you?" This got her attention, and her eyes came snapping back to his thin face as he continued. "You're not at all disagreeable. I wonder why the *ton* should think so."

Disagreeable?

She was disagreeable?

She opened her mouth to defend herself, but Blevens cut her off.

"Lady Johanna, would you care to—"

Someone touched her elbow, and she knew it was him before she even turned. A bolt of lightning shot through her at his touch, her toes curling in her slippers.

All other thoughts fled as she stood suspended in the moment, not wanting to turn and face him even as she longed to do nothing else. She wanted to savor this moment, this anticipation, for once she turned it would mark a moment in time.

It had been five *years*. Before he'd left, she was still in the schoolroom, a gangly, coltish creature prone to catching tadpoles instead of a gentleman's eye.

But she'd changed. Time had a way of doing that to a person, and she knew she was no longer the tomboy who had chased after him. She was a woman now, and with that came certain expectations she had tried her best to fulfill.

But being a lady had never come easy to Johanna, and she worried now what he would think of her. Would he compare her to Minerva and find her lacking?

Fear raced through her. What if he didn't like her now? What if he found her repulsive or worse, boring?

"Johanna."

She closed her eyes against the sound of his voice speaking her name. It rippled through her as if he'd caressed her. She swallowed the moan in her throat, and throwing her eyes open, resolutely turned toward him.

Her heart stopped.

She felt it the moment it tripped over the sight of him. He was closer now, and she could see the lines time had wrought around his eyes, the way his mouth no longer melted into an easy smile.

Ben had changed.

She didn't know why she hadn't realized it. Of course he would change. Time had passed for both of them, but her heart ached at the evidence she saw on his face.

The past five years had not been good for him, and she picked up her hand as if to reach out to him, touch him, reassure him. She realized her intention in time and moved her hand as if she had planned to adjust the dance card at her wrist.

"Hello, Ben." She was surprised by how easily the greeting

slipped from her lips, how normal she sounded. No one would suspect how her heart raced, how her mind scrambled to discover what had happened to him, what had caused him to emit such sadness.

It hit her then with such stunning velocity as to have her stepping back, pulling her elbow from the cradle of his palm.

He mourned his wife.

When she had first heard Ben was coming home, her mind had painted a picture of the way he had been. Jumping from boulder to boulder in the stream that ran between their estates, his arms thrown wide as he declared himself king of the stream, the sunlight glancing off his brown hair and throwing his face into shadow until all she could see was his goofy smile.

She forgot to remember he would be a widower now.

And a duke.

She licked her suddenly dry lips, searching for the walls she had so carefully erected around her heart when she was only sixteen and found herself madly in love with a boy who thought of her as nothing more than his best friend's little sister.

"I didn't think we'd expect you so soon. Andrew told us you'd written to say you would be delayed."

Ben's eyes traveled to Lord Blevens and back to her. "I was able to conclude my affairs in Boston earlier than I anticipated." His voice was clipped, and he offered no further explanation.

She gestured behind her. "Ben, I don't believe you've met Lord Blevens."

Lord Blevens gave a small bow as was polite, but his features had turned pinched.

"I offer you my condolences, Your Grace. Your brother was a beloved member of my circle of friends."

Ben's lips thinned as he pressed them together. "Thank

you, my lord. I'm coming to realize my brother was revered by many people."

The words did not match his tone, and Johanna studied him carefully.

She knew little of Ben's older brother as the man had been ten years Ben's senior, and her only image of him was of the bully he'd been in their youth. The rumors surrounding Lawrence Carver's death smacked of his characteristic spoiled nature. He was a man who drank to excess, gambled into debt, and trounced his way from lover to lover. That he should have been a revered friend of Lord Blevens was concerning.

Lord Blevens gave a nod. "It will do you well to remember that as you enter society."

Johanna looked sharply at the viscount as his tone had taken on an edge of which she had not thought him capable. Did he think to give the cut direct to a duke in the middle of her presentation ball?

She raised her chin to give him the disagreeable reprimand society apparently thought her inclined to, but Ben stopped her by slipping his arm through hers.

His touch startled her into silence, and she cast her gaze in his direction.

His smile was tight. "I shall keep that in mind, Lord Blevens. I appreciate your concern."

Lord Blevens eyed their connected arms as if they were those peach trousers he had lamented earlier.

"I was about to ask Lady Johanna for this dance—"

Ben smiled for the first time since she'd caught sight of him, and it was almost as if the boy she remembered peeked through the veil of his mourning.

"I'm terribly sorry, my lord. She's already promised this dance to me."

She had done no such thing, but it was apparent Ben

wished to remove her from Lord Blevens's company and even though being with Ben again had stirred up the torment and longing she had thought herself strong enough to overcome, it was far better than being trapped with the pompous viscount.

She smiled politely. "I do hope you understand, Lord Blevens. Perhaps next time."

She allowed Ben to turn her into the crowd at the edge of the dance floor, her ears registering the first notes of the quadrille. She picked up her skirts, prepared to step into place, but Ben never released her arm, pulling her in the direction of the terrace doors instead.

She faltered, her eyes careening between the doors and Ben.

"Ben?" She hated the weakness in her voice, the tinge of hope she couldn't quite repress.

"I suddenly feel the need for some air," he said and plunged them both into the darkness of the gardens.

* * *

JOHANNA HESITATED. He could feel it in the slight drag of her arm against his.

They'd reached the gardens at the edge of the stone terrace, and here the moonlight was muted through the reaching arms of the arbor. He eyed her even though the light was dim and her face dappled in moonbeams.

She appeared pensive, her brow creased and her lips parted ever so slightly in question.

He would have expected trepidation had she been with anyone else, but it was just him. She was practically a sister to him.

"It's not like I'm going to ravish you," he muttered.

Her eyes flew wide, and he would have sworn a soft exclamation slipped from her lips. How odd.

The tension he had felt in the ballroom began to ease as cool night air filled his lungs, and he didn't wish to stop now to question why Johanna had suddenly developed such a missish reaction to him. He simply wanted solitude with an old friend, the comfort of familiarity and the lack of expectation.

Because Ben was tired.

No, not tired. Exhausted. Spent. On the verge of collapse.

When word had reached him of Lawrence's death, his life had already been in turmoil. The summons to return to England was both a blessing and a curse. He could escape what his life had been like in America and all that it had entailed and return to the fields of West Yorkshire. But at the same time, he would be forced to rebuild a title and legacy his brother had let crumble in drink and gambling.

The only thing that kept him going was that soon his feet would touch Raeford soil again. His heart had never forgotten what it was like to ride out from Raeford Court in the earliest hours of the morning when the fog was still burning off the tops of the wheat fields, the sun glinting through the dew on the park. His body felt the cadence of his horse like an echo, and his heart clenched.

Soon.

Soon he would return to Raeford Court. He only had one more thing to take care of.

He needed a wife.

A very rich wife.

He plunged through the last hedge into the heart of the Ravenwood garden where a small bower was cut out of the hedgerows and a single bench was tucked into one corner. He had come here often as a boy with Andrew, hiding away from their chattering mothers. They would play Wellington and Napoleon, and Andrew had always been brilliant at charging as Wellington atop a magnificent steed.

The magnificent steed played by the bench, of course.

He smiled now when he saw it and all but dragged Johanna over to it. The night was warm even though it was still early spring, and he was glad for it as he could not bear the thought of returning to the ballroom just yet. He knew he must address the issue of finding a wife, but having a spot of fresh air couldn't hurt.

He was only sorry he'd dragged Johanna with him.

He glanced at her now.

"I'm sorry to have absconded with you, but I couldn't very well leave you with that sniveling viscount."

She adjusted her glove on the arm he'd been holding. "I will thank you for that, but I must say it was rather an abrupt greeting." She raised an eyebrow in reprimand, and he couldn't help a laugh.

"I'm very sorry, old friend." He stood and gave an exaggerated bow. "Lady Johanna, it has been an age. How are you, poppet?"

The eyebrow went flat. "If you call me poppet again, I'll knock you on your arse."

He laughed, and the tension that had wedged in his chest making it difficult to breathe since he'd disembarked in London suddenly loosened. He knew a spot of fresh air would do just the thing.

He hadn't received many invitations yet, and he'd only come to Ravenwood House because Andrew had written to say he should visit at any time. What better time than in the middle of a ball to mark his return to society?

"I am sorry to hear of your brother." Johanna's features sobered, and the tension returned with a coiling snap.

He resumed his seat beside her on the bench.

"Thank you, but you know very well I don't mourn him."

She peered out at the sleeping gardens. "I thought as much. How is your mother taking it?"

He shook his head. "I wrote her, but she never replied. I can only assume she's squirreled away in her cottage, ignoring the whole of it."

She turned her head now, and he couldn't help but study her face. Memories of Johanna had been one of the happy places he'd gone to in his mind over the last several years. When Minerva had taken to living in the separate apartment of rooms in the house on Beacon Street, it had left him with a lot of time sitting alone in his study or the drawing room. He'd filled the time with recollections of West Yorkshire and summers spent racing between Raeford Court and the Ravenwood estate.

Inevitably Johanna would tumble into a memory, and his life hadn't seemed so cold.

But she was no longer the Johanna he remembered. He had suspected she wouldn't be, but the reality of it didn't quite sit well with him. She'd grown up in the five years he'd been gone, and seeing her tonight had confirmed his worst fears.

She wore a ballgown and courted a slew of bachelors.

How appalling.

The Johanna he remembered wore muslin dresses so ill-fitting they hardly reached her knees, which made it far easier for her to ride and climb trees and chase him through a stream. Her hair was forever falling out of her braid, but now it was severely tacked back as if her head were some sort of pincushion.

It was to be expected, he knew, but a part of him regretted the loss of the Johanna from his childhood. Another part of him crumpled and fell away, and he let it go. He'd let so many things go.

"Your mother will be happy to have you home, I'm sure."

He wondered at the wistful tone of her voice and rubbed the back of his neck. "I can't say as I'm as sure as you are."

Johanna laughed. "I've heard mothers are more inclined to forgive lengthy absences than most."

His stomach tightened at the way she said it. Johanna had lost her mother before she could form memories of her. He knew that because she'd always marveled at his own mother when they were children. At the way his mother would ensure he had proper clothes for school or that he'd eaten his porridge that morning or if he were getting enough exercise.

No one had asked Johanna such things or had particularly paid such attention to her life. His mother was rather like a museum exhibit to Johanna in that way.

"I am also sorry to hear of your wife."

He turned his head at this, noting a subtle difference in her voice. It was almost as if she found his widowerhood more upsetting than the loss of his brother. He forced his teeth apart. There was no sense in revealing the truth now that Minerva was dead. It would only serve to remind him of the charade his marriage had been. It was better to leave the past to the dead.

"Thank you for your concern," he said simply.

"I can imagine there is much to be done now that you've inherited. Raeford holdings are vast from what I remember."

The air caught in his throat, almost choking him. Raeford holdings had been vast once but no longer. His brother had seen to that. Selling off parcels to cover gambling debts. Allowing what remained to fall into ruin. If the bastard had done anything to Raeford Court, he would...

What?

Conjure a ghost so he could admonish his dead brother?

He flexed his hands against the chafing truth. So much of his life had been beyond his control, and even when he thought he'd gained the upper hand, fate reminded him of his place.

But not any longer.

Now he had the title and the power to restore the Raeford holdings, yes, but more, he was going to make them flourish.

He only must find a wife with a substantial dowry. He'd rather remove his toenails with a rusty chisel. "Yes, there's quite a bit that must be done."

She turned, and he could feel her gaze on him.

"Like what?"

The question surprised him, but coming from Johanna, it shouldn't have.

He returned her quizzical gaze with his own. "Do you honestly care?"

She crossed her arms. "Well, I haven't seen you in five years, and it's all you can do to string together a handful of words to say to me. If I were the sort to be offended easily, I would be. As it is now, I just think you're as annoying as you were as a child."

He couldn't stop the smile that came to his lips, but when he would have laughed he faltered.

She was beautiful.

He didn't know where the thought came from or why it had to strike him at that moment, but it had the effect to stop him entirely. His best friend's little sister was suddenly a woman sitting beside him in a garden in the moonlight, and she was beautiful.

He swallowed and looked away. "If you insist on badgering me, I'll tell you. The farms at Raeford Court are in desperate need of updating. Do you know they haven't even switched to the Norfolk four-course rotation system yet?"

She gave an exaggerated frown. "You don't say?" Her voice dripped with sarcasm. "I should think they would know better."

He shook his head and threw out his arms as if the situation were beyond his control. "You would think so. But if there isn't someone there to lead them, they are apparently happy to continue in the way it's always been done."

"How dreadful." She wrinkled her face into a pout. "It's very good you've come back to save them."

"Just as I saved you?"

He regretted the words as soon as they left his lips, and he wished to change the subject, but something happened then. Her face changed, closing in on itself, almost as if she didn't wish for him to know what she was thinking or feeling. He turned to study her better, but she tilted her head away from him, allowing her features to fall into shadow.

"You've never required saving though, have you?" he said with a laugh.

"No, I haven't." She didn't look at him when she spoke, and he wondered why.

"Johanna—"

He was cut off by the sound of angry stampeding piercing the quiet of the night as someone hurtled himself through the hedgerow, stumbling into the bower in a mad march until stopping just before them at the bench.

"Get your hands off—"

Andrew Darby, the Duke of Ravenwood, stopped mid-sentence, his accusatory finger withdrawing.

"Ben." He spoke the word as if he had just found a leprechaun.

Ben stood, a smile coming to his face as he took in his old friend. "Andrew," he said before grabbing his friend in a fierce hug.

He broke away only to hold his friend at arm's length. "What on earth was that show of bravado about?"

Andrew rubbed his forehead and pinched the bridge of

his nose. "Ben, you cannot imagine what it is like to be responsible for four sisters."

Ben laughed. "Surely it is not all bad."

Andrew dropped his hand. "I assure you it's far worse than anything you might fathom." He gestured to Johanna. "I was told Johanna had gone off into the garden alone with some sniveling ne'er-do-well."

"Ne'er-do-well?" Ben placed a hand against his chest in mock affront.

Andrew's face relaxed. "But then I saw it was only you." He gestured weakly, a laugh tripping from his lips.

Johanna stood then and shook out her skirts with what seemed like more force than was necessary.

"Yes, it was only Ben," she said and disappeared into the darkness in the direction of the house. He thought her shoulders somewhat slumped, but perhaps it was a trick of the moonlight.

His instinct was to go after her, but he checked himself. It was only Johanna after all, but then he saw Andrew watching her carefully as she disappeared.

"Have your sisters truly been such trouble?"

Andrew gave a bark of laughter. "Far more than I anticipated, but I should have expected it as they are daughters of a duke, and my father had the sense to bestow them each with a sizable dowry."

A trigger was tripped somewhere deep in his mind, his senses coming to life at the mention of a sizable dowry. He berated himself, squashing down the thought. He could never marry his best friend's little sister for her dowry.

Could he?

CHAPTER 2

She should be glad Viv had abandoned her.

It had taken long enough for her sister's estranged husband to come to his senses and arrive in a most spectacular fashion the previous night at Johanna's ball. Viv deserved her happiness, and she also deserved to run away to Kent with her husband. If Johanna had been the type, she would have sighed at the glow the image conjured. Viv and Ryder in the country, alone together. It was the stuff of novels really.

She kicked at the dirt along the promenade path, twirling her parasol absently in one hand.

She would have liked to have been in the countryside. She wanted to feel the strong breath of her horse against the insides of her thighs as they raced across the hills at Ravenwood. She wanted to pull all these horrid pins from her hair and dutifully misplace her bonnet for a good fortnight.

She kicked at the promenade path again, sending up a lovely plume of dust.

"Johanna." Eliza's voice was firm but not scolding.

It seemed with Viv away, the second in command had

stepped in. Eliza, the second oldest Darby sister and the Duchess of Ashbourne, had arrived at Ravenwood House that morning with strict orders to see Johanna bundled off to the promenade path in Hyde Park.

The presentation ball had been a success by whatever standards such a thing could be measured, and so a promenade was the next best step to getting Johanna seen and thus seen, wed.

It nearly made her upset her accounts.

Why had Ben returned now? Why couldn't he have stayed in America?

It needn't matter though where he was in the world. He would always plague her dreams, and no matter how she tried, she just couldn't bolster the motivation to find a husband.

Because there would always be Ben.

"Don't you find promenading rather tedious?" she asked her sister then. "You weren't forced to promenade."

Eliza's smile was wistful. "You are correct. I wasn't forced to promenade. But whether or not I find the custom tedious is not relevant. Viv wishes for you to do so, and promenade you must."

Johanna couldn't help returning her sister's smile. Eliza had spent far too many years ridiculed by society for being a wallflower, and it was rather satisfying to see her happily wed to Dax Kane, the Duke of Ashbourne.

Happily wed.

Eliza was madly in love with the man and he with her.

Johanna's heart clenched, and she absently rubbed at the spot, upsetting the lace of her walking gown.

Eliza batted her hand away. "Do have a mind for your appearance."

"The cuffs of your gown are covered in dog drool."

Eliza's glance was sharp. "The state of my cuffs is irrelevant."

It was at this moment that Eliza's dog, Henry, chose to return from sniffing the hedges along the path, and sensing he was the topic at the heart of the conversation sauntered up to Johanna to nose at her open palm as if looking for a treat.

Johanna snatched her hand away. "I have nothing to give you."

Henry's ears went back, and she felt a pang of guilt. She scratched his head. "I'm sorry, Henry. It's not your fault I must endure such nonsense."

He seemed to accept her apology and trotted off to sniff more hedges.

She sucked in a deep breath and rolled her shoulders back. At least the day was pleasant, and she was outside. Surely it wouldn't be so bad.

Lord Blevens appeared on the path before them at that precise moment, and Johanna knew the universe had a terrible sense of humor.

He bowed before them with too much skip in his step, kicking up dust on his apricot trousers.

"Lady Johanna, what a pleasure to see you today."

His canine teeth were even more absurd in the daylight.

She curtsied as was appropriate. "Lord Blevens, I believe you know my sister, Duchess Ashbourne."

He bowed again. "Duchess, how kind of you to escort your sister on the promenade today."

Eliza curtsied. "Lord Blevens, I trust you're finding the day pleasant."

Johanna didn't miss how thin Eliza's lips had gone. Her sister might have been a wallflower, but she was not adverse to expressing her distaste, even quietly.

The viscount nodded. "It's quite pleasant indeed."

Johanna was going to expire from boredom directly on the promenade path.

Silence ensued as Lord Blevens flashed his canines, and Eliza stood perfectly still next to her, waiting for the viscount to discover a mildly amusing thought.

Johanna knew she would not survive this matchmaking business if this were to be how it would transpire.

Lord Blevens seemed to come to his senses as his mouth opened on what was to surely be a most declarative pronouncement, but he was prevented from saying anything by a voice behind them.

"Good day, Duchess. Lady Johanna."

Ben.

Johanna whirled about most inappropriately, but the sound of Ben's voice was enough to drive what little resolve she had mustered completely from her person.

Once again he was dressed all in black, only the snowy white of his shirt where his collar poked through his cravat lent any relief from his austere attire. Now in the daylight she could see he was paler than she was used to seeing him, and he looked almost ill.

She swallowed against the pain that bloomed in her chest. How he must mourn for his wife for it to cause him to look so worn and colorless. What must it have been like to be so loved by him? She would never know.

She raised her chin. "Your Grace, I didn't realize you were inclined to promenade."

Her words clearly took him off guard as he closed his mouth against whatever it was he'd been about to say.

Eliza slid her a tight glance. "Be that as it may, I'm pleased you've found us this morning. I didn't get a chance to converse with you last night." She turned ever so slightly to include Lord Blevens in the conversation. "Ben is an old friend of the family, you see."

Lord Blevens wiped a hand under his nose with a rude sniff. "I understand as much."

When Johanna looked back at Ben, she saw a rather predatory glint in his eyes. He must still be upset from the viscount's suggestion the previous night. Johanna knew there was no love lost between Ben and his older brother, and being reminded of how well loved the cad had been would only serve to irritate Ben.

"I trust you're settling in well," she said.

Ben's eyes met hers, and it was as though they shared the same thought.

Was she truly asking him something so mundane?

She smiled but it was really only a lifting of her upper lip. Something flashed across his features, and she felt a note of trepidation trip along the back of her neck.

Ben turned his attention to the viscount. "Yes, a very old friend of the family. I used to drop frogs down Lady Johanna's dress when we were children."

Lord Blevens's face went entirely scarlet, and he coughed uncomfortably. "Is that so?"

Johanna looked to Eliza for help, but her sister was resolutely looking anywhere else, her smile hardly contained.

Johanna squared her shoulders. "As I recall, it was I chasing you with newts, however." She turned to Lord Blevens. "His Grace doesn't care for the creatures. He said they were too likely to be the familiar of a warlock." She turned a brilliant smile on Ben. "He never did like fairy tales when were children. He was always afraid they would come true."

Ben returned her smile with one of his own. He looked almost feral.

"I'm sure you can relate, Lord Blevens. You seem to be one to enjoy a good fairy tale."

Lord Blevens only blinked.

"Your Grace!"

Their group turned at the sound of the light voice, and Johanna spied the Countess of Bannerbridge trotting up to them, her skirts clenched in one hand to allow her greater movement.

"Your Grace, I'm so glad I caught you. I was hoping I could speak to you about the books for the Weybridge School."

The Countess of Bannerbridge was a slight woman with warm features and a wide smile, which Eliza returned now. "Of course, my lady. I trust you received the samples?"

Eliza created watercolor books to help children learn their colors and the names of objects. It was a skill she had developed when Johanna proved slow to learn such things. She swallowed now at the memory as loneliness overcame her. She was lucky to have had her sisters, but there was always a part of her that seemed to be missing, having grown up without her mother.

For a moment, her thoughts drifted to Ben's mother, and Johanna couldn't help but smile, her mind suddenly flooded with memories of chasing after Duchess.

The countess nodded emphatically. "They were more than I could have ever hoped for!"

Eliza nodded, her smile growing wider. She turned back to their grouping, concern forming a line between her brows.

"Will you please excuse me for a moment? Ben, will you be kind enough to escort Johanna while I speak to Lady Bannerbridge?"

It was as if she'd offered a mouse to a cat. Ben's smile turned downright sinister.

"It would be a delight, Your Grace."

Eliza turned off the path with the countess already animated in conversation. Ben offered his arm with far more dramatics than the situation required, and Johanna did not miss the way Lord Blevens's lips thinned to almost nothing.

"Lady Johanna, I must beg your forgiveness, but I've just remembered I must be off." Lord Blevens's tone was a great deal stonier than when he'd first approached her.

She gave a nod and bid him good day, but he'd already turned his back on them.

"That was rather uncalled for."

"Uncalled for, perhaps, but quite enjoyable. Are you truly entertaining that dandy's suit?"

"As I recall, you do not have a say in whose suit I entertain, Your Grace."

She had meant the remark as a flippant comment made between friends, but it suddenly felt stilted between them. Ben's arm tensed under hers, and it was just enough of a reaction to make her thoughts run wild.

That was absurd. Ben couldn't have cared whose courtship she entertained. He had already wed the woman he loved and lost her. Johanna surely meant nothing more to him than an old acquaintance.

"Be that as it may, I offer you my guidance as a friend. Lord Blevens is not one with whom I would recommend an association."

"I shall keep your guidance in mind, Your Grace."

"And please stop calling me that."

She glanced at him. "Is there something else I should call you?"

"I had always thought *Ben* had a nice ring to it."

She pretended to consider it. "I shall see in future what I think of it."

They moved down the path several meters. It was sparsely occupied that morning, and she enjoyed the moments of quiet when she could hear the birds sing.

"Do you know what I missed most while I was away?"

Her heart yearned at his question, hoping foolishly that it was her and knowing very well it was not.

"The English rain?"

He laughed. "Not as much as you might think." He glanced toward the sky. "I missed morning song. I missed hearing the birds chatter while I harnessed my horse for our morning ride across Raeford Court."

She tripped at his mention of his childhood home. It had been a second home to her, and she could hear the chatter of the birds in the early morning as if she were there.

"I used to sneak out in the mornings and climb the oak tree at the end of the lake. Do you remember the one? It had the notched branch as if it were made for climbing?" She shivered with the pull of memory. "I would climb into its branches and be very still, hoping the birds would sing to me."

Her arm tugged as she realized Ben had stopped. She turned and looked back to find him watching her carefully. Her heart thudded at the heaviness of his gaze, and she wondered what he might be thinking.

"I bet you couldn't climb a tree now."

Her heart fell at the same time her back went up. "I beg your pardon."

He let go of her arm to cross his over his chest.

"I bet you couldn't climb a tree today. Right now."

She looked around them.

"We're in the middle of Hyde Park."

He scoffed. "You always were good at finding excuses."

Her teeth nearly snapped as she closed her jaw against the indignation. "I could climb a tree today."

He stepped closer, far too close for propriety, and leaned in. She could smell his soap. Some kind of concoction of lemon and basil, and for a moment, her thoughts turned drowsy on the pull of it.

But then he whispered, "Prove it."

* * *

WHAT THE HELL was he doing?

He'd awoken early, pushed by an urgency he couldn't name. He'd dressed quickly, his muscles already tense with unspent energy. He was used to a walk first thing, but since he'd arrived in London, his days had largely been determined for him with meetings between his solicitors and man of affairs. It was rare that he should have a morning to himself, and he'd wanted a walk in the fresh air more than anything.

He should have stuck to the squares that dotted Mayfair, but something had pulled him to Hyde Park. Perhaps it was the tug of greens and flowers and trees and the sound of water. But he knew it was likely more than that.

Somewhere deep within him he'd known he might see her along the promenade path. That was what ladies did, wasn't it? She could have been met with any of the suitors she had seen the previous night at her presentation ball. It would be expected.

And somehow his legs had carried him right to her.

He'd felt a pang of guilt at the sight of her. While he'd tried resolutely to banish the idea from his mind, he couldn't stop himself from mulling the proposition over and over again through the restless night.

What if he did marry Johanna?

She met his pitiful requirements. That she be of a good family name and come with a sizable dowry. But there were other advantages.

He might just survive being wed to her.

He thought of another marriage as one may contemplate being buried alive, and his very body resisted the notion.

When he thought of Johanna in the role of his future wife, it suddenly wasn't so asphyxiating.

But could he do that to her?

Could he seduce her into marrying him when he had no intention of giving her love? In fact, once wed, he very much hoped to see very little of her beyond what was required to sire an heir.

He felt like a first-rate bastard, and yet his mind churned with ways of wooing her.

He needed her dowry, and he needed it now.

His brother had left the Raeford title in ruins, and debts were being called every day. He had to do something or risk losing the entire Raeford legacy to creditors.

Whenever he pictured it, his stomach turned with the thought of his mother being tossed from the cottage in which she had hidden herself away for the past fifteen odd years since he'd first left for school. It was the first time she had ever experienced any kind of peace, and he couldn't think of her being expelled from her sanctuary.

So here he was playing this dangerous game.

With his best friend's little sister.

He swallowed his disgust and pushed on. "Unless you're more of a coward than I believed."

He watched as her hand tightened about the handle of her parasol. That she carried a parasol at all unnerved him, and he wondered once more where his childhood friend had gone.

But then he could have asked the same of himself.

She twirled the parasol in her grip before snapping it shut.

"Pick your tree, Your Grace."

He blinked. "You're going to climb a tree. In the middle of Hyde Park." He gestured weakly at her walking gown. "Dressed like that."

"I've climbed trees in a gown before."

"A gown which generously showcased your ankles."

She crossed her arms, her parasol dangling from one hand. "I don't see the problem with showing one's ankles. They're only joints. Why must one get overly excited over such a thing?"

"I can't imagine." He glanced in the direction in which they'd left her sister.

The duchess was ensconced in conversation with the woman who had approached them on the path. She gestured and smiled broadly, and he thought she hadn't noticed them slip away at all.

He then turned his attention to the copse of trees along the path. He could just ease them off the path and disappear into those trees and no one would be the wiser.

His eyes slid to Johanna. He had a far better chance of seducing her if they were alone.

God, he hated himself. He hated himself and his brother for putting him in this position.

"Have you changed your mind?" She raised a single eyebrow, and he couldn't help but feel goaded.

He snatched her hand and pulled her into the trees before anyone could notice.

The promenade path through Hyde Park was well groomed, but carefully placed copses of trees along the trail were left to conjure a sense of the wild where none could be found. It served his purposes, however, and soon they were shielded from the rest of the promenaders by a thick wall of trees.

He turned a circle amongst them, his hands to his hips.

"I should think you'd have your pick of them here," he muttered, studying the trees.

When he turned back, he saw she eyed the trees dubiously.

"If I am to climb one of these, I shall need a boost to the first branch like when we were children." She turned her attention to him. "I should think years spent in a shipping clerk's office may have whittled what strength you had. Do you think you're up for the task?"

He felt the pull of childish goading, and unexpectedly, a smile came to his face.

"Is that a challenge?"

He shucked his coat before she could answer, already loosening his cuffs to roll up his sleeves.

Her eyes widened at his gesture, but she gave no word of protest. Instead, she went back to studying the trees.

"That one." She indicated a moderate-sized maple with ample branches to give her a good run should she make the first branch. But as she'd already pointed out, she would need a lift to make the first hold.

He stood underneath it and peered up.

"Your skirts are going to get tangled."

She dropped the parasol carelessly at the base of the tree, her eyes already fixed on the branches. It was almost as if he could hear her mind working out her course of ascent.

"That's for me to worry over." She gathered her skirts in her hands until he could see the black leather of her walking shoes. She nudged him with an elbow. "Hurry on then."

He bent, and making a cradle with his hands, offered her a leg up.

The first thing he realized was she was a great deal heavier than when she was a scampering young girl racing through the fields, and she was obviously wearing far more clothing that must have weighed the equivalent of a bovine.

The second thing he realized was that she was right. Five years spent in a shipping clerk's office had wasted his muscles, and he'd sorely over-estimated his strength.

He heard the scrape of her fingers against the bark of the first branch at the same time his arms failed him entirely.

The only thing that saved his manhood was that he caught her against his chest on her way down, and instead of simply dropping her to the ground in a heap of gown and grass stain, he captured her in his arms and stood her up in his embrace.

And that was when everything went entirely to shit.

Because she was in his arms, and she was beautiful, and suddenly she was no longer his best friend's little sister, the persistent imp that followed him like an unwanted shadow.

Instead she was Johanna, and he knew with utter clarity that he would marry her. An instant flash of guilt overwhelmed him, and he could no longer bear one more consuming emotion just then.

So he kissed her.

And it was as incredibly magnificent as he feared it would be.

He couldn't remember the last time he had touched a woman, let alone kissed one, and all of the sensations roared through him like an explosion in a mine. Her lips were soft; she smelled of fresh, clean soap. Her body fit perfectly against his, and she was just the right height for him to tip her head back ever so slightly as he deepened the kiss.

Her lips parted for him, and he forgot to remember this might be her first kiss, and he plundered. Later he would realize how starved for affection he was, but just then all he could do was consume, and she let him.

She let him learn the contour of her lips, the taste of her kiss, even the small moans of pleasure that settled immediately in his gut in a twisted wreck of both desire and guilt.

"Johanna." He murmured her name against her lips as if to remind himself who she was, but it did no good.

The kiss went on and on, and soon his arms were

wrapped completely around her, the back of her gown fisted in his grip as if she might float away from him, and he couldn't live with the loss of her.

Their embrace was anything but innocent, and he should have relented. He should have stopped; he should have never started. But his brain no longer functioned properly, and it could not merge the woman in his arms with the young girl of his childhood memories.

The woman he held was a spitfire, never backing down from his challenge, and he reveled in her quiet strength.

Finally, a temporary satisfaction rippled through him long enough for him to ease his lips from hers, but he didn't let go. He studied her face, her eyes closed, her eyelashes fanning her cheeks, her skin gone dewy and glowing with exertion. Her lips slightly parted and swollen.

He'd done that.

He'd made her the very image of love.

And he hated himself for it.

He let go of her, the folds of her gown slipping through his fingers like sand, grain by grain, until they disappeared completely, and he could step back.

She swayed ever so much on her feet, and he reached out a hand as if to steady her, but he knew he couldn't touch her again. Not without ravishing her here completely, and he wouldn't do that.

Not because the masses of the *ton* lay just beyond the curtain of their illusory hiding spot, but because he knew when he took her it would be in a proper bed.

When. He. Took. Her.

His future slammed into him with enough force to have him stepping back, gripping the back of his neck as he sucked in a breath.

He was going to court Johanna Darby, and he was going to win her hand.

If only to secure her dowry.

He turned back to her, her name already on his lips. "Johanna—"

"Don't." Her eyes were still closed, and she held out a hand, palm forward, in the direction she likely thought he stood. "I've waited my whole life for this. Please don't ruin it with words."

His heart stopped. Time stopped. He stood in the copse of trees, and even though he knew the birds still chirped, murmured voices could still be heard from the promenade path, and the breeze lifted the leaves of the trees that surrounded them, he couldn't have recalled any of it.

He couldn't move his eyes from her. He memorized every facet of her expression, every curve of muscle as she seemed to breathe in a lifetime of expectation suddenly coming real.

He realized two things at once. One he could manage, and one he forced himself to ignore.

The first being courting her was going to be far easier than he'd expected. Getting her to accept his proposal was nearly a given.

The second item though…

She'd waited a lifetime…for him to kiss her.

For him. To kiss her.

He couldn't accept that. Not now. Not with the cruelty of his first marriage a menacing echo just behind him. But worse, could he accept it ever?

He couldn't think of that right now, so he did as she asked. He didn't speak.

It was only luck they were standing so far apart when voices grew nearer and the hedges around them began to shake. When a dog popped free of the hedgerow, he couldn't have been more surprised. The dog, however, seemed to have ascertained he'd arrived in the correct place because he went over to Johanna and nudged her hand, which caused her to finally open her eyes.

She looked at the dog first before her eyes lifted to his, and coward that he was, he couldn't meet her gaze.

He didn't need to though as Eliza appeared next through the hedgerow.

"What is going on here?" Her voice was neither scolding nor critical. She was simply demanding an explanation.

"He dared me to climb a tree."

Now he did look at Johanna, the wispy quality of her voice drawing his attention. Her lips were no longer parted for his kiss, and her eyes were focused and sharp, and it was as though the moment never happened.

He wouldn't think about how the idea saddened him.

Eliza made a gesture, and the dog trotted over to her. "Surely you didn't?"

It took him a moment to realize she spoke to him. He gave a shrug and a half smile.

"It seemed like a fine idea at the time."

Eliza's expression suggested she was not at all surprised by this.

"Come, Johanna. We must return to Ravenwood House for calling hours." Eliza shook her head. "I would worry I'd be forced to tell Andrew of this if I had found Johanna in here with anyone else."

Johanna shook her head now and moved to the edge of the copse, preparing to slip back through the hedges. "You needn't bother. It's only Ben."

She disappeared through the greenery, her voice a great deal more assured than it had been the previous night.

CHAPTER 3

When she came down the stairs the following morning, she was prepared to indulge in a generous breakfast to soothe her ravenous hunger. She wasn't sure if courting caused one to experience quite so much hunger or perhaps it happened when one's life was completely and totally changed in an instant.

Ben had kissed her.

Kissed her.

On her lips and everything.

She'd lain awake most of the night thinking of it, tracing her lips as if she could feel the imprint of his. But the physical act was nothing compared to what it had done to her emotions.

What had his kiss meant?

She had thought him firmly in mourning for his wife. He just seemed so, well, grumpy and forlorn. What other explanation could there have been?

Her whole life her love for Ben had been one-sided. It was a secret she'd kept that both tormented and thrilled her. But now Ben knew.

She'd whispered the words without thought, her body still reeling from the stolen kiss.

But now he knew, and maybe it meant something, and now he might court her properly.

The thought had her starving for sausages.

She rounded the final landing on the staircase only to stop completely.

The vestibule of Ravenwood House was filled with flowers.

She stared at them, unable to blink, as she attempted to take them all in. Amaryllis, roses, tulips, and gardenias. Peonies and daffodils. The aroma was intoxicating and heady, and she gripped the banister more tightly as she descended into the veritable jungle below.

That was when she spotted her brother. Poor Andrew stood amongst the blooms, a cup in one hand, his other on his hip in a show of strength she could only assume was meant to cower the overpowering mass of flowers.

When he spied her coming down the stairs, his frown was fierce. "You've turned the place into a hothouse."

"I've done this? You're rather quick to lay blame."

He reached out and snatched the card from the closest bouquet. A rather daring ensemble of lilies and pinecones.

"You are still Lady Johanna Darby, are you not?" he asked, his eyes scanning the card.

She swallowed, her gaze sweeping from one end of the space to the other only to find the flowers continued down the corridor. She bent over the banister, following their trail.

Andrew lowered the card to eye her again. "The drawing room and the green salon are both filled as well."

She turned at his discouraging tone and immediately straightened at his displeased look, her shoulders rolling back.

33

"I think you would be excited by this occurrence, dear brother. It seems I'm rather a success." She shrugged.

He tossed the card back on the bouquet from which he had plucked it. "You've been out for three seasons. Why should you be a success now?"

It was her turn to frown. "Do you honestly care?"

He sipped from his cup. "No. I shall be taking a much deserved and rather prolonged trip when you are safely wed." He turned and disappeared down the corridor in the direction of the morning room, leaving her stranded amongst her flowers.

She descended the final stairs and plucked a card from a random bouquet.

"Who the hell is Lord Cardove?" she muttered.

She went about the vestibule, pulling cards from various bouquets, and attempted to decipher the gentlemen who had sent them. She recalled hardly any of the names. Had she danced with these gentlemen at some point? She had three seasons from which to draw, so surely it was possible.

But Andrew was right. Why was she so popular now?

As though the universe read her mind, the front door opened at that precise moment, and Ben stepped inside.

He carried a small clutch of daisies that appeared rather sad and dwarfed by the floral chaos he had stepped into. She stood frozen at the sight of him as she had not prepared to see him so soon after their encounter. Realizing she held a fan of cards from various bouquets in her hands, she felt rather awkward when presented with his meager daisies.

Except a small clutch of daisies from Ben was better than any of the most outrageous bouquets that littered the vestibule just then. She dropped the cards in her hands on the nearest table, their senders utterly forgotten.

"Hello," she said, giving Ben her widest smile. "It seems

I'm rather a success." She glanced around her to suggest the reason for the floral madness.

Ben's smile was self-deprecating as he handed her the daisies. "I shall do my best to keep that in mind for next time."

Her insides melted at his attention, and she reached for the bouquet only to have him snatch it back.

"I'm to meet your brother this morning for a ride in the park. Might he be close at hand?" His words were innocent, but his gaze wandered the vestibule searchingly.

"I believe he's in the morning room breaking his fast."

Ben's smile was quick and devious. "Excellent."

His eyes changed then. She'd never been so aware of another's mood, and suddenly, she was an expert on eyes. Ben's were a blue so surreal she often thought them proof he was crafted by the gods. For surely, no mere mortal man had eyes like that.

And she'd never met one, so that must be proof.

He discarded the daisies on a table crowded with vases, and before she knew what he was doing his arms were around her and he was kissing her.

Again.

The first kiss had sent her into a dizzying spin of emotion, but the second kiss. God, the second kiss *melted* her.

He held her differently. He kissed her differently. Yesterday she sensed the kiss had taken him by surprise. His body had been stiff as if braced for the unexpected. But today his body curved into hers almost as if he cradled her whole while he kissed her.

And his lips. His lips were soft, so, so, so soft, and she fell into them. Into him. Into whatever was happening.

This wasn't the mere meeting of lips she had dreamed kissing would be. Ben kissed with his whole self, so she became aware of every inch of him. The hard muscles of his chest, the broadness of his shoulders, the way his hips tapered where she slid her arms around him, her fingers digging into his lower back as she tried to hang on.

There was so much Ben when there hadn't been any at all for so long, and she was lost in the whirlwind of it. She couldn't think. If she thought, she would wonder why this was happening. He was supposed to be in mourning for his wife. He was supposed to have been suffering in widowerhood.

Instead he was kissing her in a room filled with flowers and sunshine, and it was like she had finally opened a door to a part of her she'd had to hide for so long, and it was utterly beautiful.

He eased back, his lips nipping at hers as he pulled away so she chased after him involuntarily, following his receding mouth as if she may forget how to breathe if he stopped kissing her. He laid his forehead against hers, his breathing shallow and rapid.

"I can't stop thinking about you, Johanna."

His voice was rough, and something low in her belly flashed in response. It was as though her body had suddenly developed a new array of feelings and sensations she'd never before experienced. But then, Ben had never kissed her before.

"You...can't?" She sounded so stupid, but she felt stupid just then. Stupid drunk on his kiss, and it was a miracle she had strung two words together.

How was this happening? She wanted to press her palms to her pounding temples, sure she would wake up and find this was all a dream.

But it wasn't. Not the way Ben's arms fit around her. Not the way his blue blue eyes deepened to cerulean when he gazed down at her.

He shook his head so slowly, back and forth, she followed each swing of his chin, mesmerized.

"Please tell me when I can see you again."

She blinked. "You're seeing me now."

His laugh was soft. "I mean alone. Like we were yesterday."

A thrill shot straight from her toes to the top of her head at the way he said *yesterday*.

"I don't know," she managed.

He glanced down the corridor toward the breakfast room, and she realized with a jolt how likely it was they'd be caught. Surely Andrew would come back at any moment.

"Are you attending the Hattersville ball tonight?"

"Probably." She couldn't have told anyone her middle name just then, let alone what ball she was supposed to attend.

His smile was enough to convince her she was a rack of pork left unattended in the middle of a pack of ravenous dogs.

"Tonight."

A single word had never had the power to turn her knees to liquid like that.

He slipped his arms from around her and turned to the corridor before she knew he'd even let go.

It was none too soon for she heard Andrew's solid steps coming toward them from the morning room.

"I should think this all a rather obnoxious waste." Ben walked away. "I wonder why you should garner such—oh, Andrew. There you are." He gestured around him. "I was just commenting on your sister's seeming success."

Andrew popped the last of a crust of bread into his mouth and nodded. "I have a feeling you're the cause of it."

She had been pretending to admire a spray of yellow

roses, but she spun around at this, the heat flaring in her cheeks.

Ben kept his gaze locked on Andrew, but she saw the way he flexed his fingers into fists. "I beg your pardon."

Andrew gestured as he shrugged into his coat. "Eliza tells me the two of you promenaded in the park yesterday. I'm sure it's given the wrong impression. People must think you're courting Jo." Andrew shook his head. "Now every bloke on the market is going to be after her. I could have your head for this."

Ben slid a glance at her, and she felt the flare of secrecy burn within her.

Ben's smile was slow and mocking. "You should be thanking me, old friend. She's likely to make a more advantageous match now."

She rolled her shoulders back at this. "I beg *your* pardon. I could have made a spectacular match without your assistance."

Andrew eyed her while Ben laughed.

She returned her brother's gaze. "You allow him to mock me like this?"

Andrew snatched up his hat and shrugged. "It's only Ben."

She was growing quite sick of hearing that.

The sound of horses' hooves outside signaled the arrival of Andrew's steed. He opened the door and stepped out.

"Eliza is coming for you today as well, isn't she?" He looked about as if searching for some kind of answer. "I believe it should be calling hours soon or some such thing."

She crossed her arms. "Yes, dear sister is coming to chaperone me for calling hours."

But Andrew was already out the door, calling to the groom who had brought his horse around. She was staring after him so she didn't see Ben sneak up on her and catch her around the waist. She shoved against his chest before he could kiss her.

"Do you think I would allow you to kiss me after such mocking?" she hissed, her eyes darting to the door.

His grin was devilish. "I was only teasing, darling. I like the glow that comes to your face when I make you angry."

Well, she couldn't very well argue with him when he called her *darling* and told her she glowed.

He pressed his lips quickly to hers. "Tonight," he whispered and disappeared through the door.

* * *

HE WONDERED, should he lie down across the riding path, would someone be kind enough to run him over thoroughly and completely?

It was what he deserved after all.

His heart clenched as he recalled what she had looked like when he'd opened the door of Ravenwood House that morning. It was the same dewy, wide-eyed look she'd given him when he'd caught her unawares sorting through the wildflowers that grew along the hills at Raeford Court.

Sunshine was always her best look, and the morning sun had poured through the windows in the foyer of Ravenwood House that morning, illuminating her like it had that day on the hills.

He wanted to find comfort in the fact that some things never changed, but instead he only felt like a cad.

He'd kissed her again, and while he could claim it had been a reaction to seeing the flowers that surrounded her and the very real competition for her hand it represented, there was a very small part of him that worried he'd kissed her because he'd wanted to.

He didn't want to think about that this morning. He

wanted to enjoy what fresh air and greenery the park had to offer, but more, he welcomed the distraction of his best friend.

Even though looking at him sometimes filled Ben with a wave of guilt.

"How long do you plan to stay in London?" Andrew asked then, and Ben glanced at his friend.

"It would appear I'm trapped at least for the next fortnight. While Lawrence may have been skilled at social obligations, he did not seem to possess the same aptitude for financial ones."

Andrew eyed him. "Is it as bad as the rumors would suggest?"

Ben's hands involuntarily tightened on the reins. "Rumors?" While he despised the soot and smog of London, he loathed the ease with which gossip spread in town even more.

Andrew kept his gaze forward as he negotiated a turn in the path.

"I had heard Lawrence's debts were called in shortly before his death."

"The estate's affairs seem to be in order. Although rather thin and somewhat precarious, a bit of fine tuning should—"

"Not estate debts." Andrew's voice was even, the neutrality of which kept the meaning of his words from piercing Ben's chest.

"You mean Lawrence's gambling debts," Ben said, his tone just as neutral.

Andrew did nothing more than slide him a glance.

They each nodded in greeting to a passing baron and continued several meters in silence.

"There was enough left in the coffers to cover his letters, but I shall be forced to make difficult decisions in the coming weeks." He adjusted his gloves casually. "It's nothing an estate like Raeford cannot absorb."

A new kind of guilt prickled along the back of his neck. He wanted nothing more than to confide in his friend, but circumstances prevented such comfort. Besides, Minerva had taught him that a confidante was nothing more than a fairy tale, even if they should find themselves thrown together in the same hell.

Andrew seemed to struggle with his next words. "You know if Raeford is ever in trouble—"

"I assure you it is not, but I appreciate your concern." If there was even a suspicion that he needed money, he could forget the idea of securing a wealthy wife.

Andrew glanced at him again, but his expression remained stony.

"They are calling you the Impostor Duke, you know."

Ben remembered all too clearly Viscount Blevens's treatment of him the previous day.

"I had a suspicion I may have acquired an additional title."

"Lawrence was beloved even if he was a bit of a wastrel."

Ben looked at his friend now. "I think in present company you can feel free to admit the truth. My brother was a bastard of the first order."

Andrew's smile was hesitant but knowing. "I suppose that's true."

He let his horse trot ahead several feet before speaking again. "The Impostor Duke, is it? I should have thought they would conjure something slightly more creative."

Andrew laughed harshly. "The *ton*? It's a miracle they came up with something at all."

"Is it all lost then? My hopes of repairing the estate and finding a new wife with whom to sire an heir to carry on the title?" He'd spoken the words flippantly, but he felt a stab of remorse at the mention of an heir.

Once he had dreamed of children, but that hope had ended all too quickly, another choice taken from him.

Andrew cast him another knowing glance. "I'm sorry again for your loss. I'm sure it must be difficult. So much tragedy so quickly."

While he could lie to his friend about the state of his affairs, he could not lie to him about something so personal as Minerva.

"She was a bitch, and I'm not sorry she's dead." The words were like a balm on a sore that refused to heal, and he suddenly found it much easier to breathe.

Andrew, however, nearly fell off his horse. "I'm sorry?" he asked when he'd sufficiently recovered himself.

Ben nodded as they passed another baron and an earl.

"She was a bitch. Surely, you knew that."

"Isn't it unwise to speak ill of the dead?"

"In this case, I'm willing to take a chance." He smirked.

Andrew continued to stare.

"Minerva and I did not have a love match, Andrew. You know as much."

Andrew adjusted his seat. "I suppose I had thought it had been at least amicable."

"When we arrived in America, she took to her suite of rooms and barred me entrance." He met Andrew's gaze, the truth nearly spilling from his lips, but once more, he reminded himself it would do no good. So he told most of the truth. "I had barely seen my wife for nearly two years before her death. Only when social obligations demanded such contact and then it was as brief as she could possibly make it."

Andrew's lips parted on unspoken words, but now that the dam had been broken, Ben found himself unable to stop, letting go of most of it, but still holding back the thing which caused him the greatest shame. That he could still not speak, but more, he couldn't let his friend know to what depths he had been forced to sink.

"She said my touch was vile, and my presence caused her migraines." He shrugged. "We entertained no one, and I became the butt of a great deal of mockery. Do you know how difficult it is to establish oneself in a new city when one cannot entertain as it is expected?" He shook his head. "This is why I prefer plants to people."

"You never said, in your letters, you never once indicated—"

"Was I to write to you of my woes?" He laughed. "You were across an ocean, Andrew. I wouldn't have subjected you to the harsh truth of my marriage when there was nothing to be done for it."

Andrew shook his head, his lips still slightly parted as though he grappled with Ben's revelation.

"First your father and then your wife. If I believed in such stuff, I would say you had upset a god in a past life."

Ben's teeth started to grind at the mention of his father.

"I should hope I may be redeemed by penance and supplication for the remainder of my journey on this earth."

His smile was pained, and Andrew laughed.

"I should hope as much."

They had reached the end of the path and directed their horses off to where they would be out of the way.

Andrew leaned on his pommel. "I wish you had told me."

He studied his friend. Lines sprang from the corners of his eyes, and Ben wondered when they had arrived. He'd been gone for so long, and the passage of time sometimes felt real and malleable. He had only to reach out to bend it to his will. If that were true, he would undo his marriage to Minerva and—

And what?

Marry Johanna at the first opportunity?

43

He didn't like how easy the thought sprang to his mind, but it needn't matter. His father never would have allowed the match. He had had other designs for his second born.

Ben cleared his throat. "Andrew, I find myself in a rather awkward situation."

Andrew's glance was swift. "Say the word, friend. You know I would always help you."

"I wish to court Johanna."

Andrew's eyes narrowed, and his jaw appeared as though it may snap off.

"Johanna."

Ben nodded. "Yes."

"My sister."

He nodded again, pursing his lips together in a show of humility. "Yes, she is most definitely your sister."

Andrew straightened, his grip on his pommel pulling the leather of his gloves dangerously taut.

"You wish to court my sister."

Ben met his friend's gaze. "I ask for your permission to court her. I should never be so untoward to suggest I would do such a thing without your blessing."

Ben's stomach roiled with anticipation. Now that he'd acquired the title of the Impostor Duke, he knew his chances of securing another bride with a dowry this season would be nearly nonexistent. Johanna was his only hope to drag Raeford out of the mire his brother had made of it.

He watched as Andrew's expression turned to granite, and then, almost disbelievingly, it melted until his friend's lips curved into a mocking grin.

"Johanna? You wish to court Johanna?" Andrew's laugh was rich. "Have you gone mad?"

Ben's mouth opened with no sound emerging as he couldn't quite determine what to say.

Andrew laughed again. "Do you know this is Johanna's

fifth season, or some such nonsense, and she's not shown interest in a single suitor?" He shook his head. "Should you wish to court her, I'm afraid you are setting yourself on a path that can only end in doom and despair."

Ben turned in his saddle to better eye his friend. "You speak so poorly of your own sister."

Andrew's laugh was nearly a cackle. "I speak so poorly of Johanna. Surely you have not forgotten what she is like? I'm afraid she hasn't changed much since childhood. She just wears gowns now."

"Has she really had five seasons? I can't imagine Viv would have allowed her to come out at such a young age."

Andrew shrugged. "One, two, five. It all seems the same to me."

Ben studied his friend as his thoughts churned. Johanna was rather likable and quite beautiful. Yes, she had a strong personality, but by all accounts, she would have been a catch. So why was she still unwed?

Her words in the grove yesterday came filtering back to him. He had thought them the fancy of a young girl, but he wondered now if her admiration of him ran deeper.

God, what if she loved him?

He swallowed, feeling every inch a wretch.

For while he loathed the idea that someone should feel such things for him, he also understood the power they held. It would be so much easier to get Johanna to accept his suit if she'd harbored a secret love for him for years.

He swallowed again, feeling the truth in his mouth as if it were sand.

Johanna.

His best friend's little sister.

She had…loved him? For years?

He gave himself a mental shake. No, surely not.

But what if she had?

Deep inside of him a tiny flame sparked to life, born of his inability to squash all sense of hope. What would it be like to be truly loved by someone? What would it be like to have his wife step into his arms? What would it be like to have her welcome his touch? To have her whisper sweet nothings in his ear?

To know that she was proud of him.

He adjusted in the saddle.

"I find it difficult to believe Johanna has not accepted a suit before now."

Andrew glanced off at a pair of passing horsemen. "She's had offers, but she declined every one."

"And you allowed her to do so?"

Andrew's glance could cut glass.

Ben nodded. "Right. One does not *allow* Johanna to do anything."

Andrew released a breath that seemed to carry with it the weight of being responsible for four sisters.

"I suppose if you've the bullocks to try it, I give you my blessing." He caught Ben's gaze. "But do not claim I did not warn you."

Ben gave a nod. "I thank you for your advice."

Andrew shook his head and kneed his horse into moving back onto the path. "I always thought you were different, Ben. I didn't think you were foolish."

Ben squared his shoulders. "Sometimes necessity makes us all foolish."

But Andrew was already out of earshot.

CHAPTER 4

*S*he'd allowed the upstairs maid to do her hair.

She had never had a maid before. She hadn't seen the point in it. When not in town, she was more apt to steal old trousers from the footmen to wear in the barns, and what would a lady's maid have done with that?

Her hair was simple enough to manage. She favored braids, and even when she was introduced to society, she kept the braids, choosing to twist them into elaborate designs. Tonight though, she'd allowed the upstairs maid to attack her with the curling tongs.

Her thick brown hair hung like a curtain about her face before it swept to the back in a tight chignon. From the corner of her eye, she could see where the curls were already resisting the style, and her heavy straight locks were pushing to be free of their spiraling confines.

Why on earth women did this on a *nightly* basis was beyond her.

But perhaps Ben would like it.

Johanna could recall all too clearly Minerva's black hair, and the way it sprang into curls as if it were meant for the style. Minerva had worn her curls swept up in a cascade of raven beauty on her wedding day. Johanna could only imagine how much it had pleased Ben.

She coaxed a tendril back into a spiral shape at her cheek, but as soon as she released it, it fell into a straight lock. She blew out a breath, and the curls danced at the edge of her vision.

"Do you think he will show his face here tonight?" The nasally pinched voice came from behind her, and Johanna couldn't help the way her senses tuned to it.

Overhearing gossip had been the only thing to get her through the past two seasons. She surely would have expired of boredom by now had she not. She was lucky to have been the youngest of five children. It was easy to be overlooked, and in that, she'd developed a marvelous skill at subterfuge.

Just then a footman passed her carrying a tray of champagne, and she used it as an excuse to turn, grasping one of the flutes as he nearly stepped out of range. The pivot allowed her to take in the women just behind her.

Lady Devers and Lady Harris. They were somewhere in their middling years with gray just spouting at the temples of their elaborate coiffures and their hands always occupied with glasses of wine.

They had a daughter each whom they'd both managed to successfully marry off. One to a baron and one to a shipping magnate. It had been a scandal the previous season, but when it was soon discovered that Lady Harris was no longer given credit at the modiste, everyone had known the reason for such a lowly match. It appeared the Harris title was in need of funds.

Johanna could only feel sorry for the younger Lady Harris. To be matched off like not so much as a piece of cattle. How tragic.

She turned her gaze back to the dance floor as it began to

fill for the next dance, but she kept her ears trained on the women behind her.

"If he were wise, I would think he wouldn't dare."

Lady Harris scoffed. "Wise? He went to America after he was wed. I think we can safely say he shan't act with any acumen."

Johanna had been about to take a sip of the champagne. She'd never had a taste for the stuff, and as she was caught off guard by the women behind her, she choked on the bubbles and pounded a fist to her chest to make it stop.

So much for going unnoticed.

Had they been talking about Ben? He was the only gentleman who might be in attendance that night who had gone to America that she knew of. Of course, there could be others, but...

Her moment of choking seemed not to deter the ladies from their gossip as next, Lady Devers responded, "I suppose you are right. And to think he married Lady Wallington's daughter." The woman made a noise as though she found the concept distasteful.

Johanna nearly popped out of her slippers. She wanted nothing more than to see the woman's expression. For what could she mean? Johanna could recall nothing but sparkle and light when she considered Lady Minerva Wallington.

Johanna had been sixteen at the time, and although not out in society, she'd heard enough from her sisters to know the lady was the catch of the season. Why should Lady Devers speak so poorly of her now?

"I have met feral cats with more conducive personalities," Lady Harris drawled. "And you remember the rumors at the time."

Johanna's brow wrinkled in confusion. She must be thinking of the wrong person.

"Do you know I hear they're calling him the Impostor Duke?"

Her hopes fell, and she forgot about the champagne flute in her hand. It tipped, slipping from her grasp and sending a waterfall of champagne on the floor.

She was saved from making a complete ninny of herself when a strong hand shot out and righted the glass, tugging it from her lax fingers.

She looked up, a smile coming automatically to her lips as Ben studied her, concern knitted across his brow.

"Are you all right?"

She beamed. She could feel it in the way it tugged the skin around her lips, but his question had her faltering.

"Of course, I'm all right. Why would you ask—"

He held up the champagne flute, and she stopped speaking.

She folded her hands sedately in front of her. "I was momentarily overwhelmed."

Ben peered around them. "Here? In the middle of this crush?"

She nodded and raised her eyebrows as if to dare him to contradict her. "Balls. What fascinating occurrences."

He sniffed at the remainder of the champagne in her glass. "Has this gone off?" He lowered the glass. "Perhaps you've consumed too much of it. It's always the young ones. Give them their first sip of champagne, and they lose all self-discipline."

She pursed her lips. "I have not imbibed irresponsibly, Your Grace."

He flinched at her use of his title, and she suddenly remembered the conversation she'd been overhearing. She turned, but Lady Devers and Lady Harris were no longer behind her. Perhaps the arrival of the person they were gossiping about scared them off.

She turned back to Ben, placing her hands to her hips.

"Are they calling you the Impostor Duke?"

Ben's laugh was stilted with surprise. "Do you know I think they are? But I must say, only you would have the bravado to point it out to me."

She wanted very much to cross her arms over her chest, but Viv had slapped her enough with a fan and scolded her for being unladylike to prevent her from doing so now.

"It's not bravado. It's concern." She took a step closer to him to drive home her point. "Friends care about one another, and I would hope you would tell me something troubling no matter how it might hurt me."

His lips parted, but his eyes searched her face, and she thought a response would not be forthcoming when he said, "Then perhaps I should ask why you have done that to your hair."

Her hand flew to her curled hair. "What do you mean? I had a maid do it. She said it's the style of the season."

Ben shrugged. "That might be, but you forget that I've seen your hair down."

His words were simple, but his eyes held a heat and knowledge that had her stomach tightening. She snatched her champagne flute back and took a swallow. It was vile, and she could not see how the lulling effects of alcohol could surmount the awful taste.

She set the flute on the lip of a potted fern behind her. Ben had still not spoken when she turned back around.

"Where have you been? I thought you had decided to leave me to my fate alone."

"Do you know I had thought to do just that," he said now, scanning the crowd as one might observe a carriage wreck. "But I didn't exactly enjoy the idea of Andrew calling me out for not protecting your honor."

She laughed. "Andrew would do no such thing. Not for

me anyway. Perhaps for Louisa and absolutely for Eliza. But not for me."

"Then I would be forced to call myself out." His voice had turned deep, and it pulled her gaze to his to find him studying her in a way he never had before.

Almost as if he were seeing her for the first time. The ballroom around them dropped away, and she understood what it meant to be lost in the moment. Because right then it was just her and Ben, and she never wanted to be anywhere else.

Except, perhaps, in his arms while he was kissing her.

She sucked in a breath as she realized he might kiss her again. Here. Tonight. She looked about them as if to find a suitable spot for them to conceal themselves whilst they did just that.

Kissing.

Kissing Ben.

Ben kissing her.

She drew a deep breath and forced herself to concentrate. Ben would not be ravishing her here on the dance floor of a crowded ballroom.

Lud, she hadn't even considered ravishing. If his kisses were any indication, the ravishing would be divine.

"I hope you wouldn't do that."

She liked the way her words made his lips slowly curve into a smile.

He gave a polite bow. "My lady, would you be so good as to give me this dance?"

He was being silly. With her. And it made her toes curl in her slippers.

She gave an equally ridiculous curtsy. "Of course, Your Grace."

He took her arm and led her to the dance floor, and when his arms went about her, she couldn't help but think—

What if he hadn't married Minerva?

What if she hadn't spent the last five years missing him? Yearning for him? Seeing him in places where he no longer stood. Hearing his laugh when it was impossible.

He swung her about neatly, and to her, it was everything she had imagined it would be. Ben was an accomplished dancer, but she already knew that.

"Do you remember when your mother forced me to partner you during your dancing lessons?"

Ben laughed. "I kept stepping on that instructor's toes. What was his name? It resembled something one might eat."

"Mr. Hammworth."

They laughed together then.

"The poor man. He was far too short. I couldn't help but step on him." He shook his head, even as he turned her neatly in the waltz. "I think Duchess was only trying to prevent me from clobbering the man."

The laughter faded at his mention of the name his mother preferred them to call her, and Johanna was flooded with a warmth when she thought of the woman who had been a kind of mother to her, but the warmth was clouded with a tinge of sadness.

"Have you heard from your mother yet?"

"I wrote her to let her know I've another fortnight of meetings with my solicitors before I can head north."

He would be leaving. A flash of urgency erupted in her stomach. Why hadn't she thought of it? Of course, he would be leaving.

She'd been too wrapped up in him to remember.

"I do hope you'll give your mother my condolences for her loss."

His look was sharp.

"Even if she may not mourn him outwardly, he was still her son."

Lawrence had never been kind to Duchess. Just as her husband had not.

Johanna vaguely remembered Ben's father. He was more of a dark shadow than an actual person, and she'd done her best to stay out of his path as a child. Never a kind man, he was quicker to strike with a fist than scolding word.

"I write to her, you know. She's never responded, but then I wouldn't expect her to. It's only that I…" Her voice faded as she tried to find words for what Duchess meant to her. "Well, you know." It was all that she could say.

Duchess had seen her when others hadn't, but she didn't know how to tell Ben that. While Johanna had been lost in the noise and chaos of five children at Ravenwood Park, she was the center of attention at Raeford Court for a woman starved of daughters. For a girl without a mother, this had been a balm, yes, but it was more than that. So much more.

Ben's jaw relaxed at her words, and she tightened her grip on his hand as he turned her about one last time. The song concluded with a mere echo of notes in the vast ballroom, but Ben did not relinquish her arm.

As he'd done two nights ago, he steered her in the direction of the terrace doors.

"Benedict Carver, are you attempting to ruin me?"

"Would you marry me if I did?"

She nearly tripped on her own feet. His tone was playful, and she knew he was joking—he was joking, wasn't he?—but she had never even allowed herself to dream that one day he may say such a thing to her.

She tugged her arm free and stepped in front of him, backing slowly out through the terrace doors.

"Only if you catch me," she whispered and disappeared into the night.

* * *

HE WATCHED HER SLIP AWAY, disappearing into the darkness with a smile on her face that should have sent desire straight to his loins.

Instead, he was wracked with guilt.

He had been late because the meeting with his solicitors had gone long. The Raeford estate would have no more liquidity once the remainder of its debts were paid off.

He wouldn't have so much as a farthing for a broadsheet.

He needed a wealthy bride, and he needed her quickly. He'd already instructed his solicitors to apply for a special license, and with any luck, he'd be married before he left London in a fortnight.

He plastered on a smile, pretending to be happy, and plunged into the darkness after Johanna.

He had enough time alone in the dark as he searched for her to contemplate his fate. All he had ever wanted was to work the land at Raeford Court. He'd never once given a thought to marriage, an ill-advised state if his parents' marriage were any indication.

The goal had seemed so simple, and yet obstacle after obstacle had fallen into his path. When he'd married Minerva and been sent to Boston, he thought his chances of staying at Raeford Court were gone for good, but then his brother had died.

He'd tried to summon an ounce of grief, but he had none. His father had favored Lawrence, banishing Ben to the schoolroom. It had been right as Lawrence was the heir after all. But couldn't there have been a bit left over for Ben?

There hadn't been.

Whatever was left of the old man at the end of the day involved a great deal of drink and a leather strap.

Ben had felt no grief when he received news his father had died either. He'd been in his office at the docks when the letter arrived. He'd read it and gone back to work. The title and the responsibility for Raeford Court had gone to Lawrence then. It was of no concern to Ben.

But when the news had arrived that his brother had died, Ben was not ashamed to say he felt a wave of euphoria slip through him. That was, until he read the rest of the solicitor's letter. Gambling debts. Insurmountable. Some of the estate would need to be sold to cover it.

Ben would not sell Raeford Court. There were other means by which a man could acquire a fortune.

She was currently somewhere ahead of him in the dark. He could hear her laughter trickling back to him like some sort of sprite. The hedges rose up on either side of them, and the moonlight only reached certain spots. She danced through it as she made her way deeper into the garden, and it rendered him momentarily motionless.

She deserved better than him.

She deserved a love match, not to be some man's chattel. He scrubbed his hands over his face. He was doing this for Raeford Court, and all the people who depended on him. He was doing this for Duchess. Didn't she deserve to finally have some peace?

He plunged ahead and soon broke free of the hedges into a small arbor flanked by stone benches. Johanna stood in the middle of it, her face turned to the sky.

Her beauty struck him as though for the first time. Johanna *was* beautiful, he knew that, but she had always been his friend, not a potential lover. He'd never looked at her any other way, but he did so now, guilt flowing freely through him.

No one would ever tell her how her skin was like cream. Not say it and mean. No one would ever hold her in the dark of the night, his body protecting hers against the demons that lurked there.

In his mind, he saw them married and once they reached

Raeford Court they could live their separate lives. He'd be attentive, of course. He would not be cruel. But he knew he couldn't give her the love she apparently held for him.

Not after what Minerva had done to him.

"Do you know what I miss about the country?" She never broke her gaze from the sky as she spoke to him.

He came up behind her, his arms reaching, when it suddenly occurred to him—

He hadn't been with a woman in years.

Insecurity replaced guilt, and he thought frantically that he might not be able to woo her. She seemed to like his kisses well enough though, so perhaps there was hope.

But in his mind he could only hear Minerva shutting her door against him, her wails of anguish splitting through an empty house while the servants pretended to hear nothing.

He closed the distance between them and slipped his arms around her, following her gaze to the night sky.

"You miss the smell of manure early in the morning," he said as he nuzzled her neck.

She laughed and elbowed him playfully. "No, of course not." She looked up again. "I miss the stars. There are so many more stars in the country sky."

He raised his head. "I'm fairly certain it's the same number of stars, and the same sky actually."

She shook her head, and her voice was vehement. "No, they are different stars entirely."

In that moment, he absolutely believed her. He swallowed and turned her about in his arms.

She tilted her head as she turned as if anticipating his kiss, and he would not deny her. It still surprised him to be kissing Johanna. In his mind, she was still the pest who scampered after Andrew and him. How could it be that he was kissing her now?

Or even odder, that he should like it quite so much?

57

The ever present sense of guilt he had been carrying was suddenly accompanied by an overwhelming wave of trepidation. He'd never planned to marry again, not after Minerva, but he'd never thought about what might happen should he fall in love with someone.

Not that he was in love with Johanna. It was only...

It was only that her lips were so soft, and she smelled of fresh air. That she curled herself into his arms as if she belonged there. That she made the most appealing mewling noise when he kissed her.

That she didn't back away from his touch, slam a door in his face.

He broke off the kiss abruptly, his chest tightening with memory.

Johanna's eyes fluttered open, concern marring her features. He wanted to step back, drop his arms, but the urgency of finding a bride compelled him to stay still.

He laughed, and even to him it sounded brittle. "I suddenly realized who I was kissing."

The concern cleared from her expression, but she soon replaced it with annoyance.

"You mustn't worry, Your Grace. It's only me. Johanna. And it's only you. Ben."

For the first time, he realized how often that had been said of them, and he understood now how it must have annoyed her. Now that he knew she'd harbored a secret attraction to him for so long.

Now he did drop his arms and stepped back, catching her hand at the last moment to draw her to one of the stone benches.

He took the opportunity to suck in the cold night air, hoping its bracing qualities would restore his resolve. He must keep Minerva from his mind if he were to convince Johanna he cared for her enough to get her to accept his suit.

God, he was an arse.

"I feel I must tell you I've asked your brother for permission to court you."

Johanna's glance was swift, and her fingers reflexively tightened on his. "You did?"

He squeezed her hand in return and drew it into his lap where he cradled it in both of his. Holding someone's hand had never been so erotic. Minerva had never let him hold hers. After everything that had happened, hand holding seemed so insignificant and yet it was everything.

"It seemed prudent," he said.

He was busy studying their hands, so when she touched his face to turn his attention to her, it startled him.

He reached up and covered her hand with his as she held his face toward her.

"Prudent?" She spoke the word questioningly.

"Wise." Her eyes were so brown, like deep fathomless pools in which he could hide away from the rest of the world forever.

"Wise?"

"Logical."

Had he ever noticed before the way her upper lip turned up like that? Or the way her nose ended with such perfect roundness?

"Logical?"

"Yes, entirely logical."

This time when he kissed her, thoughts of Minerva did not plague him.

In fact, no thoughts at all plagued him.

He was consumed by Johanna. All of her. He wrapped his arms around her, pulling her snuggly to his chest even as he tipped her head back, deepening the kiss. The heat of her body melted something inside of him he didn't know had

JESSIE CLEVER

been frozen, cut off, dying. It was as though his very soul burst into flames just from her kiss.

And it felt glorious.

It had been so long since he touched someone, since someone touched him. Intimacy was a heady drug, and he supped from it, pulling the life-giving elixir into his body, storing it up for when the loneliness came again.

For it would come when Johanna discovered the truth of his deception.

Somewhere in the fogginess of desire, he realized he couldn't tell her. Johanna must never find out. If she did, she was sure to keep this from him.

Her kisses. Her touch. Her laughter.

God, he couldn't lose her laughter.

He gripped her waist in his hands, memorizing every curve of her. The way her hips flared, the taut muscles of her back, so strong from riding. He let his hands slip farther, daring to take after so much deprivation.

He stopped when his hand met the underside of her breast, but at the smallest touch, she moaned against his lips, and the fire inside him flared in response.

"Ben."

His stomach clenched at the sound of his name on her lips, so heavy with desire.

He no longer hesitated. He took.

He cupped her breast, and her fingers dug into his shoulders. He sucked her lower lip before nipping kisses along the line of her jaw. Finally he settled his mouth at the sweet spot behind her ear.

"Ben." This time his name was throaty and deep.

"Do you wish me to stop?" he whispered against her ear.

"No." It was hardly a whimper.

He licked her ear, causing her to buck against him before he resumed his sensual torture of her neck. He traced the line of her collarbone, his hand kneading her breast through the bodice of her gown.

"Ben." There was pleading in her voice, enough to have him ease back to look at her. "Ben, I'd very much like it if you touched me." The yearning in her eyes nearly undid him.

"I am touching you." He studied her face, so resplendent in the moonlight.

"I want you to touch me," she said again, but this time she gripped his hand in hers and moved it higher, to the place where her bare skin rose above the neck of her gown.

He watched as she laid his hand against her skin, and he could feel the heat of her through his glove. Several seconds passed as he looked at his hand, sitting so innocently on the curve of her breast. And then something quite simply snapped inside of him.

Using his teeth, he tore off his glove, and when he returned his hand to her chest, heat seared his fingertips. Glorious, delicious, beautiful heat.

"Johanna," he moaned her name before placing his lips where his hand had been.

She arched in his embrace, offering herself to him, and he took. God, he took all of it.

He traced the edge of her bodice, knowing what was just out of his reach. He wanted it with a ferociousness and suddenness that shocked him.

He wanted her.

He pulled his hand back and stood, peering down at her in the moonlight.

When her eyes finally fluttered open, shock tightened her features.

"I asked your brother for permission to court you. Not ravish you. And I will not dishonor you or him with my behavior tonight." How he managed the words he didn't know as his chest still heaved for air.

She blinked. "You're *not* going to ravish me?"

He shook his head. "I respect you too much to do so."

She'd braced her hands against the bench, and now he couldn't help but think how it set her on display for him. He reached down and snatched up his discarded glove.

"I should like to escort you back to the ballroom."

She stood, stepping close to him, and he refused to step back, no matter how his sense of self-preservation wished him to.

"You respect me too much?" The way she said the words was as though the concept were entirely foreign to her.

"Yes." He ensured his tone allowed no room for negotiation.

She nodded and straightened her bodice, brushed at her skirts. "Then I suppose I shall accept your escort back to the ballroom. Lord knows what kind of scoundrels are lurking in this garden."

If you only knew.

CHAPTER 5

*H*e respected her too much.

  She had expected to swoon with the memory of his kiss, the feel of his hands caressing her body.

She didn't expect to lose her ability to concentrate because she couldn't stop thinking about what he'd said.

He *respected* her.

As the youngest of five children, she'd never garnered a great deal of respect in the Darby household. At best, she was an afterthought, which had largely resulted in her reputation as a tag-along. It felt strange to have someone put her first. Moreover, she wasn't sure what to do about it.

Everything with Ben had always been easy, but she could feel things shifting. It wasn't just the physical either. It ran deeper than that, and she could only imagine what he was experiencing based on her own feelings.

Was it strange for him to kiss his best friend's little sister?

More than that, was it strange to wish to grab the breast of the girl who had chased him with milk snakes?

It was an odd thing to face, but he seemed to enjoy their

interludes. She hoped for more of them, and perhaps with time, the oddness would fade.

After all, he respected her.

"I really would have been fine with Andrew," she said now, eyeing her sister.

Eliza picked up her head from where she'd been resting it along the back of the sofa.

"Don't be silly. I'm only a little fatigued is all." Eliza pressed a hand gently to her stomach where she carried her second child. "I was perfectly fine carrying George, and an afternoon of chaperoning my sister during calling hours is hardly taxing." She studied the teacart at her elbow that a maid had brought earlier. "Especially when there are such delectable offerings."

"I do hope you mean the petit fours and not the gentlemen callers."

They both turned at the sound of Ben's voice, but it was Eliza who spoke first. Luckily. For at that moment, Johanna found herself somewhat overcome by the sight of Ben looking so handsome in a navy coat and buff trousers, his mourning attire suddenly gone. She had always found him attractive, but her sense of him was heightened now that she knew more of him. Carnally.

She knew what it felt like to run her fingers through the hair that fluttered at his collar. She knew the sensation of his heart beating against hers. She knew the security she felt when he held her in his arms.

The absence of mourning attire, however, nearly made her knees give out.

"I assure you. I have seen this year's offerings, and I can attest to the petit fours being of far greater quality."

Ben pressed a hand to his chest in mock indignation.

"You wound me, Eliza."

She gestured with the petit four she had selected. "I wasn't aware you were on the market this season."

Ben's gaze slid to Johanna, and she felt a hot ripple pass through her as though he had touched her.

"I have chosen not to observe mourning for Minerva. She passed some months ago now, and I find the urgency of the situation I have found myself in requires my attentions elsewhere for the good of the people who depend upon the Raeford estate."

Johanna considered him. What an odd thing to say, even odder still that he chose that morning to announce it. There were times when she'd forgotten the requirement for mourning. She forgot quite a lot when he kissed her. Smiled at her. Acknowledged her existence. That he should not mourn his wife seemed somehow out of character for Ben as he was the one going about declaring his respect for her.

Eliza wiped her hands on a napkin. "Is it as bad as the rumors suggest?"

Ben's smile was pained. "I find myself the subject of a great many gossip mongers since my return to London."

Eliza studied the petit fours once more. "It's never pleasant. I for one find it's much better to pretend they do not exist." She plucked a sweet from the cart. "So in that sense, tell me what it is *you* plan to do with the estate."

Johanna had been watching him so intently she saw a spark come into his eyes before fading as he seemed to gather his thoughts.

"The farming methods are terribly out of date. The tenants are not even employing the four-course rotation method. Yields are disastrously low. With just a little modification, the estate will be far more prosperous."

She wasn't sure why, but Johanna found herself enraptured by what Ben was saying. She'd never considered Raeford as a working estate. As a child it had simply been an endless source of exploration, adventure, and fun. As an adult, it had taken on a golden hue as she'd come to understand not everywhere was as idyllic as Raeford Court.

"I had heard some estates have been moving to selective breeding," she said then, and she didn't miss the surprised look that came to Ben's eyes. She squared her shoulders. "Do you have any plans for the herd at Raeford?"

He raised his chin and met her gaze directly. "From what I understand from my steward's report, my brother let the herd flounder. It's sparse now, but I have every intent to acquire new stock and bring back the life of the herd."

"Dear me," Eliza said from the sofa. "What sort of gentleman would allow his tenants to suffer the lack of a healthy herd?"

Ben held Johanna's gaze as he answered as though what he had to say he meant for her to understand. "Not a wise or prudent one. There's currently an arrangement in place for the tenants to trade with the Knightley estate for dairy and meat. It's not a situation I find appealing."

"Surely not," Johanna said. "What if the tenants have nothing to trade with? You know how a bad harvest can have a cascade of negative effects."

He attempted to hide a smile as she knew her response had been rather strong, but she hated to see an estate mismanaged as such.

"I am aware of the delicacy of the situation, and I hope to rectify it as soon as I can return to Raeford Court."

"And when will that be?" Eliza asked.

"I'm hoping to be on my way by the end of next week. My business here in town should be concluded by then."

Again, he spoke to her even as he answered Eliza's question.

He was leaving then. She didn't know why the thought had her stomach clenching and her mind churning. He had said he'd asked Andrew for permission to court her. Surely he didn't mean to do so in the next week.

Perhaps he would only need be in Raeford Court for a short time. It was still fairly early in the season. There was time. At least, that was what she would tell herself.

"So soon? I'm sorry to hear that." Eliza stood and brushed at her skirts. "I suppose you'd like to see Andrew. I think he's about somewhere." She gestured to Johanna. "When I told him we would be receiving callers today, he muttered something about deserving peace and quiet and wandered off."

Ben hesitated, and Johanna could feel the heat clawing its way up her cheeks. It wasn't embarrassment though. It was frustration. Why was it that everyone assumed Ben would not be here to see her? Why was it that she was so easily pushed to the margins?

Because she always had been.

"I'm actually here to see Johanna."

The look on Eliza's face was one she'd remember for the rest of her life, and it hurt so very much. Eliza would never mean to be cruel. It just wasn't in her. But Johanna had years of being pushed aside, and sometimes all it took was the slightest glance to send one beyond their own strength to endure.

"Johanna? Whatever could you need with Johanna?"

Ben had been watching her. She could feel the way his eyes moved over her as if he were picking her apart piece by piece to ensure she was all right. He apparently did not like what he saw because he straightened his shoulders and looked Eliza dead in the eye.

"I've asked Andrew for permission to court her."

He was saying that a great deal lately, and she could admit she rather liked it.

Eliza's mouth opened on no sound. Then she swallowed and tried again. Nothing.

"I've indicated to Ben that I'm open to receiving his courtship, Eliza. I hope that doesn't come as a shock to you."

Eliza's mouth snapped shut as she put her fisted hands to her hips. "I'm not at all surprised he wishes to court you, Johanna. I'm only surprised it has taken him this long to realize it."

Her sister's words were like the first warm breeze after an interminable winter.

"To be fair, he's been in America," Johanna found herself saying while she attempted to reassemble her thoughts.

"That's hardly an excuse."

Ben was unable to defend himself as Mallard, the Ravenwood butler, arrived to announce a caller.

No. *Callers*.

Soon the room was filled with gentlemen. Gentlemen here to see *her*.

Johanna. The youngest of the Darby sisters. It happened all at once, and she lost track of Ben somewhere in the crush. Eliza had gone back to her sofa, and Johanna feared it was more out of a sense of protection than of fatigue.

Viscount Blevens was there along with two barons she recalled dancing with the previous season. *The previous season*. Lud, what was this about?

She curtsied until her legs felt they may evaporate beneath her, and still they came through the door.

Earls and marquesses and was that a squire?

She paused in her greetings to peer through the mix, only to find Ben had been pushed behind the piano in the melee. The gentlemen had unfortunately brought more bouquets of flowers with them. They had just managed to dispense with the last bunch and now there were more.

Why were there so many gentlemen here to call on her?

She heard their names, but she knew she would not remember a single one of them. Finally, when the onslaught seemed to have quieted, she was better able to hear the conversations moving about her.

There were some directed at her. How was she finding the weather? Had she been to the theater? What did she think of this year's production of *The Magic Flute*?

But it wasn't those conversations that interested her. It was the ones held by the gentlemen who had found places at the periphery of the room. The ones who whispered to one another and eyed the spot behind the piano where Ben stood.

Ben.

The gossip she'd overheard at the Hattersville ball came screaming back to her.

The Impostor Duke.

These gentlemen were all here to shut out the man they called the Impostor Duke.

She made to move, but she was stopped by a commotion at the door. Her shoulders sank as she anticipated more curtsying, but it was only Andrew who stepped from the crowd.

And Dax.

Her eyes traveled from her brother-in-law to Eliza who stood at seeing her husband.

"If you will all give us a moment," Andrew said to the crowd as Dax pulled his wife aside.

Andrew stepped beside Johanna, taking her elbow to pull them both farther away from the crowd and toward Dax and Eliza in some semblance of privacy.

"Louisa is having her baby," Dax spoke softly, his hand at Eliza's elbow.

Eliza's smile was both immediate and tinged with concern.

"The doctor is already there, but Louisa's asking for you." Dax's smile rivaled his wife's. "Sebastian sent for me. He has asked that I come wait with him."

Johanna couldn't stop her own smile then. Sebastian, the curmudgeonly duke her sister Louisa had married last season, was truly a kind-hearted man, and it was absolutely like him to seek the company of his oldest and dearest friend at a time like this.

Eliza nodded. "We'll go together." She looked swiftly at Johanna. "Oh, Jo, I'm sorry—"

Johanna held up both hands. "I think I've had quite enough of calling hours for one day." She swept her gaze behind them at all the leering gentlemen.

"Calling hours? It looks like you're having a cattle auction in here," Dax said.

"I'll get rid of them." Andrew's tone was despondent.

Johanna smiled. "No need, dear brother. I'll be happy to dispense with them." She pulled Eliza in for a quick hug. "Give Louisa my love and please let me know as soon as the little one gets here."

"I will," Eliza whispered before pulling free to take her husband's arm as he guided her through the crowd.

Johanna turned to face them, these gentlemen who had thought themselves so mighty.

"Excuse me, good sirs," she called to the room. "But I find I'm suffering from a womanly issue and must beg you to leave at once."

* * *

BEN DIDN'T KNOW what it was like to have sisters, having had the dubious fortune of having only an older brother.

But he could surmise from the way Andrew's face turned green at his sister's pronouncement that sisters could be rather vexing.

Although, Ben had never seen a room clear so completely in such short fashion. Viscount Blevens hesitated long enough to sneer at Ben, but Ben only smiled and waved the man off as he made his way out from behind the piano where he'd been pushed.

He should have known by the number of bouquets she had received earlier in the week that Johanna was the object of great interest amongst the eligible bachelors of the *ton*. He hadn't thought to bring her more flowers this time, and he was irked to find the room was again filled with them.

Her callers had brought all kinds of bibs and bobs. He even saw a potted fern. What was she to do with that?

It all worked to fuel his anxiety. He needed Johanna, and if the feeling among the ton was as negative as the rumors led him to believe, Johanna was his only hope. He would have to try harder, it would seem.

He just wasn't sure he'd survive it.

Last night had been a revelation. Not only in how Johanna had responded to him, but more that he had responded to her. After the hell that was his marriage, he hadn't thought it possible. But he supposed he was still a man, and as strangely as everything else was turning out to be, he found himself physically attracted to Johanna.

Johanna.

It baffled him, but it also concerned him. He thought of his heart as a rusted bucket so full of holes it would never hold love again. But apparently there was nothing wrong with other parts of him.

He rubbed at the back of his neck as he approached Andrew and Johanna.

"Is something amiss?" he asked when the room had finally cleared.

Johanna's smile was bright. "Louisa is having her baby." Her face fell. "I wonder who is tending to poor George if Eliza has gone to care for Louisa." She paused and looked at him. "George is Eliza's son." She turned to Andrew. "Do you think George—"

Andrew held up a hand. "I'm sure George is being tended to by his nanny." His expression turned curious. "Or Mrs. Fitzhugh. You know how she dotes on him."

Johanna smiled again. "Mrs. Fitzhugh is their house-keeper. She adores little George." She looked to Andrew. "What are we to do in the meantime then?"

Andrew shrugged. "We wait. Isn't that how these things always go?"

Johanna scanned the room, and Ben turned to follow her gaze. The mass exodus had caused some minor destruction, and the room looked as though it were the victim of a trav-eling circus. Teacups were discarded on the piano. Flower petals had fallen to the carpet where gentlemen had brushed by bouquets in their attempt to flee. Napkins were draped over the backs of chairs, and a trail of crumbs led from the sofa to the door.

That might have actually been from Eliza's departure, but Ben was not one to judge.

"We wait," Johanna repeated.

Ben couldn't help the smile that tugged at the corner of his lips. Johanna was not good at waiting.

He spoke up before she could tear her skirts to shreds as she twisted them between her hands. "I would be happy to wait with you both."

Johanna's eyes flashed to his.

Andrew scratched absently at his forehead as he moved toward the door. "I must send a letter to Viv actually. She'll want to know about Louisa first thing." He stopped momen-tarily. "You should stay with Johanna. You know how she is when she's told to wait."

Ben smirked at Johanna's gasp.

"I was already thinking it." He raised a hand in farewell to his friend as he slipped out the door.

When he turned back to Johanna, it was to find she'd relinquished her skirts to form fists she placed at her hips.

"Why is it that everyone assumes we can be left alone together? Do they really think my reputation is in no danger from you?"

Ben felt the stab of guilt but forced a smile. "I'm sure they are not thinking of it in that way."

"You asked Andrew for permission to court me."

Ben considered this, his eyes searching the room. "I suppose I did."

Her expression remained unchanged. He stepped closer, slipping his arms around her waist, ignoring her bent elbows and fisted hands. She made a noise of protest, but he kissed her before she could say anything else.

It was a soft, gentle kiss compared to what they had shared the night before, and yet somehow it zinged directly through his heart. He pulled away enough to rest his forehead against hers.

"I'm sorry they all seem to ignore you, but I must admit I'm not that sorry. It gives me more opportunity to spend time with you. Alone."

He was surprised to find it was the truth. He had always enjoyed Johanna's company, even when she was more of a shadow than a welcomed partner in their adventures. She was funny and spontaneous and light-hearted. He knew how much he had needed some light-heartedness in the past several years.

She slipped her hands between them and pushed on his chest until he was leaning far enough away to see her face.

"You're leaving by the end of next week?"

He dropped his arms and stepped back, reality crashing down on his momentary happiness.

"I must return to Raeford Court as soon as possible. I should have matters settled here in town by then and can depart as early as next week."

"When were you going to tell me?" Her voice was soft, and he found it jarring.

When Minerva had asked a question such as that it was always in accusation. Johanna simply wanted to know.

He ran a hand through his hair, feeling the weight of so many circumstances on his shoulders. He wondered what he should tell her, but he recalled her words from earlier. She would be honest with him, and she expected him to be honest with her.

Mostly.

"You had inquired as to my tardiness last eve when I failed to arrive at the Hattersville ball."

She nodded as he paced to the piano, toying with the music that still perched in its music stand.

"I had a meeting with my solicitors yesterday afternoon that ran unexpectedly late." He let his hands drop to his sides as he turned to face her. "It appears Raeford Court is rather out of sorts. What I said earlier is true. The estate requires many improvements if I am to increase its yields and therefore its profitability. It will entail hard work and will likely take years to get it back on the footing it once enjoyed."

She stepped forward and laid a hand on his arm. "Do you think hearing of such things would concern me?"

He studied her face, the way her eyes narrowed as she considered what he said. "I'm not sure it should be of your concern. I was raised to believe estate matters were the husband's duty to provide a comfortable life for his wife."

She scoffed. "What nonsense. I grew up at Raeford Court as much as you did." She laughed and flung out a hand as she paced away from him. "In fact, I would say I spent even more time there after you and Andrew went off to Eton and

74

Oxford." She spun around. "I was the one who stopped Duchess from painting the marble floors in the vestibule green and blue."

He blinked. "She was going to paint the marble floors green and blue?"

She let out a breath as though expelling a particularly painful memory. "She wished to create the effect of a pond as visitors entered the front door."

He rubbed at the back of his neck. "How odd. I thank you for stopping her."

She shrugged. "Her idea held merit, I'll give her that. It would have looked beautiful. Just perhaps not in the foyer of the ancestral home of such an old title." Her smile was pained but forgiving, and he laughed.

"Duchess always has the best of intentions, and who can really fault her for wanting to see them realized?"

Johanna's smile melted into something soft and nostalgic. "I should like to see Duchess again. I miss her terribly."

Ben's heart twisted until he was sure it would rip to shreds from the sheer force of guilt. "I should think she'd like to see you as well."

She stepped closer, her footing somehow slowed.

"You're not coming back to town then when you leave, are you? With so much work to be done at Raeford, I assume it will hold your attentions for some time?"

What was she really asking him? Minerva had enjoyed manipulating him, and he'd grown used to studying each word carefully for its hidden agenda. For surely there was one.

With Johanna, he found there wasn't though. What she was asking was simple.

Was he going to come back?

For her.

His heart raced at the idea. He could have her. He knew it.

Right now he could ask her to marry him and be done with this entire charade. But even as he thought it, he caught sight of the bouquets filling the room, the debris of the scattered suitors.

No. He had to do everything he could to ensure her answer. Ensure his future. Ensure the future of Raeford Court.

He closed the distance between them and tilted her chin up with a single finger.

"Johanna Darby, are you saying you'll miss me?"

Her laugh was short and instant, and he couldn't help but smile at the incredulity on her face.

"I said no such thing." But a smile slipped to her lips as she teased him.

He searched her eyes. "I think you said exactly that."

She wrenched her chin from his grasp. "I did not." Now she bit her lower lip as if to stop the smile entirely as they both understood how much of a child she'd sounded like just then.

"I still believe you did." He crossed his arms over his chest, assuming a position of authority.

She put her hands to her hips. "It's your word against mine."

"Well, in that case, I win. They'll never believe you. You're a girl."

Her eyes widened as her mouth flew open in outrage. "I hate it when you're right."

He shrugged. "I know."

He turned and headed for the door before she could say anything further.

"Where are you going?"

He stopped at the door, turning to look at her over his shoulder. "Do I hear a note of desperation in your voice?"

Her lips thinned before she spoke. "You know I do not

enjoy being kept waiting. Do you think to leave me all alone in my own agitation?"

He raised an eyebrow. "That's up to you." He gestured to the room. "We can stay here and wait to hear word of your sister and her family, or..." He purposely let his words trail off.

"Or?" The hope that sounded in that single word had him smiling.

They may have grown older, but Johanna hadn't really changed. She still yearned for adventure. It only saddened him to realize he didn't know what that was like anymore. To throw all caution to the wind and strike out on nothing more than instinct.

It hadn't been his choice in so long he wouldn't know how.

"Or you could come with me."

He saw her take the bait. Her face transformed into a tense mixture of longing and practicality.

"Andrew said—"

"Andrew asked me to keep you company. He didn't say where to do so." He leaned ever so slightly toward her, pitching his voice hypnotically low. "After all, it's only me."

The words had their desired effect, and her shoulders went back, her chin going up.

"Then I suppose whatever is to happen will be Andrew's fault for not being more careful with his little sister." She marched to the door and flung him a playful glance. "Where are we going?"

He smiled. "You'll see."

CHAPTER 6

*S*he stared out the carriage window at the workers carrying planks and buckets heavy with sod and concrete.

"You've brought me to a building site."

His laugh was full in the confines of the carriage.

He leaned forward to peer out the window with her, and she loved how he always smelled of fresh air and leather.

"I have brought you to the greatest collection of written works yet known in the modern world. One day it shall be called the British Museum."

She sat back. "Well, that's rather lofty."

He grinned. "I know how you admire lofty things."

"I do no such thing," she said.

He laughed again. "Do please try to tell me you are not impressed with this." He gestured out the window at the building activity, and she followed his gaze.

It *was* an impressive sight.

She recalled the King's Library being completed years previously, but the new wings being built were a sight to see. To imagine the museum would be so grand one day.

"Do you think they will have enough things with which to fill the exhibit halls?" She turned her attention to Ben.

His expression was not unlike hers when she stumbled upon a particularly quiet and peaceful bend in a stream.

Awe. Wonder. Energy.

There was something about seeing such feats, natural and manmade, that made her blood sing, and Ben knew it. Of course, he did.

Her ears still rang with the endless quips she had endured from her gentlemen callers regarding the weather, the state of her gown and hair, and the way the sunshine landed dewy on her lips. She touched a gloved hand to her lips now. Sunshine should not be *dewy* no matter where it landed.

She wanted none of that and desired only to spend time with Ben. Ben knew her. He understood her. And this—

Well, this was perfect.

What better place in which to get lost while her mind worried over her sister and the baby.

"Thank you." She spoke the words softly, but even then, it seemed to catch him by surprise.

His smile was somehow hesitant as he said, "You're welcome."

"Shall we go inside?" He moved to open the door, but she stilled him with a hand.

"I haven't a chaperone."

"It's only me," he said with a particularly vexing gyration of eyebrows. "Besides, I've waited five years for this. I won't let you hold me back now with your silly nonsense."

"Five years?" She blinked. "You mean you wished to go to this museum the whole of your time in America? Why wouldn't you just go while you were here?"

His eyes darkened even as the rest of his expression remained unchanged. "Before I left, one was required to have an acquaintance in a position of power to gain entrance."

"Not something readily accessible to the second son of a duke," she muttered, reality settling on her shoulders like an itchy wool cloak.

He shrugged. "They changed the terms of admittance just as I left for America and opened the collections to anyone. I've wanted to exercise my right to enter their hallowed halls since then."

"But you're a duke now." She couldn't have lowered her voice any more or he wouldn't have heard it, but it was as though she'd fired a cannon in the close confines of the carriage.

"So they say." He glanced out the window. "Are you coming with me or will you let outdated rules of propriety keep you from having an adventure?"

She pushed his hand away from the door. "Excuse me, Your Grace." She shoved the door open and stepped down.

It was much louder once she was outside the carriage, and she paused to gain her footing. The edifice before her buzzed with workmen carrying out their trades. The beginnings of a porticoed colonnade could be deciphered amongst the scaffolding as masons climbed their heights. It would be a grand building once it was finished, but she couldn't imagine it would be complete anytime soon.

She turned to Ben who had stepped down beside her.

"Can you imagine such a grand structure right here in London?"

"You should see the buildings they are constructing in America. I've heard claims that one day they'll touch the sky."

She frowned. "Surely, you can't be serious. How is one to climb so high up?"

He shrugged. "Someone must come up with a method for transport obviously. I don't think the average person's stride could attain such a feat."

She peered back up at the scaffolding that harnessed the

skeleton of the building. It was so terribly high up, but her mind could not fathom a means of transport to such height.

She took Ben's arm. "I think I should very much like to see some old, dusty books."

He helped her traverse the rutted pavement where carts and workhorses had punctured the masonry. They climbed the steps to the library, and she welcomed the sudden deafening of sound as they stepped inside.

While it was a quiet library, the architecture was no less impressive, and she found her gaze traveling upward. It was lucky she was still holding on to Ben's arm as she could not have said in the least what the entrance looked like. Her attention was so fixed on the murals canvassing the ceiling above them, it was only Ben preventing her from running into other patrons.

She prodded Ben to look up. "It reminds me of Raeford."

Ben nodded in agreement as he led them deeper into the building. Raeford Court had splendid murals painted into the plaster of its high ceilings. Duchess had once threatened to paint over one with a shepherd scene, but again, Johanna had stopped her. She smiled at the memory.

They passed into a large central corridor, and she stopped completely as though her feet had become affixed to the floor.

Shelves of books rose up in towering magnificence toward the plaster ceiling, which itself was festooned with intricate medallions. Light poured from the tall windows set high on the walls of the balconied floor above, interspersed with even more towering bookcases.

Everywhere she looked there were library ladders and reading tables, chairs and sofas set for study and quiet reflection, and through the whole of it ran a brilliant hardwood floor inlaid with a darker wood that set off the reading tables and nooks.

"It's so beautiful," she whispered.

"It is."

At the sound of his voice, she looked quickly at him, drinking in the way he watched her with such abandon. He wasn't speaking of the library, she knew, and not for the first time in the past several days, she was overwhelmed with the wonder that this was all not just a dream.

They slipped into the stream of people milling about the room, some in obvious search of a particular work while others merely strolled, observing the quality of the building around them.

"Is it everything you imagined it to be?" she asked after some time.

They had reached the opposite end of the room where the library branched off into several smaller rooms that housed even more of King George III's collection.

"It's even better," he said.

She smiled. "You like dusty, old books so much?"

"I like you so much."

Her smile evaporated at the heat in his voice.

Her mind still hadn't come to terms with her new reality. Ben was here, with her, and he looked at her with such heat, kissed her with such possession. None of it could be real and yet it was.

He was leaving next week.

It all seemed far too rushed to consider talk of marriage, and he was very clear in the work that needed to be done on the estate. He didn't have time for a wife by his standards, and yet.

"Why are you not mourning your wife?"

She shouldn't have asked the question, and she hated how the light left his eyes at her words. She didn't believe what he had said. That duty compelled him to move on. Ben was loyal to tradition and the needs of others, and he would never neglect a custom such as mourning.

He continued to move them out of the main room and into the smaller Long Room with its crowded bookcases and spiral wrought iron staircases. It was quieter here, and she thought maybe he would answer her.

"My wife was not a kind woman, Johanna. I don't wish to speak of her to you."

She stopped so abruptly he was several feet in front of her before he realized it, his arm tugging against her stopped one. He released her and turned, his eyes on hers.

"Really, Ben? You would act so cruelly to me."

"I mean no cruelty, Johanna."

"Then why do you not confide in me? I am your friend, aren't I?"

Lud, she wished she were more, but Ben had not so much as hinted at offering for her. He had asked Andrew for permission to court her, and yet he planned to leave next week. What was the man about? Would he attempt to court her from Raeford Court?

What nonsense.

She had not waited her whole life for this to be courted via letter.

She watched him as he seemed to consider what he may say, and her heart thudded in her chest. It was as though they were poised somewhere between childhood and adulthood, and he had to make the step to determine what they would be.

Would they forever be childhood friends? Her older brother's best friend always attempting to keep her from harm?

Or would she be more to him? Would she be his confidant? Would she be his lover? His wife?

Her throat tightened at the possibility, and yet she

cautioned herself not to raise her hopes too high. He had married another once, after all.

"Johanna." He said her name as though it caused him pain, and that was enough for her to understand.

She picked up her skirts and moved around him, striding off down the row of books, welcoming the comfort of the tall bookcases and the muted quiet of the sacred space as her heart pounded and her stomach twisted.

She wasn't surprised when he grabbed her arm, and when she turned, she had her words ready. "Why did you ask my brother for permission to court me if you planned to leave? Do not play with my emotions, Ben. I don't deserve it." She hated how her words twisted with unshed tears, but she was tired of being ignored, tired of waiting in the shadows for someone to notice her, tired of always being left behind.

Something must have struck him, her words or the feeling behind them, because he looked about them as if ensuring their privacy, and holding a finger to his lips, pulled her farther down the row of bookcases until they slipped through another door.

They had crossed into some kind of storage room. Here the shelves were crammed rather than ordered as if on display. The light was not grand, and no ladders dotted the bookcase shelves.

It was also utterly quiet.

They were alone.

She readied herself for his denial, but he gripped her by the shoulders and held her attention. "I did not marry my first wife of my own free will. Minerva was a vile woman, and I do not mourn her death."

The vehemence with which he spoke shocked her, but a pain sliced through her at their meaning. "Ben," she whispered, but she couldn't say what she felt so suddenly.

She hadn't known. She'd thought he had been happily

wed, that he mourned his wife. But he hadn't. Pain and worse, terror etched their way in the tight lines of his face, and she thought she might be sick.

She wanted nothing more than to ask what he meant. Not of his free will? There were only certain circumstances that required two people to wed against their will, and somehow she couldn't believe that of Ben. He wouldn't have gotten Minerva pregnant out of wedlock. Would he?

"How do you mean vile?" she asked instead.

He let go of her to pace away, and she saw the way his jacket pulled against his broad shoulders with coiled tension.

"She denied me things a husband should expect of his wife."

She swallowed, her mouth going so dry she thought she might choke. For an instant, she felt regret at having pushed him into this conversation. These were obviously the things kept sacred between husband and wife, and she'd over-stepped.

But Ben was her friend.

"She wouldn't let me touch her. Any visit I made to her bedchamber was scheduled like I was nothing more than a visit to the modiste to her." He spun back toward her, and she recoiled at the hatred on his face.

Her beautiful, peaceful Ben so full of hate. It wasn't possible. This wasn't possible. How could she have done this to him?

"She told me she was disgusted to have been forced to marry someone so low." He spat the words now, and she regretted so much causing him to return to his pain.

Forced.

The word echoed in her mind.

"I hadn't seen her for more than social necessities in the two years before her death, and even then it wasn't much. She took to her rooms entirely when the consumption grew too great." He scrubbed a hand over his face and turned away again.

She thought it was over. That she had wrenched the last of it from him.

But then he continued, almost too softly for her to hear. "She wrote me a letter when she knew she was dying." He laughed, and the sound was brittle and harsh. "She wouldn't let me see her, so she had her maid bring me a damn letter." The laugh this time was edged with something dangerous and uncontrollable. "She said her greatest regret was in marrying me. That she wouldn't have fallen to such depths had she married someone more worthy."

His voice faded away, and all at once the past several days came crashing back to her. The whispers and rumors. The Impostor Duke. The sudden interest in her from gentlemen who had ignored her for three seasons.

They were all reminders of what Minerva had told him.

Johanna was sick.

Sick with the cruelty of humanity. Sick with the way her friend's shoulders bent as if he were trying to comfort himself.

Sick with—

She stopped the litany in her head, marched forward and grabbed his shoulder, spinning him around.

"Who the hell cares what they think," she said and pulled his head down for a scorching kiss.

* * *

HE HAD to purposefully overcome the shock to get his body to respond.

Her words combined with her actions left him stunned and yearning. Years of manipulation and hatred poured out of him as if it never existed at all, leaving nothing more than an echo of what it had been. He felt it; he saw it. And unlike the damage he had felt before then, he thought this he might be able to conquer.

He gave himself to her for the first time. All of himself.

He had never considered Johanna, but then after Minerva, he hadn't considered anyone. But somehow with Johanna it was better. More. Greater.

Perfect.

It was more than a kiss. She wrapped herself around him with her whole body. Her fingers clawing at his shoulders, her chest heaving against his. Her leg—God, she'd wrapped one leg around him, her foot pressing into his calf as if she clung to him for sustenance.

Her kiss wasn't the gentle pairing of their previous encounters. She ate him up, and a thrill shot through him like lightning.

He wanted her.

The realization had him reeling back, but she wouldn't let go of him.

"Don't," she whispered against his lips. "Let me love you."

He didn't know what happened then. His heart tripped, and his body turned to liquid. He was hers. Completely and utterly.

He wrapped his arms around her, fisting his hands into the gown at her back. She moaned, arching into him so he could get a better grip.

He bent her back, encasing her in his arms as he took what he craved.

Her.

This.

Now.

He plundered her mouth, sweeping his tongue inside when her lips parted on a gasp. It had been so long. So long since he'd been this intimate with a woman, and his body sang as though awakening from a deep slumber. He left her mouth to kiss her temple, her closed eyes, her cheeks. He found the place behind her ear he feared he liked more than she did, but when she shivered against him, he couldn't help but smile, his lips still pressed to the sensitive spot.

"Ben." His name. So full. So throaty. So incredibly arousing.

He was hard.

He pulled back, sucked in a breath when he fully realized just how aroused he truly was. What was he doing? They were in the middle of the King's Library. People swarmed just outside. They could be caught at any moment.

And then her eyelids fluttered opened, and what he saw there ended him.

She wanted him too.

"Johanna." Her name was a question and a declaration all in one, but he didn't know what he was asking or to whom he was declaring his intent.

Was it to himself or was it to her?

A smile so seductive and sultry curved her lips, suddenly he knew precisely whom he was trying to convince, and it wasn't her.

He stepped back, air swept between them, but she grabbed the lapels of his jacket before he could escape. Before he could do the right thing.

"Ben," she said as if she needed to get his attention. "While I appreciate the fact that you respect me so much, I'm really going to need you to ravish me now."

He licked his lips, willed his body to calm. "Andrew—"

"Andrew gave you permission to court me."

"This isn't courting." She had a dusting a freckles across her nose. Had he known that?

"He asked you to watch after me today."

"I would be neglecting my duties if I—"

"You would be neglecting them if you didn't."

He let his gaze meet hers then, and he found nothing there but understanding and truth. She knew what she was doing, and she knew what she wanted.

Him.

The thought had him reeling again, and he raised his hands, cupped her face. "Johanna, you have no idea what you do to me."

She used her grip on the lapels of his jacket to pull him more snuggly against her, and then, minx that she was, she rolled her hips until she pressed against his hardness.

"I think I have some idea."

She kissed him softly while his mind sifted through all that was happening. He could have her, and she would let him. She would *enjoy* it. He was sure of that.

Guilt crept along the back of his neck for he knew the truth of the thing. He needed her to accept his suit, yes, but it was more than that.

He wanted to feel what it was like to have someone want him.

Him.

Ben.

The second son who was never quite good enough.

None of those reasons made this about her, and he hated himself for it.

The light from the skylights overhead dappled her face in light and shadow, and he watched, transfixed by the way he could only see her face in pieces. Beautiful pieces that made an even more stunning whole.

He wanted her.

And right then, that was all that mattered.

He pressed his lips to hers, eliciting a moan that sent a thrill down his legs. His hands found her waist, and he fitted her snuggly against him. He swallowed her gasp, pleasure spiking through him.

She wasn't the only one who could tease.

He wasn't sure how, but he found he'd pressed her against one of the bookcases, and she came up on her toes, melding herself to him.

He tore his mouth from hers. "Johanna, you must know—"

"I do. I've read Eliza's manuals on the breeding of puppies. I know how the act works."

He swallowed, his throat closing on words. "That's not what I meant."

Her head fell back against the bookcase, pushing her hat into her eyes, which she shoved away with one hand.

"Then what is it?"

He opened his mouth, but he found himself searching for words as he studied her. Finally he said, "I promise I will make it right."

She watched him, her eyes pinched in confusion, but as he wasn't sure what *right* meant in this situation, he couldn't say more.

He took her lips as his hands began to explore like he'd wanted to the previous night. He outlined her curves and felt the responding ripple of her muscles. Finally, he let his lips follow the path he'd discovered previously. Down the column of her neck, along her collarbone. He grazed her with his teeth, and she bucked against him, her back slamming into the bookcase.

"Ben," she groaned.

This time he didn't stop at the edge of her bodice. He pushed the capped sleeve of her gown from her shoulder, freeing her bosom enough that he could wrench the fabric down.

"Oh God." He hadn't meant to say it out loud, but—

Jesus, she had a fine bosom.

Her smile was wicked when he finally looked up to meet her gaze.

"Are you just going to look? Because I'll be very disappointed if you are."

"I never knew how sultry you were."

Her grin was lopsided. "You never gave me the chance."

He felt a stab of guilt, for the past and the future, but he bent his head anyway, running his lips over one breast and then the other before sucking her nipple into his mouth.

Her hands were in his hair, her fingernails scraping in delicious trails as she arched against him.

He gave the other nipple equal attention but his hands were already moving, lifting her skirts until—

He pulled back. "You're wearing silk stockings," he gasped.

She blinked. "Yes. Ladies do tend to wear them."

He couldn't have said if Minerva had ever worn silk stockings. He only knew he'd never been privy to finding them on a lady before, and he was rather overcome at the notion.

But then Johanna reached between them, her hand caressing the bulge at the front of his trousers, and he forgot everything entirely.

"Johanna."

"You seem distracted."

He growled before returning his attention to her breasts, his hand continuing its journey up her leg.

He found the delicious space of bare skin at the top of her stocking, and he traced it with a single finger. She opened for him. Her leg falling to the side as she let him explore her.

He couldn't wait any longer. He found the slit in her pantalets and slipped his hand inside. She was warm and downy, and—

Incredibly wet.

He moaned against her breast but forced himself to concentrate.

She was so wet his fingers slipped between her folds with ease.

"Ben." Her voice held a note of question, and he raised his head to press a soft kiss to her lips.

"Trust me," he whispered.

He slipped one finger inside of her, and her eyes flew open, her fingers digging into his shoulders.

"Ben?"

"Yes, dear?" He couldn't help the grin that tipped his lips at the look of concentration that overcame her.

"This wasn't in the manuals."

"I should think not," he said before pressing his lips to hers once more.

When he slipped a second finger inside of her, her hips came away from the bookcase, driving herself into him, rubbing his throbbing penis.

"Johanna," he moaned, gritting his teeth to hold on to the shreds that remained of his control.

He hadn't been this aroused, this incredibly close to the edge since he was an unschooled dandy at Oxford. Even then, what he was doing now made him appear a right monk while at school.

Her hips began to move, and she rubbed herself against the palm of his hand, a moan escaping her lips.

He couldn't bear anything further. He slipped his fingers free and found her sensitive nub, rubbing it in ever shrinking circles with his fingers slick with her own wetness.

She pushed against his shoulders to leverage herself up, tilting her hips forward as she braced herself against the bookcase.

"Oh God, please, Ben," she gasped.

He rubbed furiously now, the bud hard under his fingers. He captured her mouth, containing her kisses. He had not forgotten that they hovered on the edge of discovery, and it only served to drive his pleasure into a frenzy.

When she came, her mouth opened against his, her arms wrapped around his shoulders, and she arched into him, her entire body embracing his. He could feel her heart pounding, see the pulse rabbiting at her neck as she sucked in a breath.

He'd done that to her.

He'd given her pleasure.

He wasn't sure how long it was before her eyes opened again, before she registered he was there, when a slow satisfied smile spread across her lips.

"Benedict Carver," she whispered.

"Johanna Darby?" He rested his forehead against hers, reveling in the way her hands clutched in the fabric of his jacket at the small of his back.

"I do believe you could write a manual of your own."

He laughed.

As unthinkable as it was, in that moment, his fingers still against her mound, as they huddled against a bookcase in the King's Library, he laughed. But then, she always could make him laugh.

He leaned far enough away to see her face. "I'm afraid I'm not one to share my secrets."

She pouted. "What a pity for other women."

He wasn't sure why as he knew she'd meant the statement playfully, but for the first time in his life, he felt like he was enough.

More than enough.

He slipped his hand free and carefully let her skirts fall back into place. When he stepped back, releasing her at the last possible moment, she almost looked as though they had done nothing more than view the library's collection.

She adjusted her hat the slightest bit, her hair still pinned in place, and he wiped his hand with a handkerchief, still unable to believe how wet he'd made her.

If only he could banish Minerva from the recesses of his mind forever.

He tucked away the soiled handkerchief and offered her his arm. "I believe it's time for us to return to the house, don't you think?"

She nodded and took his arm. "I expect my brother shall be looking for me."

When they left the library and he handed her up into the carriage, he couldn't help but think how not long ago a day like that wouldn't have been possible.

A day where he'd laughed.

A day where he'd enjoyed the company of a beautiful woman.

A day where he'd felt like anything but the unworthy second son.

CHAPTER 7

She didn't sleep that night.

How was she expected to?

Louisa had delivered a healthy, and according to Eliza, loud baby boy they named Simon Victor Sebastian Clive Fielding. Johanna had never heard a better name for a tiny earl.

Mother and babe were said to be doing well, but the new father had required a bit of shoring up at the sight of his newborn son.

Johanna smiled into the dark. She'd always known Sebastian was a softy at heart.

But while her mind wandered around the idea of her new nephew, it kept floating back to Ben.

To the things he had done to her, true, but more than that.

The foundations of several of her beliefs had been shifted, and now she was left to ruminate on them if she were not to sleep.

Ben hadn't loved Minerva. No, that wasn't it. Minerva had been cruel and withheld affection and praise. Did Ben still love her? Was that why the evidence of his pain seemed so great and deep? Or was it only that it was still so new?

Forced.

The word kept playing over and over again in her head, and she wondered at all its possible meanings. But even though forced into marriage, Ben could still have loved Minerva.

She didn't know why she needed to know whether or not he loved her, but she did. It twisted inside of her chest until it ached, and she pressed a hand to it.

She shouldn't care if he had loved his wife or not. The more important matter was whether or not he loved her, Johanna. While he had shown great affection for her, he had never uttered any words of affection or dare she say, love. A small part of her worried over it, but the part of her that had cracked open at the realization of her secret love and that now shone with the light of a thousand suns—that part ignored her practical half.

She just wanted to wallow in her newfound happiness and not think of what the future might bring.

Because Ben was leaving.

He'd said as much, and even when she'd confronted him on the subject, he had not immediately proposed marriage. He was just...leaving.

She wasn't sure if love were this complicated or if Ben were simply obtuse. For surely he understood that his words and actions had left her conflicted. She knew he cared for her, but how much?

She sighed and turned over, tucking the pillow more firmly beneath her cheek.

She could see the night sky through a crack in the drapes, and she wasn't surprised to see it had lightened to a muted gray, the in-between color the sky took on right before the sun would flood it with light.

She groaned. How was she to get through another day of callers and promenading with no sleep? It was difficult enough to listen to Lord Blevens drone on about his waist-coat collection when she'd been well rested. Now it was likely to be her doom.

If only Ben…

She sat up.

If only Ben would ask for her hand.

She sat back against the headboard, drawing her knees up to her chest and focused on the crack in the drapes.

She'd never really considered it. Oh, most certainly in her dreams. She'd pictured her wedding to Ben a thousand times over. But this wasn't her dreams. This was her future. Her very real future, and she'd never before thought of Ben in it.

Because it hadn't been a possibility until only recently.

Did she wish to marry him in truth?

Her heart sang at the question, and she knew her answer. So why hadn't he asked her?

Again, her mind worried over the same litany of questions. Surely this was doing her no good.

She shoved aside the bedclothes, determined to find something productive with which to spend her time if she weren't to sleep but also to distract her mind from useless worrying.

She had pivoted to drop her feet to the floor when the first sound pierced the quiet of the sleeping house.

She stilled, her hand on the bedclothes, her feet suspended in the air.

The sound came again.

Her gaze flew to the windows.

Someone was throwing pebbles at her window.

A smile came to her lips as she dropped to the floor and hurried to throw the drapes aside.

When she got the heavy leaded window open, it was to

find the gardens below cloaked in shadows until one shadow separated itself from the others.

Ben.

She could see the white of his teeth clearly through the dark as he peered up at her.

"What are you doing?" she hissed, struggling to keep the laughter from her voice.

"Get dressed," he called up in a whisper. "As if you were going for a ride at Raeford."

She stilled, her hands curling around the windowsill.

A ride at Raeford? But that would mean—

"Ben, I can't—"

He spread his arms. "No one is awake to see you, darling. Hurry up. I'll meet you in the mews."

She would have done anything when he called her *darling*. She waved to let him know she understood, and as she eased the window shut, she saw him disappear through the hedges toward the back gate of the garden that would lead into the mews.

She tiptoed to the trunk at the end of her bed. Why she was tiptoeing she couldn't say. Andrew's rooms were entirely on the other side of the house, and the servants were all abed. Who was to hear her in the massive house?

She threw back the leather straps that latched the trunk shut and pushed open the lid. Her worn trousers and jacket were just visible in the dimness. She tugged them free and went about getting ready. She shucked her nightdress but grabbed a chemise to put under the rough footman's clothing. Soon she had on trousers, shirt, and jacket and was stuffing her feet into boots as she made her way to the door.

Her hair hung slack over one shoulder in a loose braid as she carefully opened the door and poked her head into the corridor.

The house buzzed with silence, and soon the beat of her

own heart filled her ears. She slipped out, shutting the door carefully behind her. Her boots were well worn, and the soft leather made no noise as she made her way down the corridor to the stairs.

Ravenwood House was built around a central staircase, and she peered over the balcony, looking up and down for anyone who might see her.

Silence and emptiness greeted her. She kept going.

She made it to the kitchens without incident and headed down the corridor that would lead to the mews. She'd almost made it when a looming figure stepped directly in front of her. The startled cry caught in her throat and came out as nothing more than a strangled cough.

Mallard, their butler, held out a coat and hat.

"It's rather chilly this morning, my lady. You'll require these, I imagine."

Johanna eyed him. She reached tentatively for the garments, a smile easing to her lips.

"Thank you, Mallard," she said as if he were doing nothing more than handing her the day's post. "I shall be quick. I think," she added when she realized she didn't exactly know what Ben was about.

Mallard gave a nod. "No worries, my lady. I shall keep any questioners at bay until you've returned."

Her smile grew more confident, and she returned Mallard's nod. "Thank you," she said, and he stepped aside to allow her the door.

The early dawn air was biting as Mallard had predicted, and she was glad to nestle in the over-large coat he had given her. She wrapped her braid up into the hat that hung low on her head and waited until her eyes adjusted to the darkness.

She heard the whinny of horses before she saw them standing at the edge of the stable.

"Ben," she breathed.

He'd brought her own horse.

It stomped its feet impatiently, its breath freezing into puffs in the early morning air.

She reached for it before she'd even greeted Ben.

"I see how it's going to be. I bring her a horse, and she neglects me entirely," he muttered.

She ran her hand down the gelding's nose, transfixed by its wondrous eyes. "You don't give me the freedom a horse can," she replied, sending him a wicked grin.

He wrapped an arm around her waist and tugged her to him for a brief, intense kiss.

"I will steal my affection from you then if I must." His own smile was devilish in the muted dawn. "Shall we?" He backed away to indicate the horse.

She made to mount the gelding but looked at him. "Your Grace, you must forgive me for my impertinence, but it isn't every morning that I am awakened by a duke to run off into the dawn." She looked down. "Wearing trousers no less. Where exactly are we going?"

His smile was pure mischievousness. "You'll see."

He went around his own horse to mount it, leaving her to wonder at his cryptic words. She slipped her foot in the stirrup and pulled herself up with ease, her muscles flexing in memory. Her body sang with familiarity, and her knees tightened ever so slightly against the horse's flanks. The gelding tossed its head in eagerness.

"What is his name?"

Ben nudged his horse to start them down the alley that led between the back of the houses.

"I haven't the foggiest idea."

She looked sharply at him as she turned the gelding to follow.

"What do you mean?"

"My brother apparently won two geldings in a hand of

whist, and your horse is one of them. The groom doesn't know where they came from or even their names. I suppose you can name him if you wish."

She studied the gelding's ears, the ripple of muscle along its strong neck.

"I couldn't possibly rename him if he's already been given a name."

Ben shrugged. "Then I suppose he shall remain nameless."

She didn't very well like that either. She pondered the horse's ears until they'd reached the cross street.

"I suppose I shall call him Horse because that's what he is, and I shan't be in danger of stepping upon a name he's already been given."

Ben's laugh was soft. "That sounds so entirely like you, Johanna."

She looked up swiftly to find him watching her, his gaze soft but with a touch of something harder. Perhaps melancholy? How odd.

She smiled to banish it from his expression. "I wouldn't wish to disappoint you by being anyone else."

Her words had the opposite effect, and his expression hardened with some inner torment as he looked away. He had turned onto the street proper by then and coaxed his horse into a trot.

She looked behind them. "We're not going to the park?"

Now his expression was quizzical. "Of course not. Do you wish to ride in a manufactured greenery such as the park?"

"Well, no. But what else is there?"

He didn't answer her. He smiled, a wicked glint in his eye, as he bent over his horse and spurred the animal into a gallop. He was several meters ahead of her when she realized what he was about, and then her lips curved into its own wicked grin.

She leaned over and whispered into Horse's ear, "Let's remind him who is the better rider, shall we?"

Horse seemed to sense her intent, his muscles coiling in anticipation.

And then she gave him his head.

The thing about riding was that there was no other experience like it on earth, and just then, in the predawn hours in the deserted streets of London, Lady Johanna Darby gloried in it.

She and Horse blew by Ben within seconds, the animal beneath her stretching his legs in a way that exhibited its natural prowess, that allowed its innate abilities to spring free as if he were once more wild.

And Johanna.

She loosened her muscles, flowing until she became one with the horse, and then they were together, racing out of London into the countryside. Buildings were replaced with trees and stone fences, the cobblestones of the street were replaced with dirt roads. And finally, the haze of London lifted, and they were surrounded by crisp fresh air.

She slowed Horse to a trot, letting him shake off the exertion of the gallop and draw his own clear breath. She peered about them at the fields dotted with trees and fresh turned earth. She could see a row of cottages in the distance, but she was struck by how quickly one could escape the confines of London.

If only one were chaperoned.

Or embarking on a sinful expedition with the man of her dreams.

She turned in the saddle to find Ben coming up behind them. She could see him more clearly now in the lightening sky. His hair was mussed from the wind, his collar open at his throat as he wore no cravat. He was half-dressed, carrying about him a relaxed air she could almost feel.

This was the Ben she remembered, and her heart beat faster at the sight of him.

"Is this what you had in mind?" she asked when he drew close enough to hear her.

"Almost," he said with a grin as he trotted past her.

She followed, growing ever more comfortable in the saddle.

They crested a hill and acres of farmland spread out before her, but Ben turned off the road there, following the ridge of the hill until they found themselves approaching a line of trees that had been left as a natural divider between fields.

Only then did Ben slow and dismount, dropping the reins so his horse could nose the ground for foodstuffs. She did the same, dropping to the ground with a graceful leap, her muscles tightening in the way she had always enjoyed after a good exercise. She let Horse follow Ben's steed into the pasture to nuzzle at the ground before coming up behind the man in question and slipping her arms about his waist as he faced away from her.

"Have you brought me out here to ruin me?"

His laugh was brief and self-deprecating. "I'm afraid I have already done that." He turned, drawing her into his arms, holding her so she could see the same view he did.

The sun was on the cusp of rising, and the fields had taken on the orangey glow of near dawn. There was no wind here where they stood in the shelter of the trees, and for a moment, she could believe it was just the two of them.

"I know it's not the stars you miss, but I hope it's enough."

She picked up her head from his chest. "What is enough?"

And then she heard it, and her heart squeezed with so much love for this man.

Morning song.

It happened all at once in the way only truly spectacular

things do. The sun spilled over the edge of the horizon as the birds greeted the new day with their chirps and whistles. It was a sound so familiar from her early mornings at Raeford Court that she had to bite her cheek to keep the tears of nostalgia at bay.

She recalled his words from that night in the garden. This is what he missed, and he'd given it to her.

This.

He had done this for her.

She peered up at him to find him watching her, and she knew no matter how she tried some tears would find their way to her eyes.

She tried to smile but even that came out watery.

"Why?" she whispered. "Why would you bring me here? No one has ever done anything so kind for me."

His smile was soft, and he reached up to cup her cheek.

"Because I couldn't think of any place better where I could ask you to marry me."

* * *

IT WAS PERFECT.

He knew it would be because he knew Johanna. It didn't matter if the rest of the *ton* tried to stop him by flooding her with attention. No one could overcome the expert knowledge he'd acquired over years of friendship with her.

Minerva would have admired his manipulation. Bile rose in his throat, and he swallowed it down. He would spend the rest of his life making sure Johanna was happy even if he couldn't love her.

He'd told her the estate needed improvements. He'd made her aware of the work to be done. He'd only neglected to tell her the entire truth. Surely it wasn't as sinful as lying to her outright.

The way he and Minerva had lied to the world.

It took all his strength to keep his face relaxed, his expression encouraging and hopeful. She peered up at him, her lips parted in surprise, her eyes searching his face as if she couldn't quite believe what he'd just said.

He couldn't quite believe it either.

When he'd learned he'd inherited the title, he knew it would die with him because he would never remarry and produce an heir. Yet here he was. Standing on a knoll, surrounded by the sunrise and birdsong, asking one of his oldest and dearest friends to marry him.

Because he needed her dowry.

The thought cut as he knew he would be required to meet with Andrew to discuss the marriage contracts, and Ben would feel like an absolute bastard for deceiving his friend even as he salivated over what Johanna's dowry could mean for the Raeford estate.

Finally, it wouldn't matter that he was second born.

Finally, he could do all those things he had dreamed for Raeford.

Finally, he would be his own man.

He just had to crush the heart of the person he held most dear.

She blinked. "Did you just ask me to marry you?"

He couldn't help but tease her a little longer even though his heart was shriveling to death inside of him. "I do not believe I asked you as such. I merely stated that this would be the ideal setting in which to do so." He gestured around them at the idyllic surroundings.

She pushed against his chest with both hands as if to gain a better view of him. "But you do plan to ask me? To marry you, that is."

He still held her elbows in his grip, and he shook her a little.

"I would ask if you allowed me to do so."

She pulled out of his grasp, tugging the floppy, oversized hat she'd been wearing from her head, freeing her dark hair. It stood up in places from rubbing against the hat, and her eyes were wild as she attempted to push it down.

"But you can't ask me now." She gestured to her clothing. "Not when I'm dressed like this." She looked back up at him, her nostrils flaring now. "In trousers."

"I happen to like you in trousers."

He did too. They perfectly accentuated her bottom, and before yesterday, he hadn't known how much he would have enjoyed seeing it so perfectly silhouetted.

Before yesterday, he wouldn't have known a lot of things. Like the way his body responded to hers. That it *could* respond. When had she stopped being his best friend's little sister and started being simply Johanna? He didn't know, and he didn't really care.

He wanted her, and that made him wonder if perhaps their marriage wouldn't be all that terrible.

But it would be founded on a lie, and that was something he would need to live with for the rest of his life.

Could he?

It needn't matter for he must.

She said nothing in response, her mouth opening farther in disbelief. He took that moment to kneel before her, careful to keep his gaze locked on hers. She still held her hands in front of her as she gestured to her trousers, and he took them now in his own.

"Johanna Elizabeth Darby—"

"Stop talking." Her words were frantic, and her hands squeezed his.

He looked about them. "Why?"

"Because I'm trying to memorize this moment. I want to remember it forever."

He died just then.

Kneeling on the ground in the middle of a field outside of London, he died at Johanna Darby's feet.

And then he almost told her the truth.

Almost.

At the last possible moment, fear gripped him.

Fear of ruining this moment for her. Fear of destroying her dreams. He wanted it to be true. He wanted this moment to be real. She thought it was, and maybe that was enough.

"Am I allowed to continue?"

"Yes, but slowly."

"Johanna." He paused.

She shook their entwined hands. "Not that slowly."

He found himself smiling, even at this moment when he was nothing more than a cad. "Johanna Elizabeth Darby," he tried again. "Would you do me the immense honor of marrying—"

"Yes!" She threw herself at him.

She was on her knees, her arms wrapped around his neck, her lips on his, before he could draw another breath. Heat flooded him as she took control of the kiss, her hands slipping up the back of his neck, her fingers burying themselves in his hair.

His thoughts fell away when she touched him. The recriminations, the self-loathing. It all seemed to disappear when she kissed him, when she held him.

When she made him feel as though he were worthy of her attentions.

She shoved the jacket from his shoulders before he realized what she was doing and before long she'd discarded her own coat. The oversized garment lay spread on the ground behind her, and he couldn't help it. He pulled them down on top of it.

She sprawled across his chest, her thick dark hair falling

over one shoulder. He peered up at her, almost as though he couldn't believe she was quite real.

"You're beautiful," he said, and for once, he didn't feel like a bastard because it was the truth.

She was so, so beautiful.

And he was an idiot.

But try as he might, he couldn't bring his lifeless heart to respond, he couldn't stir in himself the very thing that would make all of this better.

If only he could fall in love with her.

He pulled her down to him, sealing their fate with a kiss that had him hardening even as it took away his breath. It was a moment before he realized she'd started on his shirt, yanking it from his trousers before she went to work on the buttons at his throat. Her hands were everywhere, and he let her explore until he couldn't bear it any longer.

He gripped her waist and rolled them until he was on top. She gave a startled gasp, but then he settled his mouth at her throat, and the gasp turned to a moan. She smelled of the wind and damp earth and life, and he buried himself in it, trailing kisses down her neck until he reached the buttons at the neck of her shirt.

He braced himself above her.

"Do you know I've seen you in this outfit probably a hundred times or more, and I've never once thought how to get you out of it?" He traced the line where the shirt parted at the neck.

He watched her swallow, attempting to follow the line of his finger.

"Would you like me to assist you?" Her eyes flashed upward to meet his, and the heat in them was scorching.

He leaned down and with a careful twist, slipped a button free. He pressed his lips to the exposed skin, and her hands flew to his head, holding him captive. He slipped another button free, another kiss. Her hips squirmed, grinding against him, and he moaned her name.

She squirmed with greater intent the next time, and he reared back, capturing her hips in both of his hands. She bit her lower lip as she peered up at him, and he stilled, drinking in the sight of her. He opened the neck of her shirt enough that an expanse of her creamy skin was visible, but it wasn't enough.

He tore at her clothing then, the shirt, the frock coat, the trousers. God, the trousers.

When he had thought to take her riding he was only thinking of how perfect it would be. He hadn't thought of the necessary attire.

She just as frantically pulled his shirt over his head, her hands tracing the muscles of his chest, eliciting another moan from him.

His hands stilled when they found the chemise she wore under her clothes.

"Attempting modesty?"

Her grin was anything but. "No matter my actions I am still a lady after all."

Right then she looked more than a lady. She was a goddess of the earth spread out beneath him, his for the taking.

He wanted to take her.

The thought was startling at the same time it wasn't. This was right. He could feel it, deep within him.

He covered her body with his, pressed kisses to her flesh until he met the obstacle of her chemise. He tugged just enough to free her breast, and he tormented the nipple until she arched against him, her nails digging into his back.

"Ben," she breathed, and he knew everything she meant with the single word.

He ran his hands up her sides, dipping beneath the thin

fabric of the chemise. He traced her soft belly, the indents of ribs, and finally he cupped her breast. Her hands scrambled, and she pushed him away enough to yank the chemise over her head.

He was rendered mute and motionless, his hands suspended from where she'd pushed them from her body in an attempt to remove the chemise.

She was naked.

Utterly and completely, spread before him like an offering.

She was giving herself to him. All of her. He would take it because he was greedy and selfish.

He swallowed and with a single finger traced the contour of breast, the valley of her breast bone, and the delicate curve of stomach. Her thighs were thick and muscular from riding, and he wondered what it would be like to have her on top of him.

One day.

They had all the rest of their lives now that she'd agreed to marry him.

The thought somehow cheapened the moment as he remembered what he was doing, and he resolutely cleared his mind. Whatever his intentions were he could honor her body with pleasure.

He stroked one thigh and then the other, his caress coming ever closer to the part he longed to touch. Would she be as wet for him today?

He captured her mouth as he let himself slip one finger inside of her. Just one. He made a come hither motion, and her hips came off the ground, grinding into him.

"Ben," she cried, tearing her lips from his. "Ben, please."

He backed away enough to see her. He studied her, the way her face was flush with desire, her lips swollen from his kisses.

She was going to marry him. It needn't matter what they did here today. He would make it right. He would always make it right.

He slid his finger out and circled her sensitive nub. He felt her tighten, felt her fingers claw at his shoulders. When he thought she might be at her brink, he slipped between her spread thighs.

He wasn't sure what to expect, but it wasn't that she would part her legs wider, pull him into her embrace.

"Ben, please," she said again, her voice not more than a whimper.

He sat up, undoing the buttons of his trousers as she watched him. He was quick about it, pushing his trousers to his knees and leaning over her once more, finding her sensitive nub with his fingers, parting her wet folds.

He pushed at her entrance, and her legs came up, locking around his hips.

"Oh God, Johanna," he breathed into her neck.

She gripped his shoulders. "Ben, I want..." Her voice trailed off.

Likely, she didn't know how to say what she wanted, but he knew how to give it.

He pushed inside of her in a single, smooth stroke, and she clenched around him in response.

"Ben." It was more breath than word, but he felt it echo through him.

"Johanna, I can't—God, I can't..." It was his turn to lack words. How could he tell her it had been so long since he'd been with a woman? He was like an unschooled young man again. He couldn't hold on.

He stroked her nub furiously, and her hips pumped against him, drawing him deeper into her.

Dear God, he was going to explode. The rush of sensation, the length of his deprivation, it roared at him relentlessly.

But finally, she came, dissolving around him in a tantalizing spiral of undulating muscles, and he was gone.

The release was intense, powerful, and it shook him.

He stayed perched above her until his arms shook with the effort, and finally he collapsed on the ground beside her, pulling her against him. Her head fell to his shoulder, her fingers absently tracing circles on his chest.

He stared up through the branches above them, but he couldn't have said what color the sky was or even what his name was just then as pleasure subsided from his body in pulsing waves.

"Are you all right?" he finally asked when he could draw a full breath.

He could almost feel her smile. "Oh, I am quite lovely. I wish I could say the same for you."

He raised his head up enough to peer down at her. "Why would you say that?"

She picked her head up and gave him a devilish grin. "Because I am not the one who must have a conversation with my brother."

CHAPTER 8

"To think I step away for a mere couple of days to bring *life* into this world, and when I return I find my little sister is to be *wed*." Louisa spoke the last word as though Johanna had done something to warrant admission to Bedlam.

"I assure you it did not occur quite so quickly," Johanna said from where she was perched over wee Simon's bassinet, making silly faces at her newest nephew. He did nothing more than stare at her, and she could tell from his expression, he thought her worthy of Bedlam as well.

"True," Eliza added from where she sat on the bed next to Louisa, a tray of sandwiches braced between them. "It was really more like a week."

Johanna looked up sharply. "You're no help."

Eliza's smile was overflowing with pride. "Oh, but you see I accomplished in days what Viv was unable to do in years."

Johanna frowned. "You speak as though I were some sort of problem which required solving."

"You were rather vexing to poor Viv," Louisa said around

a mouthful of watercress. She gestured to the tray. "Cook does wondrous things with roasted beef. Do try one."

Eliza helped herself. "I think Viv will simply be relieved to hear you have found your match. No matter how quickly it seemed to have been obtained."

That was precisely the problem. To her sisters, she had been swept up in a whirlwind romance, the culmination of which was a hasty proposal and even hastier marriage. One by special license planned for the end of the week. She only hoped Viv would be able to return from Margate in time.

But to Johanna, it had taken years for this to happen. Years of always being the little sister. Years of always being the tagalong. Years of pining. Years of yearning.

Even now she didn't quite believe it. She had had no expectations when Ben had returned. She had thought they would continue on as they had before he left for America as she had had no evidence to the contrary.

If anyone should be surprised, it should be her, but she'd been too swept up in the allure of the moment to realize what was actually happening.

She was marrying Ben.

The notion seemed odd and almost unthinkable, but it was true. He'd had a conversation with her brother the very day they'd made love at dawn under the arbor of trees. She had been expecting yelling and threats, but the house remained exceptionally quiet through the whole of their meeting. When the men had finally emerged from Andrew's study, it was to find Andrew heartily slapping Ben's back and wishing the man good luck in the future.

That was it.

Andrew hadn't spoken more than three sentences to her in the interim, and one of them had been to ask if she desired the match. She had told him most explicitly she did, and that had been it. He'd disappeared into his study to do whatever it was her brother did in there.

Johanna had called on Eliza to request her help in planning the wedding, and she'd insisted on visiting Louisa immediately. Andrew had already written to Viv by the time Louisa was feeling up to company, so here they were.

Cooing over Simon and planning her wedding. Or rather, talking about how it had come about.

"So tell me," Louisa said, brushing crumbs from her hands. "How did he propose? Was it terribly romantic?"

She could feel the heat rush to her cheeks, and Louisa pushed herself up against the pillows that cushioned her.

"Oh, it must have been good."

Johanna eyed both her sisters. "Why would you think that?"

Eliza pointed with her sandwich. "I have never seen you turn that shade of scarlet."

"Did he get down on one knee?" Louisa asked, leaning forward in her eagerness.

"Both knees actually," Johanna heard herself say, picturing the moment so clearly in her mind.

Ben, kneeling before her, slightly rumpled and wind-blown and half dressed. She had never seen anything so perfect.

"Both knees?" Eliza said as she perused the sandwich tray once more. "That's impressive."

Johanna took the seat next to Simon's bassinet. "Why do you say so? Surely Dax and Sebastian made similar overtures."

The sisters looked at one another with blank expressions before turning back to Johanna.

"Henry tried to eat Dax when Dax came to ask for my hand. There was certainly no kneeling." Eliza shook her head as she selected a ham sandwich next.

Louisa screwed up her mouth to one side as she appeared to think it over. "I'm sure you are aware Sebastian and I did not wed under the best of circumstances." She looked sheepishly about the room.

"I should think your situation would have been the most romantic of all," Johanna pressed.

Louisa looked at the ceiling. "Well, it was rather that there wasn't time for anything grand." Her smile was unconvincing, but Johanna decided to let her off the hook. "Anyway," Louisa went on, "I should like to hear about your proposal. So Ben was on his knees before you. Then what happened?"

"Then he asked me to marry him."

"That's it?" This from Eliza.

"Should there have been more?" Johanna had thought the whole thing entirely perfect, but what did she know of proposals? She'd only the one by which to judge.

"Well, what did he say exactly?" Louisa leaned all the way forward now, elbows to knees.

Johanna looked up as if she could see the entire scene on the ceiling of Louisa's bedchamber. "He asked if I would do him the immense honor of marrying him. Yes, that seemed to be what he said." She nodded as she was sure of the words. "Er, well, that was mostly it." She eyed both of her sisters as they studied her.

"What do you mean mostly it?" Louisa breathed.

"I rather interrupted him, so he didn't entirely finish the sentence. But that was what he meant." She smiled, feeling better at her sisters' obvious enjoyment of her retelling of the event.

Eliza set down her sandwich, her eyes narrowing behind her gold spectacles. "Just exactly when was this proposal to have taken place?"

If Johanna's face had heated before, it damn near caught on fire then.

Eliza sat forward. "Johanna Elizabeth Darby," she whispered.

"Far too many people are using my full name as of late," Johanna said and pushed to her feet to pace about the room.

Louisa's grin was ostentatious. "Oh, Johanna, what did you do? Was it properly scandalous?"

"I bet it involved trousers," Eliza muttered.

Johanna swung about from the window to stare at her sister. "How did you know?"

Eliza wiped her hands on her napkin. "It has always been trousers with you. Did Ben risk your reputation to propose to you?"

Johanna sighed, and she was not the sighing sort as indicated by the quick twin looks of concern on her sisters' faces. "He did at that."

Louisa made a noise that could only be described as giddy. "Oh, please do tell us everything."

Johanna came to perch on the other side of Louisa. "Only if you promise not to tell Viv."

"We promise," Louisa spoke quickly for both of them.

Johanna relayed the events of that early morning. Well, most of the events. She left out the bit that would have required their immediate marriage as it seemed rather superfluous to the point of the matter.

That being that Ben had already asked for her hand.

"I would never have expected such treachery from Mallard," Eliza mused.

"I was most grateful," Johanna said. "It was rather chilly that morning."

Eliza only shook her head.

Louisa took Johanna's hand between both of hers. "And when did he tell you he loved you the first time?"

Johanna opened her mouth only to still entirely.

Ben hadn't told her he loved her.

She looked at her sister, and her expression must have been enough because Louisa's lips formed a soft *Oh*.

Eliza waved off the question. "It took Dax months to tell me he loved me. Some men are simply too obtuse to see what is directly in front of them."

"You can only imagine what it took for Sebastian to tell me," Louisa was quick to add. "He isn't called the Beastly Duke without sound reason."

Ben hadn't told her he loved her.

The thought played over and over again in her head. She had been so consumed by everything else she had missed that. The trip to the King's Library where he opened himself up to her. The stolen kiss in the copse of trees in Hyde Park. The all too brief tryst in the moonlit garden.

It was the perfect stuff of fantasies. Perhaps it had been too perfect for she had failed to notice the most important thing of all was missing.

A declaration of love.

She glanced at her sisters only to find them smiling assuredly.

Louisa patted their joined hands. "Trust us," she said. "He'll come around eventually. I don't know why it is men are so adverse to stating their feelings."

She remembered the pain in Ben's face that day at the library, what it had taken for him to tell her how he felt and how the result was a tidal wave of pent-up emotion. Perhaps her sisters were right.

She squeezed Louisa's hand. "I suppose that's true."

"It is true." Louisa squeezed in return. "Now then, we've the wedding to plan. What did you have in mind?" She turned to Eliza before Johanna could speak. "Do you think we could secure St. Paul's in time?"

Eliza's expression was bleak. "Why ever would we wish to?"

Louisa shrugged. "You know Viv would wish the best for her."

"I suppose that's true, but why would Johanna want St. Paul's? Surely the chapel on St. Martin's—"

"Johanna has an idea or two about her wedding," Johanna interrupted.

Eliza and Louisa blinked in her direction as though they had been caught stealing sweets from the teacart.

"You do?" Louisa finally blurted out.

Eliza bit her lower lip in an obvious attempt to hide her smile. "I think what our dear sister is trying to say is that it comes as a surprise that you may have thought about your wedding. You have always been so seemingly uninterested in the topic."

Johanna sat up, arms akimbo. "I'll have you know I have several thoughts on the topic."

"Oh, do share," Louisa said, leaning back as if she were preparing to enjoy a theater show.

When suddenly faced with an audience, Johanna felt silly relaying the particulars of the wedding she had dreamed of for years.

"Go on," Eliza prompted gently.

"Well, I had wished to be married at Ravenwood Park."

"In West Yorkshire?" Louisa's eyebrows went straight up at this.

"Yes, in West Yorkshire." Johanna hoped her frown conveyed her displeasure.

"You did always prefer the countryside," Eliza noted.

Johanna nodded, feeling bolstered by Eliza's practicality. "As such, I had wished to be married surrounded by the trees and the fields and the lake, but as that is not possible, I should like to be married in the gardens at Ravenwood House."

Eliza and Louisa only stared.

"You wish to be married out of doors?" Eliza finally asked.

Johanna nodded. "Yes, I should like it very much."

"What if it should rain?" Louisa asked.

Johanna shrugged. "Then we get wet."

"How interesting." It was hardly more than a whisper as Louisa seemed to consider it.

"It's rather early in the summer for the garden to be in full bloom, but I think it should do rather nicely."

Eliza nodded and reached across Louisa to take Johanna's hand for a squeeze. "I know it's going to be simply lovely."

They were prevented from further discussion when Simon sent up a wail that would have rivaled the tones obtained by the Royal Theatre's best soprano performing an aria.

Johanna reached him first and happily scooped him up to bring him to his mother. Louisa took her son in her arms and leaned back, adjusting him so she could nurse him.

She shook her head. "It will be quite the wedding, Johanna. You mustn't worry. We'll see to everything."

Johanna kissed her sister's cheek. "I have no doubt of it."

That was true. She knew her sisters would give her the best wedding circumstances would allow. It left her to reserve her doubt for other things. The things she had not before thought to ruminate over.

Like whether or not her future husband loved her.

* * *

HE HAD EXPECTED some level of scrutiny, but when it became nearly unbearable, he finally spoke. "I worry that I might sprout horns should you continue to stare at me thusly."

He was seated across from Andrew, the imposing ducal desk between them in the study at Ravenwood House, and Ben had the sudden feeling they were children again playing at games. Andrew was some kind of judge, and at any moment, he would call down his verdict, sealing Ben's fate.

For some reason, Ben feared it would not be a desirous one.

Andrew shook his head. "I still can't believe she's marrying you."

"Is it really quite so hard to believe?" Ben tried to keep his voice even as a lick of apprehension crawled up his spine.

He had worried his best friend would find him out when Ben first came to ask Andrew for his sister's hand in marriage. But Andrew had done nothing more than smile and slap him on the back in congratulations. Ben had later realized this quick acceptance was likely due to Andrew's desire to be free of his sisters after Andrew muttered something about a well-deserved stalking trip to Scotland. Ben had no doubt his friend would slip off just as soon as the wedding breakfast was consumed.

But having to negotiate wedding contracts was another matter entirely. So he sat across from his friend and lied. Or if not lied, at least omitted the truth.

The truth being that he was marrying Johanna for her dowry and nothing more.

That he would never love her.

That while he would do everything in his power to make her happy, he couldn't do that one thing.

He wondered why it had not come up between them. She had not confessed her love for him directly, and he'd taken advantage of the situation and neglected to bring up the topic, which suited him just fine.

However, it did not help him to forget Johanna's face that day in the copse of trees in the park when he'd accidentally kissed her. The look of absolute bliss when he'd ended the kiss. He could almost feel her euphoria simply from the ecstasy spread across her features.

He needn't have spoken the words because she already believed he loved her by one simple kiss.

God, he was an arse.

But he couldn't stop now. He was so close to saving Raeford Court, the tenants who depended on the estate, his mother, the servants. So many lives were at stake, and so much depended on this match.

He must only hurt the person he cared about most.

Cared about but didn't love. He swallowed against the thought. He'd never love again. His father and Minerva had made sure of it.

Andrew shook his head again. "Yes, it is rather. She's shown no interest in finding a match in the two seasons she's been out."

"Perhaps she was just waiting for me." He tried for an arrogant smile, but the trait didn't suit him, and he felt rather foolish instead.

Andrew laughed though. "I think it's more that she finds you less annoying than the other eligible gentlemen of the *ton*."

"I suppose I shall take that as a compliment."

Andrew sat up and shuffled through the papers on his desk. "And I suppose it is as close as you'll get to receiving one from her."

He seemed to find what he was looking for and turned the document around for Ben to see.

"The stipulations of Johanna's dowry were laid out in my father's will. As such, I am not able to alter them. I hope for both our sakes' that the terms are satisfactory."

Ben peered at the figures laid out, a wave of lightheadedness washing over him. It was more than enough to save Raeford Court. Seeing the numbers in black ink had a solidifying effect, and suddenly he realized this was happening.

Both that he was marrying Johanna and that he would truly have the means to restore the Raeford estate.

No, not just restore it.

Make it even better than it once was. Just as he'd always dreamed. Finally he would be his own man, and no one would be able to tell him he wasn't good enough.

He only needed her dowry to get his projects underway, and then he would prove himself. He'd studied the latest farming methods, and he had scores of ideas for selective breeding. He would make Raeford Court flourish. He only needed time and the necessary funds.

Pain blossomed at his thoughts, pain and guilt and regret.

His chest ached, and he absently tugged at his jacket as though it were a physical pain, and he could lessen it by adjusting his garments. His mouth went suddenly dry, and it was as though he'd taken a mouthful of ash.

He met his friend's gaze directly. "That number is more than adequate. Your father was generous in providing for his daughters."

Andrew withdrew the document and set it aside. "My father was wise with his money and saw fit to ensure his daughters had the best chance at a good future. I can only hope to do the same for any of my offspring one day."

Ben sat back in his chair and affected a casual pose he didn't feel. His throat was closing. Soon he wouldn't be able to breathe.

In a split second, he suddenly wished he was his father, conniving and manipulating. No, even more he wished he was Minerva. Heartless and uncaring.

"You sound as if you're not convinced of it. Having offspring one day, that is," Ben somehow managed.

Andrew toyed with a pen. "You likely haven't had the opportunity to mingle in society enough to hear what is being said about me."

This had Ben sitting up. "What do they say about you?"

Andrew tossed the pen aside. "They say I am the Unwanted Duke."

Ben laughed loudly, drawing a frown from Andrew, but the change of topic had his tension easing.

"What do you mean you're the Unwanted Duke? Why would they apply such a title to you?" Ben gestured around him. "The Ravenwood name is old and solid with a legacy free of blemish. You're a rather fine chap, I suppose. What would there be to dissuade a bride from selecting your suit?"

"It isn't a single issue," Andrew muttered. "It's four of them."

Ben's shoulders slumped. "Oh. You mean them."

Andrew nodded gravely. "It appears the Darby sisters are far too formidable for any young society miss. I shall need to find a bride of unparalleled bravery if I am to have any hope of securing a match." He rubbed the back of his neck. "The title will require it, of course, but I haven't bothered to even look while my sisters remained unwed. What would have been the point?" He shrugged, and Ben noticed the lines around his friend's eyes, the way his mouth was bracketed with grooves now.

A lot had happened to his friend while Ben was in America, and the passage of time became very real in that moment. Ben regretted it. He regretted having missed the past several years. He regretted having left. It hadn't been his choice, but he promised himself he'd never miss another thing. Because for the first time, he had control of his future.

Well, nearly control of his future.

"You'll try to find a match now? I mean, once Johanna and I are wed?"

Andrew's gaze traveled toward the windows that overlooked the street outside as if out there he could see his future.

"I think perhaps next season I shall start to look." His smile was one-sided as he said, "I mustn't allow a courtship to interrupt my stalking trip. I have earned it, after all."

Ben couldn't help but smile. "I believe you have. But Scotland? Isn't it so terribly far away?"

Andrew shook his head, his lips tightening. "In my opinion, it isn't far enough."

Ben laughed even as he felt a hollow pang in his chest. What was it like to grow up with a family that gave you such joy and such frustration at once? What was it to have sisters that so tormented you and yet invoked in you such love that you forestalled your own future for theirs?

He didn't know.

He'd only the experience of having a father and brother who put their own comfort before others.

Ben swallowed and forced a smile. "Then I shouldn't wish to delay your departure. I do hope you can agree on a ceremony by special license. My presence is required at Raeford, and I shan't wish to delay my departure." He felt the guilt rise in his throat again, threatening to suffocate him. He forced himself to meet Andrew's gaze. "I wish it could be different but—"

Andrew waved off the rest of his words. "Your circumstances are unusual at best. Whatever is Johanna's wish the rest of the family will agree to, and I believe she has already given her consent to the special license."

Ben felt a modicum of relief to hear this. He knew the courtship had been swift. He didn't wish to upset things further with a hasty ceremony even if it were prudent.

"She has," Ben said. "But I can't help but feel some measure of regret."

It was the closet he could get to apologizing to his friend, and yet Andrew could not know it.

Andrew waved off his words. "If you continue thus, you'll apologize your way directly out of this engagement."

Ben laughed and changed the subject. "Scotland? Have you an acquaintance up there or are you engaging the assistance of a guide?"

Andrew picked up the pen he had discarded earlier. "The MacKenzie has extended an invitation."

Ben coughed. "Old Man MacKenzie? The drunkard?"

Andrew pointed with his pen. "One and the same."

Ben shook his head. "You can't be serious."

Andrew sat forward, elbows to his desk. "Quite serious and most assuredly desperate." He looked out the windows again. "I want nothing more than to flee London at the end of the Parliament session and spend a few weeks getting lost in the highlands. I'll return before the start of the next session and begin my quest for a bride."

"You're mad."

Andrew raised both eyebrows. "Out of madness comes innovation, isn't that true?"

"No."

Andrew's expression fell. "Oh. Well, it sounds like it should."

"I've never seen a man driven insane by his sisters." Ben shook his head.

Andrew scrubbed a hand over his face. "Perhaps a good nap will do just as well." He pushed to his feet. "I'm sorry to make this so brief, but I promised Viv I would lend Eliza some assistance in planning the wedding."

Ben stood as well, a laugh on his lips.

"*You're* helping to plan *my* wedding?"

"Sisters," was all that his friend could say to that.

Ben laughed. "I guess Scotland isn't too far then."

He was almost to the door when Andrew called after him. He turned back, his hands involuntarily clenching.

"I never asked, and not that it's any of my business, but... well, why do you wish to marry my sister?"

The truth reared up like a multiple-headed beast with venom dripping from its fangs. He wanted to dodge it. He wanted the lie to slip so easily from his lips. But it just wouldn't. He couldn't lie to his best friend.

Guilt choked him as he felt the enormity of what he had done. Not only was he marrying Johanna for her dowry, but he'd compromised her as well. He'd tried not to think of that day on the hill under the trees, the sun just slipping over the horizon.

He tried not to think of it for so many reasons. For the fact that it had felt so terribly good to hold Johanna in his arms, to feel her quiver beneath him, her fingers digging into his shoulders. The physical act had been both exquisite and explosive, and he'd never experienced the like before then. Whenever he thought of the magic of that day, the ghostly memory of Minerva swooped in to steal his happiness, the ever-real guilt of fooling his best friend choking him.

But it was more than that that had him avoiding the truth of what he'd done.

He'd compromised his best friend's little sister. If his honor was not already damaged, it was all but destroyed now.

Still, he couldn't stop the truth from tripping from his lips.

"Johanna reminds me of sunshine and laughter." He laughed and looked at his feet, pinching his nose between two fingers. Finally, he raised his gaze to his friend. "I know it sounds absurd, but Johanna reminds me of what it was like to have hope once."

Andrew considered the pen he still held in his fingers before tossing it aside.

"It's not absurd at all." He swallowed, and Ben braced

himself for what might come next. "Ben, I—" Andrew stopped and shook his head. "I want to apologize for what happened even though none of it was caused by myself."

Ben gave a soft smile. "Do not apologize, friend. You've done more than you know to help better the situation."

"By giving you my sister?"

Ben tried to keep his smile from turning watery with guilt. "Something like that," he said and bid his friend farewell, thinking that maybe if he didn't look at the man he had betrayed, he wouldn't give in to the guilt.

CHAPTER 9

She awoke on the day of her wedding to the man of her dreams to the sound of torrential rain attacking the windows. She jumped from bed and yanked back the curtains, hoping she may be wrong about the cacophony that had awakened her.

She was not.

A veritable typhoon had descended upon London, and on the very day she had dreamed of for so many years.

Was it an omen?

Hogwash. She didn't believe in such drivel.

Still, one could hardly have a ceremony in the garden in such an onslaught. She rang for a footman and dashed off a note to Eliza. She dressed quickly and was already stepping into the corridor when the footman arrived.

She handed him the note. "Please have a messenger get this to my sister Eliza's residence as quickly as possible."

The footman had barely given a nod before she made her way to the rear of the house and down the servants' stairs. She had never been in the servants' domain of the house other than to sneak out the previous week to ride with Ben at dawn, and thus, she had never experienced the total power with which she held to silence a room.

She stepped into the kitchens, abuzz with not only the normal morning preparations but the added ordered disaster that was her wedding day.

Servants stopped, suspended in mid-motion. Water boiled into the silence, but the clinking of metalware and glasses ceased almost at once.

"Good morning," she said as brightly as possible.

Cook merely blinked.

"Is there a problem, my lady?" This from a timid scullery maid Johanna had only come upon once, cleaning the grate in the upstairs drawing room.

"Yes, it appears it's raining."

The servants present all turned their gazes to the small windows set high in the stone walls around them before looking back at her as if this were the first they were hearing of it.

"I mean to say it is raining, and the ceremony is to take place in the gardens. I was wondering if there were any available men to help me construct a type of shelter under which the ceremony may take place."

Cook blinked again.

The scullery maid opened her mouth without speaking now.

This was not going as planned.

"My lady." She turned at the deep, ponderous tones that could only belong to one person.

She smiled. "Mallard. Good morning. We seem to have a problem."

Mallard gave a small nod. "Yes, my lady. I've already sent two of the footmen to assist Cribbs with the construction of an adequate shelter."

She beamed. "You knew I would wish to have the ceremony in the gardens no matter the weather?"

Mallard nodded again. "Of course, my lady." He spoke the words with no inflection whatsoever, but in her heart, his words rang with undying love.

For such a stoic pillar of loyalty, he really was quite thoughtful.

She smiled and returned his nod. "Thank you, Mallard." She turned to leave and stopped. "Thank you so much for your service today. I realize it's rather unexpected."

The gathered servants blinked and said nothing.

"I mean, a wedding at Ravenwood House. And put together with so little notice. I just wish to thank you."

Cook blinked. The scullery maid stared. Mallard stepped forward. "Your gratitude is hardly necessary, my lady. It is a servant's duty and pride to rise to the occasion."

She wrinkled her nose. "Even in the rain?"

For the first time, she witnessed a crack in Mallard's calm facade when his upper lip twitched ever so slightly as if he were attempting to hide a smile. "Especially in the rain," the butler intoned.

Johanna smiled and with a quick nod scurried back up the stairs.

They had planned to have the ceremony relatively early so as to have a semblance of a wedding breakfast before they must depart for the first leg of their journey north. She knew the urgency with which Ben wished to return home. She could feel the same urgency pulsing in her stomach every time she thought of Raeford.

Soon.

Soon they would be home.

She had never felt whole the way she did when she was with Ben at Raeford Court. But more, soon she would see

Duchess again. The notion filled her with anticipation and longing.

But home would mean something entirely different now she realized with a tumble of her stomach. She stopped on the stairs, pressing a hand to her middle as reality crashed around her in a cold, restoring waterfall.

It would be *their* home.

Raeford Court.

The place where she had spent so much of her youth dreaming of this very day. It was happening. Now. In the rain.

She couldn't stop the smile that sprang to her lips. Who cared if it rained or snowed or they suffered blistering heat? As long as they were wed.

She picked up her skirts and dashed the rest of the way to her rooms. She'd shed her morning gown and was unwinding her braid when the knock came at her bedchamber door. She expected the maid she had requested help her and called absently over her shoulder, "Come in," but the door was already opening.

Louisa spilled in, a laugh fading from her lips as Eliza trotted in behind her, snapping the door shut.

Johanna spun away from the mirror she was using to unwind her hair.

"Louisa!" She rushed forward and seized Louisa's hands. "You mustn't be out in this!"

Louisa laughed again, and Johanna could tell the sisters had likely been laughing since they'd arrived at Ravenwood House, and a rush of happiness swamped her. She wanted this. She wanted her sisters laughing. She wanted to marry Ben. She wanted all of it. The rain mattered little.

"No one should be out in this," Louisa replied, her words wobbling with her smile.

"But what about Simon?"

Louisa shook her head. "He'll be all right with Williams for an hour. I just fed him, and he tuckered right out the poor little one." She shook her head. "All of this eating and sleeping is exhausting to someone so little."

Johanna looked to Eliza for confirmation of this as Johanna had hardly any experience with babies.

Eliza waved off her look of concern. "It happens all the time. He'll likely sleep for a good hour or more before he even realizes his mama is missing." She seized Johanna's elbow. "Let's get you ready. Ben will be here soon."

Louisa had insisted on having a new gown made for Johanna even though Johanna thought it rather silly. It was just a garden ceremony and it was just Ben.

Oh dear. She was doing it too now.

Her sisters helped her into the pale yellow gown, and she ran her hands down the length of it as she stood in front of her dressing mirror.

"I feel like a butterfly," she murmured and didn't miss the look of happiness her sisters exchanged behind her.

She did feel like a butterfly with the soft fabric of such a buttery, sunshine yellow. She knew if she only lifted her arms she might float away. A matching pelisse draped over her shoulders and fitted snug along her middle, sharpening the lines of her silhouette until she felt as pristine as a butterfly's wings.

Another knock came at the door just as Louisa finished pinning the final braid in Johanna's coiffure, and Andrew poked his head in, a hand over his eyes.

"I do not wish to see anything I might be unable to unsee, but Ben has arrived. He would very much like to start before the road north turns to mud."

"We're all finished here, Andrew," Eliza said, her voice touched with pride and laughter.

Johanna stood as Andrew dropped his hand. Several years

separated Johanna from her brother, and she had always seen those years a gulf preventing them from being truly close. But just then, when Andrew saw her in her wedding costume for the first time, she knew what it must feel like. To be a part of something. To be cherished by something. To be loved as a sibling can only love.

She was not just the tagalong anymore. She was Johanna and suddenly she felt whole. Of course, she did. She was marrying Ben. She had never felt more complete than when she was with him.

Andrew swallowed. "Johanna, you look lovely."

She smiled. "Thank you, Andrew."

Louisa made a noise that could only have been meant to relay her happiness, and she pulled Johanna into a quick hug.

"Oh, you're getting married, my little sister." She pulled back. "I'm so very happy for you." There was a pause, and Louisa leaned in closer whispering, "Is Ben him? The man you spoke of? The one who has your heart?"

Only once had Johanna come close to admitting her secret to anyone, and it had been Louisa to whom she had spoken. Johanna nodded, her smile bright, and Louisa hugged her tighter.

Eliza came next, her hug not as tight nor as long, but when she pulled back, her eyes were wet with tears.

"I wish Viv were here to see this."

"Hold your tongue."

They all turned swiftly to the door at the demanding voice that was unmistakable.

Viv, her rumpled traveling cloak spotted with rain, stood in the doorway, a brilliant smile on her lips.

"Viv," Johanna breathed. "You made it."

"Of course, I did. Am I not married to the best phaeton racer in all of England?"

Louisa gasped at the same time Eliza muttered, "Lud."

"You didn't come here in Ryder's racing phaeton, did you?"

Viv laughed and shook her head. "No, but your expressions were marvelous." She stepped forward and took Johanna's hands into both of hers. "Let's see you married."

This was much easier in theory than in truth. Several minutes later Johanna stood in the terrace doorway off the drawing room, which was the closet exit to the makeshift shelter Cribbs and his men had assembled in so short a time.

"You're going to get soaked," Andrew muttered, peering up at the relentless rain and the gray sky thick with clouds.

"No." She beamed. "I'm going to get married." She looked at her brother who would give her away to the man she loved. "We must make a run for it. You remember how, don't you?"

His smile was swift, and for just a moment, she saw her brother as he once was before the weight of the dukedom had fallen on his shoulders.

"A farthing says I make it first." His grin was mischievous.

"A guinea," she cried and leapt into the rain.

Her sprint was less than spectacular as she was too busy laughing and pulling up the skirts of her now ruined gown as she splashed through the garden to the shelter. She tumbled inside just behind Andrew to find the space crowded with family.

Her heart soared as she took in Dax and Eliza, Louisa and even the dour Sebastian who didn't appear so dour today. Viv and Ryder stood just behind them, and Ryder winked playfully in her direction.

And then there was Ben.

Her beloved Ben. The tips of his rich brown hair touched with raindrops, the navy of his suit crisp and clean, and his boots mottled with mud.

He looked perfect.

Except—

He wasn't smiling.

Her heart squeezed, and she rushed forward, taking his hands into hers.

"It's all right," she said quickly. "A little rain never ruined anything."

Surely it was this that had him so upset, and at her words, his pained expression lifted somewhat.

He licked his lips and swallowed. "You're so beautiful," he whispered, and she was certain only she could hear his words.

"I'm soaked," she whispered back, but while she laughed, he only smiled absently, his eyes filled with what could only have been pain.

Pain?

She tried to ignore it, but at his closed expression, she couldn't help but think of what her sisters had said earlier in the week.

Did Ben love her?

It was too late to ask now, and it wasn't as though he *didn't* love her. Otherwise, why would he be marrying her?

He took her arm and turned them to the priest standing at the front of the shelter.

The man was in middling years with gray streaking his black hair, and a pair of silver spectacles perched low on his nose.

"Shall we begin then?" His voice was firm and coaxing in the small space, and Johanna forgot all about Ben's expression.

"Dearly beloved—"

"Wait."

Later she would remember the sound of Ben's voice. The way it seemed to split time in two, drowning out everything else around them.

Johanna turned only her head toward him, but she already knew what she would find.

Because a part of her knew this was all too good to be true.

He'd changed his mind.

That was it surely.

He had been swept up in the moment. He had been overcome with the loss of his wife. He wasn't thinking clearly. This had all been a mistake.

She was a mistake.

But when she finally saw his face, it was much worse than that.

Regret.

That was what she saw on his face, and her heart cracked in two.

"Wait," he repeated. "Johanna, I must say something."

Her family shuffled in the cold and damp behind her, and in the sudden quiet, she heard Sebastian murmur, "He's worse at this than I was."

Even Sebastian's awkwardness could not ease her trepidation in that moment.

"What is it?" She tried to smile, but she knew what was coming.

It was the same thing every time, and it was so very hard to believe in good things now.

Ben had remembered who she was. Just Johanna. His best friend's little sister. Nothing more.

She would always be relegated to the margin. The forgotten sibling. The motherless child.

She had so hoped it would have been different with Ben.

Ben opened his mouth but said nothing, and impatience flashed through her. She stepped back.

"Ben, you mustn't say anything. I understand—"

"Johanna, I'm only marrying you for your dowry."

* * *

SHE WASN'T sure why there wasn't a sound to accompany her world splintering into a thousand irreparable pieces. There should have been. She was sure of it. But there wasn't.

Instead there was deathly silence.

Silence as each of her siblings and respective spouses all gathered what her soon to be husband had just said.

He was marrying her for her dowry.

Ben.

"You're a fortune hunter?" Sebastian spoke first, his voice cold and unfeeling. "I thought you said he was an old friend of the family."

This was probably directed at Louisa because she heard her sister mutter a curse, and Sebastian was silent.

Johanna never moved her gaze from Ben's face. She watched as the pain rippled across his features. First as his lips parted without sound, as his nostrils flared and his eyes pinched, as his forehead wrinkled. As he tried again to speak.

Yet all she could think was he hadn't told her he loved her, and now she knew why.

"Ben, what is this about?"

This broke her gaze, sending her attention to Andrew. Her breath caught in her throat. She'd never seen Andrew so angry. He appeared taller and broader, and his hands flexed into fists. Oh God, he was going to pummel Ben.

"I'm so sorry, Andrew. I cannot apologize enough for what I've done. I've—"

Andrew took a single step forward, and in it she saw a world of menace. She snatched Ben's hand.

"Please excuse us. I must speak with Ben."

She didn't wait for a response. She pulled Ben out into the rain, the sound of it deadening the eruption she left behind as she plunged once more through the puddles of the garden.

When they reached the drawing room of the main house, she was soaked once more but now a chill set her teeth to rattling.

She willed it to stop as she turned to face this man she had thought she loved.

"Ben, what is going on? What do you mean you're only marrying me for my dowry?"

He reached for her, but she backed away, leaving a trail of water on the carpet like a scar.

She knew her dowry must have been significant as it had caused quite a stir when Sebastian had refused Louisa's when they had wed, but she had never suspected...

"Ben, are you a fortune hunter?" Saying the words hurt her throat, and she swallowed hard, willing the lump there to dissipate.

"Yes." At least he met her gaze when he admitted such.

She made a sound that even she could not describe, and it was as though life left her body. She crumpled against the sofa behind her, her hand going out to steady herself, and Ben reached for her.

"Don't you dare touch me." Her words were like daggers, and she hoped they cut him.

He stopped instantly, his hands still outstretched but his feet frozen to the carpet, puddles forming about his boots.

"Johanna."

She couldn't look at him even as her name tripped from his lips like a plea for help.

This couldn't be happening. This couldn't be true. The world as she had believed it swarmed around her as if taunting her to pick out the lies. A thousand questions swam at her at once, and yet she couldn't speak a single one. She blinked furiously as if it might clear everything, and it would all go back to how it was supposed to be.

She should have been married by now.

"Why?" she whispered, the only word she could force free. "I was going to marry you. Why admit the truth now?"

He reached out his hands as if searching for something to save him. "I couldn't go through with it. I couldn't trap you." He made a small step toward her, but her expression must have stopped him because he didn't go far. "I was trapped once." His voice dropped, so very low. "I was trapped, and I remember how that felt, and I couldn't do that to you." He looked around them. "I thought I could." He gave a harsh laugh. "I thought I could do it for Raeford, but I couldn't." He looked back at her. "I couldn't do it to you."

His words jumbled together, too many thoughts ricocheting through her head.

That same horrible sound erupted from her throat, and she sank onto the sofa, her gown soaking the cushions beneath her. She put her face into her hands and finally allowed her eyes to shut, feeling the drugging call of darkness.

But she was too angry for darkness. She was worth more than darkness.

She surged to her feet and rounded on him. "Explain yourself." She had to grind her teeth together to keep from adding a foul word to the end of her command.

She would not sink so low even if he should deserve it.

His lips parted, and his head shook, and his hands reached out, but he offered her nothing until he said softly, "I'm broke."

A line so deep appeared between his eyes, and in it she imagined the pain he felt at speaking those words.

Ben was a proud man, and his pride found its roots in the Raeford title. In the land and the estate and the legacy.

"How broke?"

The line grew more distinct. "My brother wasted it all. Without your dowry, the estate will be without liquid assets by the end of next week."

"And my dowry?"

His eyes started to slide shut.

"Don't hide from me," she seethed.

He opened his eyes, met her gaze. "It's sufficient to rebuild the estate."

"Rebuild it how? I will not allow my family's money to be used to pay your bastard brother's debts." She was not above calling his dead brother any name he deserved.

Ben shook his head quickly and took a step toward her. She took a step back. It wasn't that she loathed his touch, though she did, and it wasn't that she was a coward. It was that she feared if he drew any closer, she might cause him physical harm.

She was slighter than him, so much so, and she knew she could do little by way of damage, but she wanted nothing more than to hurt him just then. Physically. She wanted him to feel the agony she felt, the way it gnawed at her bones, the way it stopped the air from filling her lungs, the way it made her want to give up.

He had been trapped once.

None of this made sense.

"I've paid all of my brother's debts. That's why there are no more funds. I had to give it all to his creditors." He licked his lips. "Johanna, without your dowry, I cannot make the improvements the estate needs to stay alive. Raeford Court will crumble, and I'll be forced to sell if I do not have your dowry to save it."

Of anything he might have said, this was the only thing that could pierce her pain.

Raeford Court.

Her beloved Raeford Court.

The place where she'd gone to be seen and heard. The halls in which she'd chased after Duchess, telling her not to paint over the Baroque murals. The fields through which she'd raced her brother and his best friend.

The only place where she felt whole.

The place which mere hours before she had thought would be home.

She swallowed and turned away, her hand going to her forehead where a headache brewed.

"What improvements?" If she were to give this man her dowry, she wanted to know what he would do with it.

"Improvements?"

She whirled, pinning him with her gaze. "What improvements, Ben?"

He looked to the floor and back up. "The tenants are not using the four-course rotation method. This is the first thing that should be done. We can increase yields a hundred fold if they start using the fallow fields. That's the first step. Drainage will be a consideration if all of the fields are in use at once. The next step is to bring back the herd. There isn't enough to sustain the tenants, let alone bring in a profit. I wish to cultivate a new herd and employ strategic breeding methods to increase the yield." He spoke as if he were reading from a list.

Because Raeford Court meant as much to Ben as it did to her, and he'd done his research. He wasn't going to let the estate fail.

She crossed her arms over her stomach. "I want regular updates on your progress, and I shall accompany you on any visits to the fields as I see fit."

He blinked. "Johanna, what—"

"You're taking my dowry. I get a say in how it is used." The words clogged in her throat, and she wanted to press a hand to her chest, but she wouldn't let him see how much he hurt her.

It wasn't supposed to be like this. In her dreams, Ben had always finally come to his senses, realized the amazing thing that was there. Her. He realized he loved *her*.

And yet here she was. Negotiating her future like nothing more than a financial transaction. The pain was real and deep, and she thought she might never recover.

His mouth snapped shut, and a beat passed between them before he said, "You will still marry me."

"Of course, I'll marry you. That's not in question. The only thing we're discussing is my role in the improvement of Raeford Court."

"Your role."

She nodded. "I do not wish to see my family's money friv- olously spent. I will demand to see the ledgers to determine if the improvements are seeing the cash flows they are supposed to produce. Is that agreed?"

It was a moment before he nodded. "Yes, of course."

She swallowed. "Then that's settled. We should return to my family to see the deed done. We've already tarried too long. The roads have likely gone to mud."

She moved to step around him, and he reached for her. She recoiled.

"Don't." She hated the sound of tears in her voice. She'd made it this far. She need only make it a little further.

Her eyes flashed to his, and she willed herself to stay strong. To not give up.

Years of neglect swam underneath her until it firmed into a foundation of solitude. She could live without his love, but she didn't know if she could live without him. Not anymore.

She studied him, the way his face was etched with pain.

"Was none of it real?" She didn't want to know. She wanted to believe that some part of him wanted to kiss her.

That some part of him wanted to be with her. That some part of him loved her.

But she saw the way his face folded. Saw the way his brow furrowed against the truth. So much was written clearly across his face and yet he did not speak.

She turned away from him, but he caught her arm. She wrenched it free and pinned him with her gaze.

"Johanna, you mustn't do this." The line was back between his eyes, and somehow she couldn't quite believe it was filled with concern for her.

She raised her chin. "I can be in love with you when you're married to someone else, or I can be in love with you and married to you. I've already tried the former, and I found it not to my liking. The latter is all that is left to me."

It was like she had punched him in the throat, cutting off his breath. She could see it in the way he broke his gaze away from hers and stumbled back.

"Johanna, I never meant to—"

"No, no one ever means to." She let the words hang between them, but she never let go of his gaze. "My family is waiting."

He didn't say anything more, nor did he try to reach for her again. He followed her into the rain and back to the shelter where her family was waiting. She wasn't surprised to find Andrew pacing and Eliza trying to calm him. Ryder held Viv back with his hands on her shoulders, and Louisa whispered frantically to Sebastian that now was not the time for comments.

"I'm very sorry. There seems to have been a misunderstanding. All is well now. Shall we proceed?" Her smile was tight as she stepped up to the priest who looked as though he'd just witnessed the second coming of Christ.

"Johanna." Andrew spoke her name through clenched teeth. "If you think I'm going to let this wedding continue—"

She snapped. She felt it like a physical thing. The very center of her came apart into a spiral of glass that shattered to the four corners in a blinding ray of light.

She turned, her finger raised to poke her brother in the chest.

"You get to decide nothing." The venom behind her words surprised her, and she blinked at the realization of what the neglect had done to her. It had done this.

She'd pushed her own feelings to the side for so long that now they erupted into this horrible, vile person she didn't recognize. But she couldn't stop.

She pressed forward.

"For too long, I've gone along with what any one of you has said. I've followed when you led. I've gone when you called. I've done everything that was asked of me. But now this is a decision that affects only me, and I will not have you deciding it for me." Her voice shook with anger. "This is my turn. My turn," she repeated softly, and then she was out of words.

She looked at each of her sisters in turn, their astonished faces filled with regret and guilt and surprise, but Andrew's expression hurt the most. In his face she saw only understanding.

He stepped back without saying a word.

She was married then, to the man of her dreams, but when the priest invited the groom to kiss his bride, she pulled her hands free from Ben's and walked out into the rain.

Alone.

CHAPTER 10

*H*e waited in the carriage for them to depart.

He felt hollowed out as though someone had taken to scraping the insides of him raw. The rain pelted the roof of the carriage, and in its rhythm, he sought escape. But it wasn't to be.

The events of the past week rolled over and over again in his mind, and each time he recalled them, they pulled a little more out of him.

He played the game so well, and he might have succeeded entirely if he'd not succumbed to the weight of his own honor.

But he simply couldn't do it.

When Johanna had stepped into the makeshift shelter, soaking wet, breathless, and smiling, when she'd looped her arm through Andrew's…

He'd fallen apart.

Everything else he could bear. The duplicity, the scheming, the machinations. Five years of marriage to Minerva had taught him exactly how to get people to do as one pleased. It had all worked so perfectly, and he had so expertly arranged it.

But that moment was too much.

His best friend and the young girl he had come to respect as a woman in the past week. It was too much. He'd let his own ambitions cloud his judgment, and this was where it had gotten him. Sitting alone in a carriage waiting for his wife, a wife who likely hated him, listening to the sound of the rain and hoping it would drown out his thoughts.

But Raeford Court would be saved.

The thought didn't carry the appeal it once had.

The door wrenched open unexpectedly, and he turned to see the rain was a relentless curtain now. A footman stood with an umbrella, but it did little to protect Johanna as she vaulted into the carriage without anyone's aid.

She'd changed at some point. The yellow gown she had been wearing for the ceremony was gone, and in its place was a plain muslin gown of gray or lavender. It was too dark in the carriage to see precisely, and she'd covered her shoulders with a cloak that she now wrapped tightly about herself like a shell.

The carriage lurched into motion as soon as the door clicked shut.

He wanted to hold her.

The realization struck him like a sickening blow, and he had to turn away. He stared out the window seeing nothing, the sound of the wheels on the cobblestones serving as a better distraction than the rain.

He suddenly wasn't sure if speaking the truth had been the right thing to do, and this more than anything that had come before undid him.

Somehow in the past week he'd come to enjoy her company. No, it was more than that. He'd come to crave it.

The feel of her in his hands, the taste of her kiss, the sound of her laugh.

He knew without her saying so that all of that was denied to him now, and he hadn't expected it to hurt so much.

He wasn't sure how long they sat in silence, but they'd left the built-up streets of London for some time before she spoke.

"I would have married you, you know. You had only to ask." Her voice was devoid of tears, neutral and unfeeling.

He turned to face her, and he found her expression matched her voice. He swallowed. "I didn't realize that," he said even as the words stuck in his dry throat.

"Raeford Court means as much to me as it does to you, I expect. I would ask that in the future you be truthful with me rather than manipulate me into getting what you want."

Her words stung, but they were true, and that hurt all the more.

"I will. I promise."

"You'll forgive me for not believing in your promises." Her expression remained neutral, her tone flat, and he knew she did not mean to hurt him, but she did nonetheless.

He deserved as much.

He nodded and turned back to the window.

The carriage rocked on, but the progress was slow. The rain had turned the road north to nothing more than rutted mud flats, and Ben could hear the driver urging the horses on.

"You didn't answer me," she said after some time.

He looked at her, but the light in the carriage was quickly failing, and he saw little more than the outline of her face.

"Was any of it real?"

The words pierced him as they'd done the first time she'd asked.

He swallowed. "You've asked me to tell you the truth."

She nodded.

He looked down at his hands, pressing the tips together and apart as though the gesture could make it easier to speak.

"My wife was not a kind woman, Johanna. She taught me things I would never wish you to experience. But I'm sorry to say the thing she taught me best was how to get what you want out of others."

She turned away from him. He caught the sharp motion out of the corner of his eye, and he couldn't help but look up then. She made no sound, but even in the darkness, he saw the way her shoulders shook.

He'd made her cry.

Brave, strong, invincible Johanna.

He reached for her.

He couldn't have stopped himself, and nothing she could do could stop him either. For she tried. The moment he touched her shoulder, she reared back, her hand going up as if to deflect him, but he was stronger than she was, and he simply wrapped his arms around her, tucking her head under his chin. It frightened him how quickly she gave up the fight, but what frightened him more was the way she cried then.

He'd never seen Johanna cry.

In his memories, she was always the triumphing pirate or the powerful witch, weaving unbreakable spells in their childhood games.

He'd never seen her as vulnerable, and he thought now that was likely how he'd been able to pull it off for so long.

He didn't think he could break her, and now he had.

"Johanna, I'm sorry. I know you don't believe that, but it's true. I am. I never meant to hurt you. I—" He licked his lips. "I only meant to save Raeford Court." The selfishness in his words burned his ears, and his heart ached at what he'd done.

But he would do it again. He knew that. Anything to save Raeford Court.

Her fists struck his chest, but the motion was weak, and he thought her heart was likely not in it.

"Why didn't you just tell me? Why did you make me believe—"

She didn't finish the sentence, and he thought back to that day in the copse in Hyde Park.

He'd made her believe he returned her feelings.

He eased her away from him, and with one finger under her chin, tilted her face up to his.

"Johanna, I will never be able to tell you how sorry I am, but—" He lost track of his words when he took in her face.

The girl and the woman had somehow become mixed in his mind, and he couldn't decipher one from the other.

"I cannot love another. Not anymore. Never again." The words spilled free and with them a weight he had been carrying.

She blinked, her eyelashes dotted with her tears. "You...what?"

Her lips were slightly parted, her eyes wide. She'd lifted her chin at some point, and he no longer could feel her smooth skin against his hand.

"I cannot love another. My first marriage was enough for me, and I will never love. I...can't."

She blinked, and the tears on her eyelashes dropped onto her cheeks. "You can't...love?" She wrinkled her nose ever so slightly at the question.

"I can't endure what I did then, Johanna. I simply can't, and I won't." He pushed a lock of hair that had fallen loose from her coiffure behind her ear. "I can promise you I will do everything in my power to make you happy and provide a good life for you, but I just can't love you."

She slipped entirely away from him then, her eyes wider now, her lips firm.

"You wish to live without love?" Her voice had gone soft and wondering, and her words unsettled him.

"I do not require such sentiment. I need only know Raeford Court will survive beyond me."

Her eyes searched him, but they needn't bother. He'd already searched himself. No matter what his physical response was to her, his emotional response remained the same.

In that there wasn't one.

The sounds she had made when he had told her the truth, they spoke of a depth of feeling he could only wonder at. He was wrong about how he felt now. He had already been hollow. The events of the day had only served to deepen that state.

He was dead inside where other people flourished, and worst of all, he did not regret it.

His father had made sure of that when he'd demanded the impossible of Ben.

Now Ben would ensure Johanna was comfortable and well cared for, and beyond that, it would not be his concern.

His thoughts paused, skittering on that last one.

He hadn't thought of it really. What Johanna would do when they wed and she realized the truth of their marriage.

Would she seek a lover?

He dismissed the thought as none of his concern as his stomach tightened on the notion.

She tasted of sunshine and warmth and happiness. He could know those things and yet not feel them. He didn't want those things for himself, and yet the thought of someone else having them gave him pause, an unfamiliar coil of heat churning in his gut.

JESSIE CLEVER

She didn't say anything then, her lips parting and closing on an unspoken thought. She turned away, and he let her go.

The silence rang in the carriage so much louder than the shouts of the driver or the torrent of rain.

They didn't make it much farther that day, and blissfully the carriage sloshed to a stop outside an inn. He stepped down from the carriage before the footman had a chance to open the door and put down the step.

His boot sank into mud, and he knew the step would be useless. He turned back, his arms reaching for Johanna as she shrank into the bench, away from his touch.

"You must, Johanna," he called over the sound of the rain. "The mud is fierce, and you're liable to lose your slippers in it."

A kind of silence had overtaken her in the last of their ride north. It was a silence so complete, he might have thought her a ghost. It was far worse than the fury and the tears. It was as though she reflected the emptiness he felt inside himself.

So he was surprised when she moved toward him, sliding across the bench and reached to brace herself with a hand on either side of the door. She slipped into his arms, her own going about his neck, and he didn't want to think about how good it felt to hold her again. Just the weight of her was a reassurance in his arms, and he took his time crossing the muddy yard.

When they slipped beneath the overhang at the front of the inn, his feet struck the wooden platform there that kept the front door free of mud. She was already moving to slip from his arms at the sound of his boots hitting hardwood, and he had to let her go.

She clutched herself, arms wrapped tightly around her middle as she waited for him to open the door to the inn. He glanced back at the carriage to see their things being

152

brought down, and he ducked inside to speak to the proprietor.

The owner nodded his assurances that the best room would be made up quickly, and Ben went in search of food next at the public room reached through a connecting door. When he returned to the front room, Johanna had finally wandered inside, her arms no longer rigid about her middle. Her face was calm as she spoke with a woman who had stepped behind the owner's desk, likely the mistress of the inn.

He didn't catch what words were exchanged, and the woman slipped off before he could approach.

"I've requested trays be brought up with supper," he said when he reached Johanna.

She only nodded when he expected her to deny her hunger. They stood there, dripping in the front room of the posting inn, a clock somewhere ticking in the distance, the rain still falling outside.

Their poor tiger soon appeared with the luggage they'd brought with them. The remainder of their things would come by cart later. In this weather, he feared how much later. He told the young man to find hot food and drink next door, and he plodded off, a sleepy, contented smile on his face.

Ben picked up their things as the proprietor returned to show them to their room. The wooden steps creaked beneath their feet as they climbed to the upper floor, but he was pleased to see the establishment was clean if worn. When they reached the upper floor, a door was open on either side of the hallway.

The proprietor gave a nod and went back down the stairs, leaving them to stand in the hallway. Well, leaving Ben apparently as Johanna moved into the room on the left side of the hallway.

"You can leave my bag there. Thank you," she said.

He eyed the room across the hall, one eyebrow going up.

"I requested a separate room from the proprietress. I'm sure you understand," she said at his look.

Her words held no bite and yet they might as well have been daggers for the way they shredded him. He realized he had been planning on spending the night with her. He had been looking *forward* to it.

What an idiot he was. Of course she wouldn't wish to spend the night with him. And yet—

"Johanna, there are certain matters that must be seen to tonight." He met her gaze directly.

Her smile was soft and sad. "Oh, but you mustn't worry about that, Ben. You've already seen to consummating this relationship, haven't you?"

She took her bag from him and closed the door softly between them.

* * *

SHE OPENED the door of the carriage even before the wheels had fully stopped on the gravel drive outside Raeford Court.

She didn't wait for a footman to help her down or a step to ease the journey. She simply jumped. She heard a sharp intake of breath and looked up as she brushed out her skirts.

She smiled for the first time in days.

"Mrs. Owens," she said when her eyes lit on the Raeford housekeeper. "It has been too long." She nodded in the woman's direction.

The poor housekeeper shook her head as if to clear it before giving the required curtsy to her mistress.

"Your ladyship, er, I mean..." The woman coughed discreetly. "*Your Grace*. We are pleased you have arrived safely."

Mrs. Owens never appeared to change in all the years

Johanna had known her. She wore her black hair parted in the middle and pulled back flat along her ears. She had an enormous hooked nose that suspended over slightly protruding front teeth, and while her hips were wide, the rest of her was outrageously thin, giving her a body shape that never seemed to be in the correct proportions.

And Johanna loved her for all of it.

Johanna approached the older woman and pulled her hands into her own.

"Please, Mrs. Owens. Such formality."

The poor woman blanched, and Johanna had to bite back a smile.

Mrs. Owens had on more than one occasion chased Johanna out of Raeford Court with a broom.

It had been well deserved. Johanna would not deny it. But the poor woman must be feeling a multitude of emotions just then, every one conflicting with the other.

Johanna could only understand all too well. She, too, was swamped by emotion. Suddenly she felt set to rights again, her feet once more on Raeford land, but there was something else. Something more her heart sought, but for now she must attend to her duties.

The woman blinked furiously now at Johanna's outrageous sign of affection, but Johanna did not care. She was the duchess now after all, wasn't she?

She squeezed Mrs. Owens's hands. "I do so appreciate all you have done to ready the house for my arrival, and the servants appear resplendent." She gestured up the front steps of the house where the servants stood at attention, their uniforms pristine, their posture impeccable.

For a second, she was distracted by the looming edifice of Raeford Court behind them. It was built by the first Duke of Raeford some time in the seventeenth century so the original part of the house was heavy with Jacobean tapestries and symmetrical leaded windows. A much later duke had added the east and west wings in the Georgian style to create the Romanesque court between them for which the estate had been renamed. The entire thing led to a disconcerting mixture of styles for anyone caught unawares in the house, but to her, it was simply magical.

Her eyes drifted automatically upward until they met the cap-house at the top. Shrouded in weathered copper, she knew just what one could see from up there for it had been her favorite hiding spot as a child. Her heart squeezed at the sight of it, and she knew she'd visit it later.

She returned her attention to Mrs. Owens.

"I must run," she finished and gave the woman's hands another squeeze.

The housekeeper gave out nothing more than an aborted squeal of surprise as Johanna picked up her skirts and ran.

It was likely the very last thing a duchess should have done, especially considering this was how she was to be introduced to her staff, but after three days in the carriage with Ben, she couldn't take another moment so cloistered.

She didn't look back, even as she heard him call out from where he'd just stepped down from the carriage. She didn't care. She knew only that she had to get away. She had to *breathe*.

She was grateful the simple gown she'd chosen to travel in had allowed her such freedom of movement. After the first day in the rain, she'd swapped her slippers for leather half boots, and they ate up the gravel beneath her feet as she streaked off in the direction of the stables.

The fresh Yorkshire air whipped past her, and she felt the tie of her bonnet loosen, but again, she didn't care. She reached the stables in seconds and tripped through the door, faltering to a stop.

"I thought I heard a carriage on the drive."

She turned at the familiar voice to see the stable master, Smothers, walking a mare toward her down the main corridor of the stables.

He handed the reins of the horse to her, and she took them, her eyes wide.

"Oh, don't give me such a look, Your Grace. As if I wouldn't know you'd been keening for a ride once you arrived." His smile showed the tooth he lost when a gelding had found the attention Smothers was giving to his lame foot not to his liking.

She smiled and said nothing more as she led the horse from the stables. She wasn't more than a few feet from its entrance when she vaulted into the saddle, her hands sweeping down the flanks of the horse as she leaned forward. The ripple of muscle beneath her hands soaked into her as the horse's breath matched her own.

"Let's run," she whispered, and the horse tossed her head as if she sensed the energy coiled inside Johanna.

And then they did just that.

She wasn't sure when she lost her bonnet, and it didn't much matter. Her hair pins went next, and soon she was flying, free of the constraints London and now her role as duchess demanded. In an instant, she was just herself again, her body becoming one with the horse beneath her as they sailed over the fields of Raeford Court.

Thank heavens the day had dawned with ample sunshine, the first hints of summer pushing their way north. She turned her face up to the sun as they crossed the field that was bordered on the south by the stream that separated Raeford from Ravenwood.

Her heart gave a jolt when she remembered how much she missed her sisters, but she knew she would see them again. Whenever they should visit the family seat, in fact. For now though, she was finally her own woman, no longer held in the shadow of her sisters, marked by a tragedy over which she'd had no control.

It was only that she thought she'd feel better about it.

She eased the horse into a trot as they neared the edge of the field and let the sounds and smells around her invade her senses. She heard the stream through the trees that marked the edge of the estate. A bird call split the air, and she looked up, but the sun was too bright to catch the bird in flight. The horse trotted on, and soon she could hear the tumble of water over the small falls where they'd played as children.

She nudged the horse in that direction, but something made her pause. She eased the horse to a stop and sat there for several moments, taking in the sun, the fields, the stream, and the trees. It was all so peaceful, and yet her stomach still roiled with unease.

She had thought the uneasiness that had plagued her the past three days would subside once she reached the familiarity of Raeford Court, but it was apparently not the case.

It was one thing to feel the fury that had swamped her at Ben's revelation, and then another when she realized everything that had happened in the past two weeks was a lie. But when he had revealed to her the truth, that he could never love, that upset the rest of it.

Because he hadn't said he could never love...*again*.

This was the thought that had tumbled end over end in her mind the last three days in the carriage. Ben had never loved Minerva, but something had forced them to wed. Something terrible and dark and horrifying. She knew it to be so from the pain that etched its way across Ben's face when he spoke of it.

She'd been numb and confused for the past three days, with despair, betrayal, and worst of all, hope spiraling through her. When she thought she would be strong enough to carry on, she would catch Ben watching her, and hope would flare inside her. Stupid, pointless hope, and she tumbled once more into the mire of her emotions.

What had he meant when he said Minerva had taught him to get what he wanted from anyone? Why had they been forced to wed? What torture had his first marriage wrought?

Her horse shifted beneath her and tossed her head at the lack of movement. She nudged the horse into a canter in the direction of the main house but changed direction almost immediately. When she reached the dowager cottage that lay nestled in a grove of trees just beyond the main house, she dismounted and pointed the horse in the direction of the stables. The mare trotted off, her head high in hopes of her oat bag.

Johanna passed through the gate at the front of the small cottage, noting the spots of overturned earth and discarded trowels and flower pots. The entire front garden looked as though a team of gnomes had been at work, and she'd frightened them off with her arrival.

The front door was wrenched open before she could reach it.

Duchess stood in a plain muslin gown marked with splatters of paint and stains of earth. Her graying blonde hair was a riot of curls springing from her head, and around her neck hung a collection of colorful beads.

She said nothing. Instead she stepped into the sunshine and wrapped her arms around Johanna. Duchess was considerably taller, and it was something from which Johanna had always drawn comfort. No matter what happened, she could always count on Duchess's embrace and the way Johanna's head always fit snugly against the woman's bosom.

And with that embrace, Johanna's heart finally settled. For it was to Duchess she had always run when she needed someone to see her, hear her, and it was to Duchess she now returned.

"I'm so sorry, child," Duchess whispered finally, and this had Johanna straightening.

She peered into the woman's unnaturally blue eyes, so like Ben's. If one did not know Duchess, it would be easy to assume the woman was mad. The wandering look in her eyes evidence alone of some kind of mental drifting. But Johanna knew better. Duchess had the look of a woman who had been forced to learn to protect herself above all else.

"Sorry for what?" Johanna asked.

But Duchess only shook her head and tucked Johanna's arm through her own, leading her off the front path and into the maze of gardens she kept herself around the dowager cottage. There were more discarded pots and trowels, mounds of overturned earth and uprooted shrubs. It was as though the garden were never quite finished, or perhaps Duchess was never quite finished gardening.

Finally they reached the odd collection of chairs Duchess had placed at the rear of the house where the afternoon sun lit the garden in yellowy warmth. The chairs, Johanna was told, had come from discarded dining room furnishings from the main house. Duchess had painted them a rainbow of colors once, but now they had faded and chipped into a splash of hues set amongst the slumbering garden.

Johanna took her favorite chair, a wooden contraption Duchess had attempted to mend when one of its arms had fallen off. It was half blue and half yellow and the replacement arm was a violent orange. It somehow suited Johanna.

Duchess knelt in the center of the space where a small fountain had once stood, the bottom of which was all that remained. She had had it turned into a Japanese rock garden. She had never traveled to Japan nor met anyone from there. She'd simply read about the gardens in a book depicting the travels of an eighteenth century explorer and decided they sounded peaceful. She'd had the guts of the fountain removed immediately to install her own rock garden.

She had taken to perching on the edge of it and running her fingers through the sand as she did now, her eyes fixed on something no one could see but her.

When next the other woman looked up, Johanna was surprised by how sharp her gaze was.

"Ben was hurt by his father too," Duchess said, her voice strong and clear. "You should know that. The man hurt Ben so much."

Johanna straightened. She knew Ben's father had been cruel, but she never knew how cruel. As children they'd avoided the main house when Ben's father was home. They had avoided Lawrence as well, but he'd never been interested in torturing them. He found other things much more playful sport.

"How do you mean?" she asked, hoping Duchess would stay with her long enough to answer.

Duchess shook her head, her fingers trailing through the sand. "He tortured Ben. He tortured Ben by hurting the thing he loved."

Johanna's chest squeezed. "He hurt you," she whispered, but Ben's mother did not respond. Duchess had returned her gaze to the rock garden.

"I'm sorry for so much," she whispered, her eyes watching the sand curl between her fingers.

"Me too," Johanna whispered, and they said nothing more.

This was how things were with Duchess. Johanna only knew a glimmer of what the woman had suffered at the hands of her husband and then her eldest son, but it was enough to give her her freedom where it could, even if it meant cryptic conversations such as this.

Still it bothered Johanna. She'd known Ben's childhood

161

hadn't been easy, but was there more to it than what she knew? Than what Ben had told her? Did it have something to do with his ill-fated marriage?

She could still feel the echo of his touch on her. The way he had pulled her into his arms in the carriage when the reality of what had happened overcame her strength to resist it. He had been so tender and yet so demanding at the same time. He had spoken in riddles much as his mother did, and she was left…wondering.

Duchess looked up suddenly, her eyes wide. "I suppose you're the duchess now," she said, her smile wide. "It will get mightily confusing should we both be called Duchess."

Johanna laughed, relaxing back in her chair as the tension of the past three days subsided. "I think you should continue to be Duchess, and I shall continue to be Johanna."

Duchess nodded and smiled again before her attention slipped back to the sand at her fingertips.

"I like it when you're Johanna," Duchess said some minutes later.

"Me too," Johanna whispered, but she knew Duchess was no longer listening.

CHAPTER 11

*H*e wasn't surprised to find Johanna in the dowager cottage garden with his mother. He also wasn't surprised to hear the elation in his mother's voice, the way her face shone when Johanna spoke to her.

Johanna had that effect on everyone.

He left them be. He'd come to see his mother on the morrow. He would be at Raeford Court for the foreseeable future now, and he had plenty of time to make up for the years they'd been apart.

He wondered if his mother truly understood what had happened. He'd written to her, and he knew from Mrs. Owens's letters, the housekeeper had repeated the current state of affairs to the woman regularly. Lawrence was dead, and Ben had married Johanna.

Did the thought give his mother peace? Would she now feel safe to emerge from the place she had taken to hiding in her head? He rubbed his chest where an ache had started two weeks ago and grew with alarming fortitude.

It would have been better had he married someone he didn't care for. Maybe then he could have been happily ensconced in his study, preparing the agenda of repairs that must be made, arranging meetings with his steward, planning visits to the tenants.

Yet here he was, walking the fields of Raeford, unable to get his wife out of his head.

He had already found what he'd gone into the fields to find, and he tossed it between his hands now.

Johanna's bonnet.

He'd stood transfixed as she'd leapt from the carriage and raced off in the direction of the stables, her skirts held improperly high. He wasn't surprised to see her emerge, moments later, mare in hand. She was off before he could get to her, and when her bonnet had come free, the sight of her had hit him squarely in the chest.

Johanna was home.

That should have been consolation enough for what he had done to her, and yet he somehow had managed to feel even worse.

He wandered back into the house by way of the kitchens where Cook had plied him with her famous honey biscuits, made from honey produced from the estate's own apiary. It had been his idea to start the apiary, a project he had only been able to accomplish with the help of the softhearted gardener, Willoughby. Willoughby had been gone for some years now, but every time Ben tasted honey from their own apiary it sent him back to that day so long ago when he thought he may still have a part to play at Raeford Court.

He ambled into his study more than an hour later and was pretending to read the report from his steward when a soft knock sounded at the door.

He looked up expecting Mrs. Owens and was surprised to find Johanna.

In a nightrail and dressing gown.

Carefully, he set the report down on his desk, his eyes never leaving her.

His body responded to her in a way he still thought impossible, and yet here he was. Lusting after his wife. Still his heart felt nothing, and he knew he was the worst kind of cad. She was his wife though, and by rights, he could do with her as he pleased. But he couldn't live with himself if he took her body when he had no intention of returning the feelings she had for him.

She shut the door behind her and came toward him, stopping several feet in front of his desk.

"I've come to inquire as to the plans for improvements. Do you plan to start on the morrow or do more immediate tasks require your attention?"

He had never heard her speak in such formal tones, and another piece of his memories died.

He leaned back in his chair. "I plan to tour the tenant farms tomorrow. Most were here when I was a boy, but there are several new families to whom I wish to introduce myself."

She nodded. "Then I should like to go with you. As the new duchess, I should like to make their acquaintance."

"Of course."

An awkward silence, so unusual for them, descended then, and he felt a headache pressing at the backs of his eyes.

"Johanna—"

"Ben—"

He stopped and watched her. She stopped and watched him. He gestured for her to go on.

"I visited your mother today. She seems in good spirits although I didn't venture to mention Lawrence."

He nodded. "I should think she grieves in her own way, if at all."

She nodded and looked down at her folded hands.

"I wonder if she feels peace now. Now that they're both gone," she added.

She spoke with no malice, and he knew she was of the kind to let the past be the past. He wished he were so lucky.

He stood and moved to the front of his desk, leaning back against it as he crossed his arms over his chest. She didn't move, and he took that as a sign they had reached some sort of detente.

"I assume you have no problem with my mother remaining in the dowager cottage."

Her eyes flashed. "I find it hurtful that you should even bring up the subject."

He suppressed a grin. "I meant to inquire whether or not you had designs to return my mother to the main house."

She pursed her lips. "Oh." She unfolded and refolded her hands. "I think your mother is happiest in the cottage." A smile touched her lips. "She appears to be doing some gardening, although I fear she'll forget she was doing so and the cottage should look as though a league of ground creatures has invaded."

For a moment it was as if they were their old selves. Just Johanna and just Ben. He didn't realize how much he could long for something that had dogged him for so much time and had suddenly vanished.

He wasn't sure how long they stood there, but slowly Johanna's expression became muddled, as though an unpleasant or confusing thought had filtered through her mind. She seemed to clear her head though for her features lightened as she stepped closer to him.

"Good night then, Ben." She leaned forward and on tiptoe, pressed a kiss to his cheek.

He knew the gesture was automatic, one she had thought very little of performing, and yet he could tell the moment when she realized she'd stepped too far.

She smelled like Raeford.

Like fresh air and horses and trees and the stream. She smelled like memories and home and everything he longed to have returned to him. Peace and happiness and laughter.

His heart jumped at her nearness, and he willed himself to maintain control.

She'd paused with her lips hovering over his cheek, and she backed away slowly.

She was barefoot.

He didn't know why he would realize as much now, but suddenly, he became very interested in her feet.

"Good night," he said when he thought his voice would hold steady, and he looked up to find her watching him.

Her eyes moved back and forth across his face, and he wondered what she might be sorting through.

A naive part of him wished she were looking for a way to awaken his heart, to bring back the part of him Minerva had killed. The part that could love her.

He released his arms and grabbed hold of the desk behind him to keep from reaching for her. He couldn't do that to her. He couldn't toy with her emotions that way. He couldn't tell himself it was all right because she loved him.

But God, he didn't want to be alone.

Seeing Raeford Court for the first time in five years had hit him harder than he'd expected it to. It was as though he'd been gone an entire lifetime and yet somehow it felt like not a day had passed. It left him whirling and wandering, and all he wanted was to lie in her arms, feel her comforting embrace take hold of him.

"Good night," she said again and still she did not move toward the door.

"You already said that."

The tension was palpable, and he realized had his honor not won out, he would be taking her upstairs now, taking her to bed. *His* bed. He would be spending the night lost in her arms.

"I did." She nodded briskly and turned for the door.

His heart ripped apart, and he turned back to the reports on his desk, determined to let her go.

But the sound of the door opening never reached him, and he turned back.

She stood, her back to him, her hand on the door knob. He willed her to go through it. He willed her not to test what was left of his resolve.

She spun around. "Ben, what did your father do to you?"

The words smothered any desire that might have kindled inside of him.

"My father?" He set the papers he'd picked up back onto his desk. "What has my father to do with anything?"

She worried her lower lip and came toward him. "It's just that your mother mentioned something, and I think—" She licked her lips, her fisted hands going to her hips. "I think it's time you were honest with me. For once. Please, Ben. What did your father do to you?"

He settled back against his desk, shaking his head.

"I'm afraid the story is not terribly interesting."

"I'll decide if it's interesting or not."

He studied her face and was surprised to find the hardness that had entered her expression. She always had been one to defend them. She was strong like that.

But he wasn't. Shame burned inside of him when he thought of what he'd done, what he'd succumbed to. He would tell her the truth. Just not all of it.

"When I entered my majority, I made a request of my father. I wished to see to the running of Raeford Court. I knew the title and thus ownership of the estate was out of question as that would pass to Lawrence, but I asked that I might have a cottage on the estate and be given free rein to see to its health."

She shrugged. "Any number of second sons would ask for such a posting."

He nodded. "I had thought the same. I knew I wasn't cut out for the vicarage, and I hadn't the stamina for the military. Raeford was the only thing at which I excelled, and I knew I could make it something better for the title. My father thought differently."

"What happened?" She'd stepped closer again, and he caught the ghost of her scent.

"My father sent a letter down to Oxford informing me that he'd secured a post in a shipping office in Boston for me."

"He told you this in a letter?"

He nodded and rubbed the back of his neck. "My father was very good at ensuring he delivered bad news with crippling accuracy."

She stepped forward, her hand reaching out and settling softly on his chest. "But Ben, that's awful."

He wasn't sure if her words or her barely-there touch undid him, but he suddenly felt the desk more sharply at the backs of his thighs as his knees weakened.

"Yes, it was rather poorly done," he said.

She shook her head, and the hand that lay on his chest turned and gripped the lapel of his jacket.

"How can you give him such latitude?"

He searched her eyes as he said, "Because I'll be damned if I give him anything more."

Something passed between them, and he recalled the look of fury on her face when Andrew had tried to stop their wedding. He wondered not for the first time if he and Johanna were much more similar than he had first believed.

She let go of his jacket and stepped back. His body

yearned toward her, and it was all he could do to stay leaning against the desk.

She considered him, and he expected her to say more, but she seemed to come to some kind of conclusion as she turned once more to the door.

But once again she stopped, her eyes riveted to a place behind him. He turned to follow her gaze and found her bonnet on his desk where he'd placed it when he'd first come in. He picked it up now, ran his hand one last time over the brim before handing it to her.

"Your bonnet, Your Grace," he said, forcing a smile.

Her lips parted as she took the hat, her fingers tentatively tracing the brim. "You rescued my bonnet." Her words were not more than a whisper.

He shrugged. "I know how much you enjoy losing them. I thought you might like another go at this one."

When her eyes met his, he saw the confusion of her emotions, and he hated himself for doing that to her.

An apology was already on his lips when she said, "Thank you, Ben."

He could do nothing more than nod.

"I'll see you at breakfast," she said and slipped out.

Sleep eluded her.

She lay in bed until she was certain the mattress would forever contain the imprint of her restlessness, and finally when the sky lightened from black to gray, she threw back the covers and got up. She donned her dressing robe and in bare feet padded into the corridor and turned right toward the main part of the house.

The personal quarters were all in the Georgian wings, but what she sought was at the heart of the original house. She found the stairs without error and climbed to the top floor. She was quiet as she moved past the closed doors for she wasn't certain which rooms were still occupied by servants, and she didn't wish to disturb them. Someone ought to have a good night's sleep.

She found the alcove that hid the circular stairs that led up to the cap-house. The metal was rough and cold against her bare feet, but she hardly noticed. It was lighter here, and she could almost sense the sky hovering above her somewhere. She grasped the wrought iron railing and climbed higher until finally she broke free into the cap-house.

Glass encircled her, and through it she saw the morning fog as it lay blanketing the fields of Raeford. It spread out before her like an offering, and she could do nothing more than collapse on the bench installed in the uppermost part of the cap-house.

Unlike other Jacobean houses, the cap-house at Raeford had been built higher than the surrounding parapet and even as she sat, she could still see beyond the house, the morning sun just beginning to crest the distant horizon.

She wrapped her robe more tightly against herself and pulled her knees against her chest. And then she waited.

She'd always wondered what it would be like to watch the sun rise from here. She could no longer count the number of times she'd stolen away to the cap-house as if it were some magical place and in it she could be seen. After all, with so many windows, how could she not be?

But she had always been invisible.

She understood that now.

For a brief moment in time, she thought Ben had seen her, but it had all been a trick of the light.

She had spent the journey north wrestling her feelings for Ben, and yesterday's ride across the fields and visit with Duchess had done little to sort herself.

It was one thing for Ben to have lied to her, to have pursued her for her dowry rather than her heart. It was another to carry the memory of the things he had done to her.

More than once now she'd awoken, shaken with the thought that she had felt the brush of his kiss, so real, so certain, and yet it could only have been a dream.

It always would be a dream now.

She wasn't sure which was worse. To have craved his kiss and never felt it. Or to have tasted it and to face the reality of never having it again. She thought the latter was the worse punishment.

But last night had complicated matters.

She had known Ben's father preferred Lawrence, but she had never realized the depth of his hatred nor the lengths at which he had gone to show his distaste of his second born. To have something so precious ripped from him without ceremony must have been devastating.

To be forced to leave England so soon after, crushing.

The news of his brother's death must have sent him reeling. She knew Ben enough to know it would give him pause no matter how cruel the man had been, but she was sure Ben must have felt a surge of emotion at the occurrence.

What had he felt when he realized Raeford was his?

And then, when he realized it would all be taken away from him?

Again.

She swallowed at the sudden pain in her chest. The cartwheel of emotions he must have endured in the space of a few weeks' time was unimaginable to her.

It did not excuse what he had done, and she still didn't know if she could live with the memory of what they had shared or with knowing the fact that it had all been a charade.

Still her thoughts were haunted by his revelation that day in the carriage after he had so recently shattered her entire world.

Minerva.

The sky melted into tones of pink and orange as the name tripped over and over again through her mind.

What had Minerva done to him? Johanna had formed an image of Ben with his wife that she was now coming to understand had been entirely fabricated from her own wild imaginings.

But he hadn't loved her. Why had he married her?

Ben had gone from the cruelty of his father, the torture meted out by his brother, to the prison that was his marriage.

She shook her head as if a physical gesture were needed to clear her thoughts of the tumultuousness that had been Ben's life till now.

Till now.

Everything was different. Everyone who had hurt him before was gone. All of the people who had the power to control him, to determine his future, were gone.

Maybe now he could heal. Now that he had returned to Raeford, he could find the peace that would allow him to heal, and maybe, just maybe, one day he might learn to love.

Love her.

The thought seemed ridiculous. Love in real life was not the love of fairy tales and novels. Ben had been hurt over and over again. How could she expect him to ever recover?

The sun slipped over the horizon at that exact moment, and light spilled over the fields of Raeford as though someone had tipped over a cup full of sunshine. It pierced the early morning fog that had already begun to dissipate, and soon she could see the fields themselves, only dappled now with lingering haze.

Movement caught her attention, and she leaned forward, pressing a hand to the glass.

Ben.

Ben on horseback as he raced across the fields and toward the dawning sun. She could almost feel the wind against her cheeks, the way it would pull at her hair, the horse undulating between her thighs as she let her body flow until they were one.

But the rush of euphoria at the sight of him once more on horseback racing across Raeford fields evaporated at the memory of their last race.

When he had proposed and she thought she could never be happier in all the rest of her life.

Her hand slipped from the glass, and she made her way back downstairs to dress for the day.

By the time she arrived in the breakfast room, the sun had fully risen, and she was surprised to find Duchess at the table consuming an alarming pile of scones and clotted cream.

"Good morning," Johanna said softly as she entered, worried she'd startle the woman as she so intently spread jam and cream across a broken piece of scone.

"Good morning," Duchess sang and offered the bite of scone to Johanna.

Johanna smiled and bent to press a kiss to Duchess's cheek. "No, thank you. Ben and I are riding out to the tenants this morning. I should probably eat something a little more robust."

Duchess looked crestfallen but then gave a shrug. "I suppose it's too sweet for some tastes, but not for mine." She gave a wicked smile before popping the sickly sweet morsel into her mouth.

Johanna couldn't help but laugh. Her heart warmed at seeing Duchess so playful and in the main house no less.

She helped herself to the sideboard, piling a plate with eggs and sausages. It had been months since she'd spent a day riding, and she knew she would need the sustenance. Her muscles practically hummed in anticipation of the day's exercise.

"You're to visit the tenants. How lovely," Duchess said around another mouthful of cream. "I remember doing so. Some of them are so kind." She pointed with a bit of scone. "Some are right arses."

"Mother." They both started at Ben's sharp tone as he entered the room. "Do not say such things about our tenants." His smile melted into a mischievous grin. "Johanna should figure it out for herself."

Duchess laughed and wiggled her brows. "Oh, I seem to have ruined the fun. Dear me." She went back to scooping clotted cream on her scone.

Johanna couldn't take her eyes away from Ben though. He was dressed much as he had been that morning he'd come to sneak her out of Ravenwood House. He wore no collar, and his hair was mussed with sleep and wind. He was without jacket now, and his shirt sleeves were rolled up, exposing muscled forearms.

She knew what it was like to have those arms wrapped around her. To press her mouth to that spot exposed by his lack of collar.

He caught her gaze then, and she nearly swallowed her tongue. Except his eyes slid to the side, taking in his mother, before returning to hers.

His mother rarely took a meal in the main house. At least, she hadn't when Johanna had been there as a child. It was telling that Duchess had chosen to break her fast with them that morning. She returned Ben's gaze before forcing her attention to her plate, poking at her eggs.

"I trust you slept well."

It was a moment before she realized Ben spoke to her.

She smiled, but even she knew it would fool no one. "Splendidly," she lied.

He nodded as he helped himself to a plate. "It should prove to be an arduous task if we are to visit all of the tenants in a single day."

She peered across the table to where her husband had taken a seat at the opposite end.

Her husband.

They spoke as though they were colleagues collaborating on a particular task.

So mundane.

So abject.

So...

Heartbreaking.

She swallowed her eggs. "I am up for the task if you are."

"What are you thinking of doing with the estate, dear boy?" Duchess asked then.

For a moment, they were tossed back in time. She knew Ben felt it as well from the sharp glance he sent down the table at her. His mother had always called him dear boy whereas Johanna could not recall the woman calling her eldest anything other than Lawrence.

It was almost as if they were children again, and nothing bad had happened to them yet.

"I'm going to make Raeford flourish once again, Mother," Ben said as he filled a cup with coffee from the urn set on the table.

Duchess paused, bite of scone in one hand, a knife dripping jam in the other. "Isn't it flourishing now?"

Johanna paused in her chewing and caught Ben's eye. They were never quite sure how much Duchess really knew and how much was an act she conjured to protect herself from further harm. Sometimes her statements held too close to the edge of reality for either's comfort.

"It is not as grand as it once was," Ben finally said.

Duchess set down her knife. "Oh dear. Should I practice restraint when it comes to the clotted cream then?"

Ben eyed the enormous bowl of clotted cream and the dubious crater Duchess had excavated just that morning.

"I should think the clotted cream is not in danger."

Duchess's sigh of relief could surely have been heard in Cornwall. She scooped more of it onto her plate.

"Well, if that isn't a blessing, I don't know what is."

Johanna laughed even as the domesticity of the scene struck her in the throat, causing her to reach for her coffee.

She caught Ben watching her, and she returned his glance, her chin up.

This was what she had now. This businesslike relationship with the man she had once loved above all else—still loved?—and the affections of a woman whose sanity would always be in question.

But it was the choice she had made and in that, she took refuge. For once, she had something of her own doing, and it would need to be enough.

It simply must be.

CHAPTER 12

*B*y the third tenant farm, he was ready to pack it in for the day.

It was obvious his steward's reports were padded at best. At worst, the man was outright lying about the conditions of the farms. Ben wondered if it were a loyalty to Lawrence or an instinctual dislike of the second son inheriting the title.

The steward had been in place since Ben's father, and Ben couldn't help but wonder if it were not all second sons the man abhorred or if it were Ben in particular.

The drainage issues in the west fields were far more dire than the reports let on. A good rain could wash out an entire year's crop of wheat, leaving the farmer without food stuffs, feed, and profit. The last of the dairy herd was indescribable. The lone dairy cow he'd come across was shared between the three farmers on that end of the estate.

The situation, to put it simply, was unacceptable.

The tenants all approached him with a wary eye as soon as they rode onto their parcel of land. The only saving grace was Johanna. She slipped from her saddle, bright smile already on her face and a parcel of flowers from the hothouse Duchess kept.

Johanna insisted on seeing the woman of the house, and she more than once marched right past the man who'd come out to greet them. Ben wasn't sure what she said or did, but by the end of the visits, the wife had always emerged, usually with a smattering of children surrounding her, a smile on her face and an arm full of flowers, Johanna promising to visit again soon.

She'd been born to this.

In his mad dash to find a wealthy bride, he'd never considered how *good* Johanna would be as a duchess. Yes, she was the daughter of a duchess and knew the requirements that came with the title, but it was more than that. She had a way with people he couldn't fathom. It was as though she'd been studying them her whole life and had developed an innate ability to assess a person immediately and determine what it was that would appeal to them most.

He wondered not for the first time what it must have been like to be the youngest of such a big family. How often she might have been inadvertently neglected. How much time she had spent simply observing people. She had won over the three tenants they had visited thus far, and he could only imagine what more she could do.

As they made their way to the next tenant farm, he felt something shift, and he tried to recall what she had said on their wedding day. It hardly seemed like nearly a week had passed since that awful day, but in that time, he'd come to understand something better.

Johanna had married him for her own reasons, reasons he was not privy to but was coming to understand. He suspected it had much to do with the running of Raeford Court as she took to it so naturally. He felt a slight stab of annoyance at this, but he pushed it away.

Raeford Court was his, and he needn't feel so protective of it. Johanna had a role to play as his duchess, and she was doing it with aplomb. If she wished to monitor the progress of improvements, so be it. It was the means of her livelihood now as well. It was only right that she show a concern.

She held her horse at a walk several feet in front of him, leaving him to his own thoughts, but he couldn't help but let those thoughts stray to her. She sat a horse well, and he remembered their younger years spent racing one another across the fields. He wondered if she'd still raced after he left for America.

They had arrived at the next tenant farm by then, and he found much of the same. Drainage issues, a lack of livestock, and even a broken fence. He went to inspect it, trudging through the swampy field with the farmer, the sound of Johanna's laughter trailing behind him. She'd taken to rolling hoops with the tenant's children, and he worried she'd get stuck in the swamp the poor drainage had turned the fields into.

The fence was beyond repair. A storm had knocked down several trees along the length of it, and it would be best to replace the entire thing. Nowhere in his reports was there any mention of the decrepit fencing. He assured the tenant he would see to it before the livestock was replenished and began the arduous journey back to the farmer's cottage.

He'd only made it several meters when Johanna's laughter caught up with him. He looked up to find her racing down the small hill toward the road, a hoop spinning crazily in front of her. The eldest daughter of the farmer chased after her, her braids bouncing behind her.

The scene was so terribly domestic it stopped him where he was, his boots sinking farther into the mud.

He watched, his chest growing uncomfortably tight, but it

wasn't the sight of Johanna with the child that undid him. It was the look on her face.

Pure, uncomplicated joy.

Johanna was truly having fun with the little girl as they rolled the hoop back up the hill. He couldn't remember the last time he had been that unfettered. The last time he had let himself simply be for the joy of it. No expectations, no responsibilities, nothing.

He wasn't sure how long he stood there watching his wife play with the small child, but it was long enough for him to make up his mind. He tugged his boots free of the mud and crested the hill just as Johanna was returning with the hoop.

Her open expression dimmed at the sight of him, and he wondered what his own expression suggested.

Currently, he was feeling anything but joyful with his boots full of mud, his fields quickly becoming a bog, and his fences requiring costly repairs.

He forced a smile. "Ready to move on, wife?"

Her lips quivered against a smile at that last word, and she eyed him skeptically. "Certainly...husband."

He bid farewell to the tenant and his wife, assuring them he would return in short order to address the repairs. They turned onto the road, and he stared straight ahead of them, mentally picturing the rest of the tenants along this stretch of the lane.

He cursed and pushed up his hat to rub at his pounding forehead.

"I take it you were not expecting things to be as they are," Johanna said after some time.

He scrubbed his hand over his face. "Not at all."

They had nearly reached the next tenant farm when something seized him.

"Race you to the stream." The words were out before he knew what he was doing.

Johanna's glance was swift and startled, but he'd already spurred his horse into a gallop. He didn't wait for her as he turned the horse toward the fields. The agile animal vaulted the ditch by the road with ease, and when its hooves hit the open field, it took off.

Euphoria.

That's what Ben felt as the horse gained its footing, found its stride. As its gallop reached its full potential. They tore across the fields, the wind whipping past them, and he felt his body sink into the horse, become one with the animal.

He hadn't ridden like this since he left for America. He'd risen early that morning hoping for a ride, but the fog had been too thick. He'd managed a few sprints, but it was not this. This complete and total release of all inhibitions.

He vaguely became aware of the sound of hoofbeats behind him, but he didn't turn to see if Johanna had caught up. He knew only too well her skill, and any deviation from his trajectory would give her an edge.

He bent over his horse, urging the beast to give it his all. They hurtled over the last hedge that delineated the tenant farms from the main house, and it was as though the horse knew where they were going, a fresh burst of speed tearing through the creature. They passed the lake, it's surface glassy in the calm day, but he didn't have time to admire it.

The edge of the forest that bordered this end of the estate loomed before them. He had to slow enough to prevent injury to him or the horse, but he had to keep his speed if he wished to win. It was an arduous task that required skill and cunning, and no matter how he had practiced when they were younger, Johanna had always bested him.

He began to slow, the tree line nearing, but it was already too late. Johanna tore past him. The only thing he could note was that her bonnet bounced loosely against her back, her hair wild, having come undone from its pins. The distraction caused him to pinch the horse with his thighs and the animal slowed even more in confusion.

He'd lost, quite soundly, but he didn't care. For a moment just then, he was a young man again. For just a second, he was free, young, and happy. For just a moment…

He watched her slip through the trees, reducing the speed of the horse with ease and grace, and soon they disappeared into the denser wood that shielded the stream. Belatedly, he remembered to urge his horse forward to follow them, his thoughts muddled and confused.

Why couldn't he be happy again?

All the pieces were there.

Raeford, Johanna, and the stream where they'd once pretended to be pirates.

If only so much hadn't happened. Shame flashed inside of him, and he stamped it down.

The stream was unchanged.

It hit him hard, and he sucked in a breath. Here it was as though time had stood still, and maybe all of the bad things that had happened hadn't really happened at all.

The stream narrowed into a gentle waterfall over a tumble of rocks, creating a pool deep enough for swimming. The tumble of rocks scattered for several yards in each direction, giving ample flat surfaces that had served as the decks of pirate ships and even a fort. He smiled at the memory of Johanna standing on the rocks opposite, a stick held loftily in the air as if it were a sword, the sash of her dress tied around her head like a pirate scarf, demanding Ben walk the plank.

This meant he had to jump from the waterfall into the pool, and it was never really a threat, but it didn't matter when he was twelve. It only mattered that he made a bigger splash than Andrew when he jumped.

He was so lost in his own memories, he didn't see Johanna slip from the trees behind him until she was nearly to the edge of the stream. The banks were steep here as years of erosion from the waterfall had made them so. She'd left her horse to graze in the grasses at the edge of the forest, and she turned her face up to him now, shielding her eyes from the sun with a flat hand.

"Would you like to tell me what happened back there?" Her tone was light, but he didn't wish to speak of it. Not here.

He slid from the saddle and let his own horse find the grass at the forest's edge before stepping over to the bank. He grabbed Johanna's hand without really thinking of it and started the careful trek down the bank to the stream.

She didn't try to pull her hand away, but he thought she wished to. They had traversed the tricky descent of the stream bed for years, and she didn't require his help. It was only that he wished for the feel of her hand in his just then.

He stepped out onto the first flat rock and stopped, letting the early summer sun warm his shoulders. The water rushed over the falls behind him, and birdsong trickled from the forest. But there was no other noise except the sound of their own breathing, and suddenly he was weightless.

He sank. He sat directly down on the rock, pulling Johanna with him. She didn't protest that he would ruin her gown, and for that he was grateful. He couldn't ever imagine Johanna complaining of her gown being ruined, and he would have really not enjoyed finding her preference for dress having changed now.

He lay directly back on the rock, feeling its heat through his jacket as his hat fell back against the rock. He closed his eyes and draped an arm across them to block out the sun.

When Johanna touched him, he started and opened his

eyes. She leaned over him, her fingers just tracing the line of his jaw.

"Do you want to tell me what's going on?"

Her hair fell about her in a curtain, the sun illuminating her like an angel in a Renaissance painting. He thought if he touched her she would evaporate, disperse like a mirage, and he'd be left all alone. So he didn't touch her. He lay there and wondered how they had come to this.

"The reports from the steward appear to be inaccurate," he finally said.

She frowned. "And this is cause for running away?"

He tugged his jaw free from her wandering fingers. "It's cause enough for running away *today*. I think I shall find a new steward and attempt to visit the tenants on another day." He snapped his eyes shut against her assessing gaze.

"So what is it you plan to do today?"

He cracked open a single eye. "Am I not doing something now?"

She lifted both eyebrows. "Oh, I see. We are to play at sea lions then." She flopped onto her back beside him, her arms splaying to either side. "I'm ready."

He laughed, the sound so unexpected that it sounded odd to his own ears. Sea lions was another game they had played. They would lie on the warm rocks until they could no longer bear it. The first person to jump into the pool lost the game.

He nudged her. She elbowed him.

"You will not get me to jump into the pool, Your Grace."

He rolled over. "Who said anything about jumping?"

He tucked his arms around her, prepared to lift her and toss her into the pool himself, but he stopped, arrested by her beauty, by the fact that she was there, that she was in his arms, that she looked...content.

"Johanna," he whispered, his fingers tracing the curve of

her cheek, the line of her jaw. "Johanna," he said again and lowered his head, pressing his lips to hers.

* * *

IN ALL HER DREAMS, she had never imagined them here.

Like this.

The stream had always been the place of childish games, and the way she felt about Ben was anything but childish. She had always pictured them at the main house. Her favorite dream had always involved the cap-house. Ben would find her there and slip behind her on the window bench, pulling her snugly against his chest while he whispered words of love in her ear.

Getting pinned against a rock was not the first romantic notion she'd had.

But when his lips touched hers she suddenly wondered why she hadn't thought of this before.

The rush of the water around them drowned out the rest of the world. The sun warmed them, and the steep walls of the stream shielded them from the outside world. It was all so perfect.

Except it wasn't.

She pushed gently against his shoulders until he released her lips.

"Ben." She searched his face, so many questions wrinkling her brow.

Was this all she would have?

His touch, his kiss, his embrace. The physical parts of him when she longed for the other bits. His heart, his devotion, his…love.

He seemed to study her, his eyes moving over her face as if he were seeing her for the first time. Abruptly, he sat up, raking his fingers through his hair as he pushed his hat the rest of the way off his head. It tumbled to the rocks behind him, and he didn't bother to pick it up. He sat, his arms propped on his bent knees as he peered down at the pool of water below them.

She sat up too, quietly, softly, and watched him, the tension visible in the tick of muscle at his jaw.

She let several seconds pass before she spoke. "Ben, what happened between you and Minerva?"

The tension caused the muscle in his jaw to jump, and he looked to the opposite side of the stream away from her.

She pulled her knees up and wrapped her arms around them, waiting.

There was a soft breeze and it brought with it the smell of earth and tree. It played with the ends of her hair, and she gathered the mass of it in one hand and pulled it to one side, tucking it in the crook of her neck to keep the wind from blowing it in her face.

Still Ben did not speak.

She studied the tension in his shoulders, the pulse of that muscle in his jaw. "It must have hurt, Ben. Deeply. The things Minerva did. Have you never spoken with someone of it?"

Silence.

She dropped her knees and crossed her legs, her hands finding the buttons of her riding skirt as if to distract herself from her own lack of progress with her husband.

"I know what it's like. Not to have someone in whom you can confide. You might remember I've carried a secret for a very long time. One I did not feel I could tell even my sisters." She put a little self-deprecating laughter into her voice. They both knew where her secret had gotten her. Alone in a marriage to the man of her dreams.

He turned now and met her gaze, but still he didn't speak.

She kept going. "It's hard being the youngest of the Darby sisters. I used to think it was because I had no memory of our mother. Nothing to share with them when they spoke of her. But I think it's something more than that." She moved her gaze away from his as she looked out over the stream, her mind going back through the memories of her childhood. "They each have something. Viv was always the eldest and taking care of everyone. Eliza had her watercolors, and Louisa had me." She shrugged. "I had nothing. Or at least I didn't until I discovered Raeford." She met his gaze then. "And you," she nearly whispered.

He broke his gaze away, and her heart cracked at the rejection.

What had she been expecting? He'd made his stance perfectly clear on their wedding day. He didn't love her and couldn't love her. There's was a business arrangement, and that was all.

She pushed to her feet, brushing sand from her skirts.

"I suppose we're done for the day, so I'm going to return to the house now. I promised Duchess I'd help her make yarn from the goat hair she's collected."

He didn't stop her, and somehow her heart broke even further. She didn't know how she could possibly be hurt any more, but apparently, she wasn't done. She climbed the steep bank out of the stream bed.

She paused at the top to brush the dirt from the knees of her skirt and searched her pockets for a piece of ribbon to tie back her hair. She'd left her bonnet on the horn of her saddle, and if she failed to find a ribbon, she'd simply tuck the mass of it under her hat.

Giving up the search, she snickered to draw the attention of her horse from where it stood nibbling at grasses along the bank. She had already started to reach out a hand when Ben grabbed her.

The movement was fast and startling, and the air rushed from her lungs. He spun her around and pressed her against the trunk of a tree, the bark biting into her back through the thin fabric of her gown.

His face was tight with the memory of pain or the ghost of his wife's cruelty, she couldn't be sure. But it frightened her to see it there. Her beautiful Ben so wracked with torment. She could do nothing but lay her hands against his chest as he bore down on her.

"I don't want you to know the things that happened to me," he growled. "I don't want you to be ruined because of it. Do you understand me?" He shook her a little now, her head bouncing softly against the tree at her back.

"Ben." Tears had somehow made their way to her voice, and she didn't know why.

Was she crying for Ben or was she crying for herself?

He bent his forehead to hers. "Johanna," he groaned. "Johanna."

Her name was like an oath on his lips, and she wanted to hear it again and again.

He cupped her face in his hands, traced the column of her neck down and back up to spear his fingers through her loosened hair. Only then did he back away enough to meet her gaze.

"Johanna, you're the last piece of my life that reminds me what it is to have happiness, and I don't ever want that to change. Please." His voice was pleading, and something deep inside of her thrummed in response to it.

She gripped his wrists. "Ben, I won't change. I promise. I'm strong enough for you to tell me the things—"

"No." Again, he shook her just the smallest amount as if he had to shake her to get her to understand.

"Oh, Ben." The tears were thick in her voice now, even though her eyes remained dry.

His eyes had turned dark and relentless as he seemed to drink in her face, as though he had to hold her and see her to assure himself she wouldn't disappear, taking with her the last of his happiness.

"I need you." The words were part growl and part whisper, and they thrummed deep in her belly. "I need you," he repeated, his eyes searching her face as though he couldn't understand the words himself.

This time when his lips met hers she welcomed his kiss. She pressed into him, coming up on her toes to wrap her arms around his neck. He pressed her back into the tree, his hands gripping her hips to hold her in place.

Desire shot through her, complete and unexpected, and she remembered their all too brief encounter on the hillside. Her nipples hardened at the memory, and she pressed herself more fully against him.

His tongue plunged in her mouth, sweeping over her teeth and tongue, and she reeled at the sensation, her fingers digging into his back as she tried to hold on. He swept his hands down, cupping her buttocks to fit her snugly against him.

He was hard. She could feel the bulge of him low against her belly, and the notion thrilled, sending her passion into a frenzy.

"Ben," she moaned against his lips. "Ben, please."

His hands scrambled to lift her skirts, and her head fell back as his lips found their way to the sensitive place behind her ear, to trace the line of her jaw, to follow the column of her neck. His beard scraped against her soft skin, and she thought she'd expire from the sensation.

Finally, she felt his touch through her stockings, his caress traveling higher.

"Ben, please," she whimpered.

He pressed kisses along the collar of her riding habit, and she wished her costume wasn't so modest. She wanted him to touch her everywhere. To feel his lips pressed to her most intimate places. To places only he would know.

When his fingers brushed the bare skin above her stockings, she bucked against him, her legs threatening to give out.

He tightened his other arm around her, lifting her slightly against him so she held him and he held her.

His fingers explored, tracing the soft curve of her thigh, and the tension coiling at her core grew unbearable.

"Ben," she moaned. "Please, please. I want you to touch me."

His answer was only a groan as he slid his hand higher, his fingers separating her folds. He was so close, so close to that spot that ached for him.

But he didn't touch her.

He pulled back, the motion leaving her bereft and gasping.

"Johanna, forgive me." His voice was thick, his eyes searching.

"Ben."

She thought he would leave her then, panting and wanting against the tree, but he didn't. She dimly became aware of movement, the rustling of fabric, the—

Oh God, he was undoing the front of his trousers.

Heat spiked through her, and she couldn't tear her eyes from where he furiously worked at buttons, his own desire apparent in the way his hand shook.

It all happened so quickly. His hand slipped beneath her skirts again, but instead of it finding the place where she ached, it moved to cup her buttocks, lifting her against the tree. She arched, raising her legs to wrap them around his waist.

"Ben." It was hardly more than a sigh as he pressed against her, as she felt his hard length against the place that ached for him.

"Johanna." Her name. God, the way he said her name, she could hear it a thousand times and never grow tired of it.

He slipped into her, full and glorious, and she stretched around him, the pulsing growing furious.

"Ben, please."

He moved, sliding out almost to the tip before slamming into her. Her back would be raw from the tree bark, but she didn't care. All that mattered was that he kept going.

The tension grew, the heat flared, her body yearned toward his.

"Ben, I need—"

But she never finished the sentence because just then he slipped his hand around to the front and touched her.

She exploded, a cry of utter desire spilling from her lips. He didn't stop, pounding into her until she thought she could bear no more. Somehow the tension began to build again. His thrusts grew harder, sharper, longer. Her legs wrapped more tightly around him.

"Look at me," he whispered, and she shook her head against the tree.

"Ben, I—"

"Look at me. See me, Johanna."

Her eyes flew open at the exact moment the second climax hit her, and her entire world erupted around her. Her muscles squeezed around his hardness, and she felt his orgasm, impossibly stronger than hers and the sensation was heady and exhilarating. She wrapped her arms tightly around him as if she could possibly hold on as the tremors racked their bodies, and eventually her legs slid to the ground.

They stood there, still entwined although their bodies no longer connected, trying to catch their breaths, the breeze suddenly cool against her sweat-dampened skin.

"Ben, I—"

He pulled away from her, his hands furiously doing up his trousers. She stood, shaken and confused against the tree.

"I'm so sorry," he said before he snatched the reins of his horse and vaulted into the saddle, spurring the horse in the direction of the house and leaving her utterly alone.

Again.

CHAPTER 13

*B*en threw himself into the estate improvements.

It was either that or torture himself by being in the company of his wife.

He hired a new steward immediately. Firing the previous one provided far too much pleasure for him. It was almost as if Ben were firing his father when he terminated the lying, inept steward. He wanted to feel a rush of joy at shedding the estate of his father's lackey, but he didn't. He only faced more sadness as the real state of the land came into focus when the new steward assessed the tenant farms.

It was much worse than he had first believed.

He set the steward, Blanstock, to begin the migration to the crop rotation system of planting while Ben went in search of the new herd. Excavation for new drainage started the week Ben left for Harrogate, where he had a lead on an estate selling off some of their herd after a plentiful spring.

He'd written a note for his valet to give to Johanna. He knew it was rude and unforgivable, but he couldn't bring himself to face her. It was more than what he had done that day by the stream. That he could live with. It was the fact that she had opened herself up to him, and he hadn't been able to reciprocate.

No, more than that. He'd shut her out completely. Taking her physically so he wouldn't be forced to give himself emotionally.

He was a first-rate bastard, and so he'd taken to avoiding her.

Somehow in his mind he'd figured that if he no longer plagued her with his presence it was somehow making it better for her. He knew damn well he was just a coward, but there was too much at stake.

Raeford was finally his, and he could put into motion all the plans he had engineered five years ago. He buried himself in work, trying to remember that this was what he wanted, and yet he still felt hollow as if he were still waiting for something to happen.

He hadn't felt this kind of despair since his days working in the shipping office, and it frightened him. Raeford was supposed to be everything he had ever wanted.

So why was he still left...wanting?

The week he had planned to spend in Harrogate managed to turn into two. From there he'd heard of a gentleman farmer selling off his herd just south of Leeds. He sent letters home, notifying Johanna of his whereabouts, but his missives contained nothing personal. It was better that way, or at least that was what he told himself.

Soon weeks became a month, and summer unfolded across Yorkshire. Blanstock reported that the crop-rotation method was in full swing, the tenant farmers keen to increase their yields and hopefully their profits. He sent word back of the status of the herd to alert Blanstock to prioritize the mending of the fences.

In all that time, he never once saw Johanna. She never returned any of his letters, but he didn't see why she would.

It didn't mean he didn't notice their absence, didn't feel the lack of communication from her like a knife in his gut.

It was late June before he returned to Raeford Court, and as he rode up to the house, he cut across the field to follow the line of the lake. It was much as it had been that day when he'd raced Johanna to the stream, like a sheet of glass stretching out before him. He need only peer over its edge to see his reflection. He rode on to the house without stopping.

It was late when he entered his study, and he was dusty and tired from the road. He wanted to feel the buzz of success at having secured a new herd, but all he felt was weary.

A lamp burned low on his desk, and he wondered how the staff knew he would be returning that night. He hadn't sent word ahead because he hadn't been sure himself. Soon a rustling reached his ears and he spun about. The lamp had not been left for him. It had been lit by his mother apparently.

His mother who now took a knife to the seat cushion of the chairs nearest the fire.

"Mother," he said softly, not wishing to startle her with a weapon in her hand.

She looked up, her riotous silver-tinted hair falling in her face. "Dear boy! Home so soon?"

His mother had always been this way, slightly out of touch, and while he understood the reason for it, he still felt a pang at the loss of having a mother with whom he could converse and confide.

The thought sent a wave of guilt through him, and he wrestled out of his dust-coated jacket, forcing his thoughts away. "Yes, but what precisely are you about here?"

She held the cushion aloft on the point of her knife. "I've decided these chairs require reupholstering. Floral patterns really are rather out of touch, don't you think?"

"Do you think perhaps you should leave that up to Johanna? She is the duchess of the house now, is she not?"

His mother peered at her knife. "I suppose she is."

She dropped the cushion unceremoniously back onto the chair. The knife remained upright in her hand, glinting in the lamplight.

"And perhaps you should give me the knife." He eased forward, hand extended.

"Why?" She studied the knife. "Do you have reupholstering plans?"

"I had it in mind to configure a leather satchel for when I must travel."

She turned the knife back and forth. "Oh dear boy, I'm sorry to tell you this knife is no good for leather. I can get you another—"

"Please, Mother. I like the look of this one."

She frowned but turned the knife so he could take it by the grip.

"Thank you," he said on a hearty exhale. Now that the knife had been secured, he took time to look her over.

She was dressed much as always. She wore a plain gown draped in an apron embroidered with sheep and daisies. Around her neck was tied a knitted scarf of vibrant pink, and he recalled what Johanna had said about his mother wishing to make yarn from goat hair.

"That's a beautiful scarf, Mother."

Her expression lit up at this, and she fingered the wool at her neck. "Johanna, the darling, helped me. Isn't it lovely?" She flipped one end at him.

He couldn't help but smile even as a little more of him died. "Yes, it is quite lovely."

His mother sat down on the chair she had just desecrated, heedless of its mutilated cushion.

"You know, you really mustn't go away so much or for so long. Johanna gets very lonely without you."

His mother's words stabbed with far greater accuracy than her knife ever could.

"Lonely?" He leaned back against his desk as he studied his mother.

Surely she was mistaken. Johanna had never been one to need the presence of others, and even with what he now knew of her feelings, it did not suggest she would cling to him.

She hadn't come after him that day at the stream, and that was proof enough. She might have loved him, but she would not pine for him.

He still felt like an arse.

His mother leaned forward and whispered as if imparting a great secret. "I've seen her, you know. Walking about the house, especially at night. I'm not sure the poor girl can sleep." His mother straightened, shaking her head.

He crossed his arms over his chest. This sounded entirely unlike Johanna, but he was willing to amuse his mother.

"Is that so?"

His mother's eyes widened. "She thinks no one knows, but I do. I like to walk the portrait galleries at night. It's almost as if the dead dukes and their wives come to life." She held up her hands, fingers spread. "It's almost as if you can feel their ghosts following you."

He couldn't stop the look of horror that came over his features. "Why would you do that to yourself?"

Her laugh was sharp and full. "Oh dear boy, why would you not? It's great fun to scare yourself now and again." She shook her head, sobering. "But Johanna is not up for the fun of it. I know that much."

"How is it that you know that?"

His mother used the arms of the chair to push herself to

her feet. She came toward him, and he heard the distinct sound of clicking beads. He looked down, knowing what he would find. Strings of azure and indigo beads were wrapped around her ankles, visible beneath the too short hem of her gown.

When she reached him, she placed both of her hands on his shoulders and peered up at him. "Dear boy, you know I love you, don't you?"

"Of course, I do."

She patted his shoulders and cast her hands into the air as if she were giving a blessing. "I'm glad you do because I must be honest with you now." She dropped her hands and met his gaze. "You're being a right bastard."

It was moments like this when he was sure his mother knew exactly what was happening around her, and her character was all a charade to protect herself from the life she had been forced to live with his father and brother.

He pinched the bridge of his nose between two fingers.

"And how is it that you know this?"

His mother pressed her hands together in front of her as if in prayer. "Because Johanna's been crying."

She said the last word like an incantation and threw her hands into the air again.

He was paying attention now. "Crying?"

His mother nodded emphatically. "At night. When she roams the halls." She pointed a finger accusingly in his direction. "While you've been gone. Leaving her all alone." More head shaking. "She cries for you, you know."

Her words cut him, but it was all nonsense. Johanna didn't cry for him. Did she?

He straightened and went to his mother, rubbing her shoulders and pulling her into his embrace.

"It's all right, Mother. I'm sure you misheard. Perhaps it's those ghosts following you."

She tugged free of his arms and poked him in the chest. "It is you who misheard, dear boy. Your wife is sad, and as your mother, I can sense it's your fault."

He frowned. "How do you know it's my fault?"

She shook her head. "I tried to save you from the worst of it. Lord knows I tried. But still…" Her voice trailed off, but it didn't matter. Her eyes caught the lamplight, and in them, he saw an unfathomable sadness that caught him by the throat. "I tried, Benedict," she whispered. "I tried so hard. You shouldn't have been forced to pay for your brother's sins. I tried. And yet, somehow you came out broken."

She pressed a fist to her mouth as if to hold back the sadness that welled into her eyes.

"Mother—" He choked on the word as a swarm of emotions overcame him all at once.

But his mother was already poking him in the chest again. "You made her cry. You go tell her you're sorry."

His shoulders slumped. "It's not that simple," he heard himself say.

His mother shook her head. "It's always that simple."

She turned and walked to the door without saying another word, but he called out to her.

"Mother?"

She paused but only turned her head back to meet his gaze.

"How do you know for certain Johanna was crying?"

She pointed to the ceiling above them. "She goes to the cap-house where she thinks no one will find her. But I find her," she said, pointing at herself with a single thumb. "I will always find my Johanna."

His mother slipped out the door then, but he didn't hear her receding footsteps, almost as if she were a ghost herself.

* * *

Forty-four.

The number of days Ben had been gone.

Forty-four.

It seemed like an interminable time and yet nothing at all. She couldn't decide which it was, and she'd had plenty of time to think on it as she hadn't been sleeping well.

She had no trouble falling asleep. It was easy to do so after the long days of work an estate of this size demanded. She'd created a kind of routine for herself to hold back the hopelessness that threatened to consume her.

In the mornings, she took to visiting Smothers in the stables. She'd become attached to her mare, Grindel, and over the weeks Ben had been gone, Johanna took to riding her every morning. She never went to the stream though. It was easier to stay away from there and the memories that moved within her still.

She spent time before luncheon with Duchess. The woman was forever starting projects and leaving them half done. Johanna had managed to get the cashmere scarf finished, but it had been a herculean effort.

They took luncheon on the terrace that led down into the courtyard when the weather allowed. It often stretched into more than a meal when Duchess would tell stories from Ben's younger years. Johanna wasn't sure how much of them were true, but it made Duchess happy, so Johanna let her talk.

Afternoons were for estate work. She'd taken to visiting the tenant farms on a rotating basis. She brought preserves and pots of lavender cream she made from the estate's own lavender blooms. She knew which families were expecting children and which had sent off the last of their children to apprenticeships or marriage. She almost had a grasp of which farms required the most work to see the new rotation system put into effect and which flourished under the hand of a knowledgeable farmer.

On the afternoons she wasn't visiting tenants, she worked with Mrs. Owens. It had been some time since a duchess had taken proper care of the house, and many of the rooms were in need of much attention. They sorted linens and expelled moth-eaten draperies. Rugs were beaten or replaced. Furniture was polished and repaired.

Several rooms were beyond even her reckoning, and she made a note to invite Louisa to visit when the family was able to. Louisa would know what was to be done.

But even though her routine kept her occupied, she still had many hours left to roam the estate. She spent time in the gardens and reading on the terrace. She and Duchess learned how to roast a duck, an experience neither of them would be repeating.

But mostly she just walked. Her favorite walk took her along the edge of the lake. The far side was bordered by trees, and she'd find a shady place amongst them on a hot afternoon. More than once, she'd fallen asleep only to awaken startled, the memory of the past few weeks leaving her for just a moment and painfully, blissfully, she thought Ben was still with her.

But he wasn't.

It was the same when she went to bed at night. She'd fall asleep quickly only to awaken when the whisper of a memory streamed out of her reach. She'd wake with a gasp as though she'd physically been trying to catch whatever it was that eluded her. At first, she'd tried to go back to sleep, but it was useless.

The first few nights she wandered the rooms in the Jacobean part of the house, taking in the gold and orange filigree and stenciling work on the dark wood panels, the endless symmetry of the leaded windows.

Soon her feet carried her only to the cap-house. Barefoot, she'd climb the circular staircase and nestle into her window bench. She had resigned herself to her nightly expeditions and had placed a blanket and some pillows on the bench. The nights grew chilly when there were no clouds to cover the sky, and on those nights, she was grateful for her foresight.

The little glass house was like a window into a world she wasn't quite a part of. The night sky was a map of places she'd never see, and she traced their patterns across the glass. She made up stories about the shapes she drew between the stars. She knew she could probably find a book in Raeford's library about the constellations and their meanings, but what fun would that be? It was much more enjoyable to make up one's own story.

So she spent over forty nights like that. Nestled on her window bench in her cocoon of blanket and pillows and tried very hard to think of when her husband might return. If he would return.

That thought was the saddest of all. Ben simply must return to Raeford. It was his home. If she were keeping him from it, she would leave. It was as simple as that.

If only she knew.

That night she once more found herself in her cap-house. It was chilly, and she drew the blanket more snuggly around her. The stars blinked above her, little lanterns floating through the darkness. She'd gone to bed early that night, exhausted from following Duchess about all day. The woman had taken a keen interest in the possibility of re-weaving the carpets in the first floor drawing rooms. It was all Johanna could do to keep her from unraveling all of the floor coverings.

She'd awakened soon though, a gasp leaving her lips, and she'd sat up, wondering if a noise had awakened her. Was

Ben home? Had she heard him through the connecting door of their rooms?

She'd taken the duchess's usual rooms, of course. She hadn't really thought about it at the time, but now, having looked at that closed connecting door for more than a month, she rather thought about moving bedchambers.

She'd left her bed when it was obvious sleep would not be returning and made her way to her nest in the cap-house.

She traced a trio of stars now across the glass and thought of her sisters, wondering what they were doing just then. She missed them more than she had expected to, and it surprised her. It had felt so good to stand up for herself on her wedding day, but her victory had lost its luster. Now she only missed her sisters, missed being part of a family.

Perhaps that wasn't entirely true. Perhaps it was just that she was very, truly lonely.

A noise at the bottom of the circular staircase startled her, nearly sending her off the bench.

"Johanna?"

She stilled, her fingers digging into the side of the bench.

Ben?

She leaned over the edge of the bench as her heartbeat sped up and peered down between the railings of the stairs.

Ben.

She could just make him out in the moonlight, and her heart squeezed. He wore no collar, and his shirt was open at his throat. His hair was mussed, and his shirtsleeves rolled up to his elbows. He stood at the bottom of the stairs, a hand on the railing and one booted foot on the last stair.

It took two tries to get the word out. "Yes?"

"Would you mind terribly if I joined you?"

She wondered if he could see her face, and she tried to hide her smile.

"Yes, I would mind, but it's your house."

She wasn't sure why she teased him. He had left her so abruptly by the stream, and it had left her dazed and unsettled. She wasn't sure where they stood or how she should act or what might scare him off again. It only made sense that she fell back on the way they once were. Friends, teasing one another endlessly.

If only she could get him to talk to her.

She'd tried though, hadn't she? It hadn't ended particularly how she had planned.

"Then prepare to be boarded," he said with a menacing pirate lilt.

His heavy boots made the metal of the stairs ring in the small space, and when he rose into the cap-house, the small glass room felt suddenly much smaller.

He smelled of leather and earth, and she soaked in the sight of him.

"Where have you been?" She neither meant to ask the question nor did she need to. He had sent regular letters letting her know of his whereabouts, letters she had resolutely not returned. Their sterile nature made her stomach twist, and she'd shoved them in a drawer as soon as she read them.

He stopped at the top of the stairs, his elbows resting on the railing on either side. He leaned forward and peered out and up through the glass wall.

"I've been all over Yorkshire securing us a new herd."

She didn't like how her heart thrilled at his use of the word *us*. She knew he only said it because she'd made demands in regards to her dowry, but she couldn't help but hope for more.

It was like her daydream, being there in the cap-house with him. Only it was so much worse. In her dream, he came to her, knelt at her side and kissed her before slipping onto the bench behind her and pulling her against his chest.

Now he stood as far away from her as the small room allowed, exaggerating the wedge that was planted firmly between them.

"Have you?" She was finding it incredibly difficult to feign an interest in dairy cows.

"I have." He finished coming up the last of the steps and sat on the bench at her feet, but he didn't touch her. He tried so hard not to touch her, in fact, that he looked awkward and bulky.

Pain constricted her breathing, and she tried very hard to keep the tears at bay.

"Johanna," he said, and he raised a hand as if to lay it on her upturned knees but thought better of it, returning his hand to his lap. "My mother tells me you've been having some nocturnal adventures."

She raised an eyebrow. "Has your mother been in the portrait galleries again?" She shook her head. "I told her not to let her imagination run wild like that. Do you know she's been trying to reweave the carpets in the drawing rooms?"

Ben's laugh was soft. "I caught her trying to reupholster the chairs in my study."

She sat up. "Oh Ben, no. Not the Chippendales."

He cringed. "I'm afraid so."

She deflated against the pillows at her back. "I suppose they are only chairs."

"I'm sure they can be fixed," he offered.

She waved him off. "It's quite all right. As long as Duchess is happy."

Her words seemed to upset him, but she couldn't imagine how. His face tightened, and he raised his hand to touch her again, once more returning his hand to his lap.

"Johanna, I owe you—"

"Don't." The word came out more sharply than she'd intended. "Benedict Carver, if you apologize to me one more time, I will push you down those stairs." She nodded to the circular stairs in question.

He sat with his mouth open on his unspoken apology as his eyes moved to the stairs.

"Those stairs?"

She nodded. "The very same."

He crossed his arms over his chest. "You couldn't get me down those stairs."

"I certainly could." She shoved the blanket off of her, intending to stand and prove just how capable she was when he finally touched her.

It was just his hand on her arm, his touch gentle. She stilled completely.

"I didn't come up here to play games, Johanna." His voice was unusually tired, and she felt guilty for keeping him from his bed.

She slipped out from under his touch, tucking her arms against her middle. "I shouldn't keep you up. We can speak in the morning if you wish." A horrible thought struck her then. Would he be there in the morning or was he planning to leave again? She wasn't sure, and she didn't know how to ask.

He was already shaking his head though. "Johanna, my mother said something. Something I—" He looked up suddenly and captured her gaze. "Johanna, are you happy here?"

The question seemed ludicrous, and she opened her mouth to tell him so when she stopped suddenly. All at once she remembered the many nights she'd awoken with his name on her lips only to find herself alone.

Ben continued. "I know this hasn't turned out the way you had planned or hoped, and I know you don't want another apology from me, but I will continue to apologize until the day I die for hurting you." When he looked up, she saw the pain he felt in the tightness of his lips, the furrow of his brow. "I never meant to hurt you. You must know that. And I would take it all away if I could. If you would be happier living at Ravenwood—"

She didn't let him finish the sentence. She chucked a pillow at him instead.

"Johanna!" She threw another. "Johanna, stop! What is the matter—"

But she didn't hear him. A floodgate had released inside of her, and everything she had held back over the past several years stormed out of her at once. She grabbed the last pillow and came up on her knees to beat him with it.

She was so terribly small compared to his large frame, and her blows were futile, but with every impact, she felt a release of everything that had been blocked inside of her.

He caught her wrist, preventing her from striking him again, so she pivoted, using the last thing she had available to her.

Her body.

She straddled him, using her free hand to grab a handful of his shirt, pulling him close.

"You are an idiot, Benedict Carver." Her voice shook but not with tears this time. This time she vibrated with the force of her fury and her fear and her love. "I don't want your past, and neither of us can tell what the future will bring. I want you." She tried to shake him, but he was far too strong, and her fist thumped uselessly against his chest. "I want you, Ben. Right now. Right here. For today and tomorrow and however many days we have left. Why can't you see that?" Her voice grew soft as the fight went out of her. "Why can't you see that the rest of it doesn't matter?" She shook her head, let go of his shirt. "Why can't you see how much I love you, Ben?"

His face hadn't changed through any of her rant, and she

slumped back, one arm still held in his grip, the other falling to her lap.

The funny thing about a secret love was that one always had hope as long as the object of said love never knew of it. But once it was out, once it was known, the magic of it went away, and one was left with only the harsh reality.

She hadn't expected Ben to tell her he loved her. Far from it. She knew where he stood. Perhaps she just wanted a little piece of hope to come back.

She moved to slide off his lap, but he caught her around the waist, pulling her snuggly against him. The air left her lungs as she grabbed hold of his shoulder with her free hand, trying to steady herself.

"I can't love you." He said the words through gritted teeth. "You must know that."

She couldn't help it. She touched his face, thinking her fingers could somehow erase the pain there.

"Oh Ben," she whispered. "What happened to you?" She didn't ask the question of him, and somehow he knew that.

"I want you, Johanna. Just as much as you want me, and maybe that can be enough. You don't want my past, but it's a part of me. There's no denying it or pretending it's not there. If the present is what you want, then you can have it. All of it. Just don't ask me to love you." And then he crushed his mouth to hers.

CHAPTER 14

*H*e could just make out her features in the moonlight, but it was enough, and suddenly he wanted to see all of her. Here. Now.

He also didn't want to let go of her, which made getting her naked rather more difficult. He tore at her dressing gown as she fumbled with his shirt. She tugged it free of his trousers, and he leaned back just long enough for her to get it over his head. She did the same to allow him to pull her nightrail over her head and toss it aside.

She was suddenly naked against him, her breasts pressed to his chest, her lush hips beneath his palms. He was already hard, but he wasn't surprised.

He thought staying away from her was the right thing to do. He thought he could forget it, or at least, allow his body to forget her. But he'd been wrong. He'd never forget the way she fitted against him, the way she never hesitated when she was in his arms. It shook something in him. The way she so casually accepted him and his attentions.

For a moment, something in him cracked, and he wondered, if perhaps, he was good enough for her.

But then she sucked his lower lip into her mouth, and he forgot anything of substance.

Her hands were at the fastenings of his trousers next as he pulled the ribbon from the end of her braid, sending her thick dark hair swinging down her back. He grabbed fistfuls of it, its silken strands so soft against his work-roughened hands, and he used it to pull her head back to allow him access to her neck.

His trousers loosened, and he felt a moment of relief from the growing pressure there, but then she slid her hands inside.

He pulled back, snatching her hand.

"Johanna," he breathed. "I'm not sure that's a good idea. Not right now."

His gut tightened, thinking he may have hurt her feelings, but then her grin turned saucy. "Promise me I can try it later."

He swallowed. "Jesus, Johanna."

She kissed him, pulling her hand free to push him against the glass. It was cold against his back, and she was fire against his chest, the dichotomy of sensations thrilling. He let his hands wander down her torso and around to her generous buttocks, cupping her to pull her more fully against him.

This time she pulled away and cradling his face, tilted his gaze up to hers.

"I'd really like it if you took your trousers off this time," she whispered, a wicked glint in her eye.

He turned, depositing her on the window bench and made quick work of his trousers. She'd retrieved the pillows she'd used to beat him with and lay sprawled against them now.

He slipped between her legs as if he'd always done it, settling in the cradle of her thighs. He brushed the hair from the sides of her face and captured her lips in a tender kiss.

When he backed away, her eyes were open and watching him.

She touched a single finger to his cheek, scraping it along his beard.

"Do you know I've dreamed of this?"

The words shot through him with unexpected precision. He felt them, tearing through the scars so many others had left inside of him.

"Johanna, you don't—"

She pressed that single finger to his lips, silencing him.

"I dreamed of us here in the cap-house." She looked beyond his shoulder as if glancing out the glass. "Only it was dawn." She returned her gaze to his. "You know how much I've always cherished the sunrise. Please promise we can do this again some morning." Her eyes were dark and fathomless, and he knew she thought of the morning he had proposed.

He could only think of it as the moment of betrayal, but her eyes reflected nothing but happiness. He mumbled against her finger.

She lifted her finger just long enough for him to say, "I promise."

She placed the finger back against his lips. "I dreamt that you worshiped me with your body."

He was so distracted by her words, by the pools of desire in her eyes, he didn't realize her other hand had found its way around to his back, and her nails dragged a line up his spine, sending all his muscles into convulsions.

Her grin turned lopsided, and he knew she must have understood what she was doing as she released his lips to slip her other hand around him.

"I did?" He managed.

Her hand dipped lower, and he sucked in a breath.

"You did." Her eyes suggested only too well what exactly she had imagined them doing, and he felt something foreign and unreal wash over him.

She had imagined them, like this. She had imagined *him*.

Worshiping her body.

Him.

The crack inside of him grew, and he felt a lightening in his chest, as though a weight he hadn't known he'd been carrying had shifted. Doubt still plagued him though, and he didn't prod at the feeling anymore.

He kissed her softly, first her lips and then her cheeks before slipping over to her ear.

"What exactly did we do?" he whispered in her ear before sucking her soft lobe between his teeth.

He reveled in the way her fingers dug into his back, her hips lifting off the bench and pressing against him.

"I—" The single word came out strangled, and he couldn't help the smile he pressed to her neck.

"I'm sorry. What was that?" He nipped the soft place where her neck met her shoulder, and she bucked against him.

She moaned something so garbled he wasn't even sure what it was meant to be.

He dipped lower, tracing a line of kisses to her collarbone. The first two times they'd made love had been rushed, and he'd been unable to savor it. Like the way she breathed his name when he pressed his lips to a particularly tender spot. Or the way she ran her toes along the back of his calf when he licked the spot behind her ear.

He wanted to remember everything, every nuance, because he knew this couldn't last. At some point, she would wake up and realize to whom she was married.

No, trapped.

He'd trapped her into this marriage. Not unlike the way he'd been trapped.

"Ben," her voice was soft and wondering, pulling him out of the mire of his thoughts.

He pushed up his hands to lean over her. "You're avoiding answering the question, Your Grace."

She blinked up at him. "There was a question?"

He eased down, his lips hovering over her skin as he made his way down her body. He knew she watched him. He could feel her gaze burning into him as he made his way lower and lower still. But he never touched his lips to her. Never gave in to the temptation.

"Ben? What was…what is…that is…" She stammered, her hands reaching for him, but he ducked out of her grasp, leaving her to twist the blanket beneath her in her fists.

He'd reached the soft skin of her thigh and finally, he softly pressed his lips to it.

She moaned.

"What is it that you dreamt of, Johanna?" he whispered against her skin. "What is it that you want me to do?"

Her head came off the pillow, and she glared at him.

"I don't know," she pleaded. "But please do it quickly."

He hid his smile against the inner softness of her thigh, moving his lips higher. Her hips thrashed against the blanket, and he reached up to hold her still.

Only then did he allow himself to put his mouth to her hot core.

She jerked against him, sending her against his tongue.

"Oh my God, Ben," she moaned.

He plied her with his tongue, stroking her sensitive nub until she squirmed relentlessly against him. He didn't release her; he only stroked her harder, faster.

"Ben, I—" She made a noise not unlike a growl. "Ben, you can't—"

And that was when she came apart. He pressed his tongue to her as her climax rocked through her body. He held her, steadying her, until he felt her muscles relax. Only then did he sit up. Only then did he allow himself to look at her in the moonlight, satiated and well-loved because of him.

It was several seconds before her eyelids fluttered open, and he felt a moment's hesitation now that she was looking at him.

But then she held up her arms to him, beckoning him to come to her.

The crack inside of him split entirely open.

He could count on one hand the number of times he'd made love to a woman, and two of those had been with Johanna. The other times were furtive gestures in the dark, nothing more than fumbling and frustrations. Minerva had only allowed him to touch her long enough to satisfy any notions of consummation, but had things progressed the way they should have, he doubted anyone would have questioned it.

But it wasn't like that with Johanna.

Everything about her was light and open and accepting.

Accepting of him.

He went to her, lowering himself until her arms were around him. She shifted her hips, and he slipped inside of her. She gasped, and he stilled, but when he caught her expression, a smile unknowingly came to his lips.

She looked happy.

She looked more than happy; she looked content. Her lips were spread in a soft smile as her eyelids fluttered shut as though she couldn't contain the feelings coursing through her.

He thrust against her, deeply and slowly, and she moaned. "Ben."

The way she said his name was like a breeze on a summer day, light and full of promise.

He thrust harder, increasing his pace, and she tilted her hips, drawing him deeper inside of her.

"Johanna." He didn't know how much longer he could stand it. She was so tight, so wet; she stroked him with her moist heat.

Her fingernails dug into his back, and her eyes flew open at the exact moment he felt her explode around him. He came in a rush of sensation, his muscles turning to wax as he collapsed against her.

He struggled to move so he wouldn't crush her, but she stilled him, her arms tightening around him.

"Stay," she said. "Please."

He kept his weight on his forearms. "I'll hurt you."

"No, you won't." Her voice had turned soft and dreamy. "You'd never hurt me."

Her words stabbed him, and the guilt that had become so familiar to him increased tenfold. He withdrew and slid to the side, pulling her with him so she stayed cocoon in his arms.

Her head fell to his shoulder, but her eyes never fluttered.

"Johanna." She stirred, her breath catching. "What happened after I worshipped you with my body?"

Her hand found its way to his chest, slipping through the mat of hair there and tracing the line of his breastbone.

She opened her eyes, and he lost himself in them. They were so pure, so dark, so endless.

"We lived happily ever after, of course."

The words fell on him like a fog. He could see them, even believe he could touch them, but when he reached for them, they disappeared.

He pulled her closer, tucking her head beneath his chin. "Some people aren't destined for happily ever after."

She wiggled and pushed against his chest, her gaze meeting his. "Everyone is destined for a happily ever after. You must only be brave enough to reach for it."

He made to shake his head, but she sat up and began to rummage through their discarded clothes.

"Johanna—"

"Do you know what else I dreamed of?" she asked, finding her dressing robe.

"What?" He held his breath, unsure of what she might say next.

She turned and leaned in, pressing a soft kiss to his lips. "Waking up in your bed."

* * *

She did, in fact, wake up in his bed.

She was also nearly underneath him. In his sleep, he'd turn, tossing a leg over her hip, his arm around her waist like a steel band.

She woke to the overwhelming sense of being loved, and as reality crashed into her, her eyes smarted with tears as the events of the night before rushed back to her.

Ben might claim he couldn't love her, but she knew that wasn't it. He was holding himself back, protecting himself. She knew what his father had done, denying him a place at Raeford Court had hurt him gravely, but the fear she saw in his eyes when faced with something more, something intimate and real and lasting, must have come from something else.

Something more had happened to Ben. Beyond the cruelty of his first wife and the disregard of his father. Something that had made Ben *afraid* to love, not unable to.

She clutched the arm he had wrapped around her, as if by holding him tightly she could keep him with her, mentally

JESSIE CLEVER

and physically. If only she could keep him present and with her, she could make him forget the terrible thing that had happened.

He'd sworn he couldn't release his past, and yet he would not speak of it to her. What else did she have left to do?

He stirred against her, his nose nuzzling her temple, his lips finding her cheek.

"Did I wake you?" he mumbled against her skin.

She smiled, a rush of heady sensations coursing through her.

Regardless of the challenges that still lay between them, she had this, now, with him, and it was even better than she had ever imagined.

She turned in his arms and kissed him softly, reveling in the scrape of his beard against her soft skin.

"You did not wake me, Your Grace, but now that you've awoken…" She let her words trail off as she ran a hand up his back.

His eyes flew open, his gaze catching hers. He reached up, pushing her hair behind her ear, the gesture so simple, so intimate her heart squeezed.

"Johanna," he breathed her name as her hand stroked down his back and lower. Much lower. "You cannot possibly —" She squeezed, his words ending on a guttered gasp. "Again? This morning?" His eyes were wide now, searching her face.

She pushed him onto his back with a hand to his chest and came up above him on her elbow.

"I always want to as long as it's with you," she said and bent to kiss him, but he stopped her.

"Johanna." His tone had lost its playfulness, and fear gripped her. Fear that he had changed his mind. Fear that he regretted what he'd done the previous night. Fear of so much.

But then his eyes drifted away from her face and took in the room about them.

"Johanna, is that sunlight?"

She followed his gaze to the windows to find warm, strong sunshine spilling through where the drapes didn't quite meet.

She sat up. "It appears to be. What time is it?"

She looked around. She'd never been in Ben's rooms and found it utterly foreign to her and quite delightful. The bedchamber was tastefully furnished in blues and golds, dark woods polished to a high gleam. It suited him. Simple and warm.

What she didn't find, however, was a clock.

She heard him pushing back the bedclothes and felt a pang of loss that he should so easily leave her.

She was still quite naked, her long, thick hair loose around her shoulders. She wasn't so conceited as to believe she was beautiful, but she thought herself at that moment maybe more appealing than seeing to the time.

Ben snatched up his pocket watch from the night table.

"It's after ten," he said once he released the cover. He turned back to her, his face tight. "I was to meet Blanstock at half nine." He gained his feet, casting his eyes about the room as if looking for his clothes.

Blanstock was apparently more appealing than his wife. Of course, he was. She had never before been one to experience moments of low self-esteem, but just then, she rather thought she'd wallow in it.

She pushed back the bedclothes and searched for her dressing robe. She wasn't sure her nightrail had made it down from the cap-house.

"I will leave you then," she said, shrugging into her robe as she moved to the connecting door.

"Leave me?"

She turned at the incredulous note in his voice.

He stood with his trousers on one leg. "Don't you wish to come as well? The herd is coming today. We were to check the mended fences before it arrives."

The moment of self-doubt evaporated.

"You want me to come? With you?"

His grin was somewhere between playful and chagrinned. "It is a part of our bargain, I believe."

She tried to hide her smile, but she was entirely unsuccessful. "I'll be quick."

She dashed through the connecting door. Waiting for her maid would have taken too long, so she scurried about, finding the gown she had worn the previous day. It would have to do.

She scrubbed her face and brushed her hair into a suitable braid. In all, she'd taken not more than fifteen minutes. She'd hardly gotten her half boots tied before she flew out the door and down the stairs.

She stepped into the breakfast room to find Duchess lingering at the table, newspaper in one hand, scone in the other.

"Did you see that man Peel has been elected Prime Minister?" She shook her head. "Who knows what will be in store for us now?"

The question stopped Johanna in her stride, her arms suspended in the air as she had been about to reach for a plate. She'd need her strength if they were to be in the fields for the remainder of the day.

"You follow politics, Duchess?"

She dropped her hand, folding the newspaper unceremoniously under her elbow. "I do when it affects Raeford Court. The world is not as it once was, my girl, and I should like to know what this man plans to do about it."

Johanna canted her head. "Do you mean the economic

troubles? Ben is working to ensure the estate is as resistant as possible to downturns like what we're witnessing now."

Duchess shook her head and popped the last bite of the scone in her mouth, chewing thoughtfully as she picked up the newspaper once more.

Johanna continued to the sideboard, scooping up some eggs and sausages to fortify herself for the long day ahead.

She'd hardly taken a seat at the table when Duchess set down the newspaper once more.

"What is it that my dear boy is doing?"

Johanna swallowed her eggs. "He's moved the tenant farmers to the four-course rotation method. It should have been done ages ago, but it seems to have been neglected."

Duchess screwed up her mouth in disapproval. "Yes, I think we all know how it was neglected." She picked up the newspaper only to set it back down again. "What will the four-course crop nonsense do?"

Johanna speared a sausage. "If the method is used properly, it will increase crop yields exponentially, thus increasing a parcel's profit."

"For the estate or for the tenant?"

"Both." Johanna filled a cup with tea and took a quick swallow. "Ben wanted the tenant farmers' buy-in to the new methods and increased their profit shares in the selling of the crop."

Duchess's smile was quick. "That's my dear boy."

Johanna turned to the door. "Your dear boy is rather late. He was to meet Blanstock this morning. I can't imagine what's keeping him."

She'd left him nearly a half hour before, and he still hadn't appeared in the breakfast room.

Duchess picked up her paper again. "I wondered why he only grabbed a scone and rushed out of here. That boy. He needs to eat to stay healthy and strong."

Johanna stared at her mother-in-law. "He's already been here?"

Duchess peered around the newsprint. "Been here and scurried out like a hound after a rabbit."

Johanna pushed to her feet, nearly knocking over her chair. "Please excuse me, Duchess." She pressed a swift kiss to the woman's cheek. "I must go." She paused at the door, turning back. "I'm not sure I'll make luncheon today. I—"

Duchess waved her on with a smile. "I know, darling. Ben is home. Isn't it grand?"

Johanna couldn't stop her smile. "Yes, it's quite grand."

As long as he hadn't left without her.

She didn't want to think such things of him, but a part of her understood his reluctance to let her in. Raeford Court had always been his dream, and now that it was his, he might be feeling protective.

He was protective of so many things.

She broke out into the sunshine of a warm, summer day in Yorkshire, and she realized almost at once, she should have brought a bonnet. There wasn't time to go back for it now. She made it to the stables within seconds, rounding the corner of the paddocks only to stop, arrested by the sight of her husband standing in the stable yard, his horse in one hand, Grindel in the other.

He was speaking to both Smothers and Blanstock, but he stopped when he must have seen her. He turned a smile on her and held up Grindel's reins.

"The herd will be coming from the west. They're likely to reach the Gibbons parcel first. Should we start there?"

He was asking her. He was letting her decide. She opened her mouth once, but sound did not emerge. She wasn't sure what it was, but he was offering her something. Something that was important to him.

She took Grindel's reins. "I think that's a fine place to start."

Smothers made a grumbling noise. "You should be wearing a hat, young girl. Out in the sun all day, you'll make yourself sick." He plucked his own floppy felt hat from his head and plopped it down on top of hers. "Not very well suited for a duchess, but I'd rather see you safe than ill from the sun."

She stood on tiptoe and kissed the man's bearded cheek.

"This is the finest hat I've ever worn," she said, adjusting its brow to shield her eyes from the sun. "Shall we?"

She turned and vaulted onto Grindel's back without assistance. Blanstock stared blankly between her up on the horse and Ben. She rolled her shoulders back.

"Well? Shall we?"

Ben shook his head with a smile and mounted his horse, leaving poor Blanstock to scurry up on his gelding behind them.

Smothers raised a hand in farewell and ducked back into the stables.

They had trotted out of the stable yard when Ben finally looked at her.

"You've charmed the stable master and my housekeeper. What is next?"

She turned in her saddle to face him. "I've charmed Mrs. Owens? This is the first I'm hearing of it." She pictured the dour-faced housekeeper with whom she had spent so much time over the past several weeks.

"She cornered me when I came down this morning. I was informed that the house has never been in better order." His smile was one-sided. "It seems you have impressed her with your domestic economy."

Johanna returned her attention to the drive ahead of

them. "I wasn't aware I had such skill. Viv would be pleased to hear it."

Ben's laugh was rich and full, and for the first time since arriving at Raeford Court, she thought things might just be all right.

CHAPTER 15

*H*e had thought witnessing the arrival of the new herd would feel differently.

But he was so entirely distracted by Johanna's obvious elation at seeing the bovines flooding the newly repaired pastures, he couldn't recall how he had felt at all. The rest of the day had been much the same. Instead of finding the joy he thought he would in the culmination of his lifelong ambition to see Raeford improved, he found himself watching his wife.

Marveling in the way she so easily found joy in everything she viewed. Envying her that easiness. How quickly she came to the good in something and how swiftly she found something over which to express happiness.

He wondered at it, and more, he thought of a possibility he hadn't in a very long time.

What if he tried to find such joy again?

He had once, a very long time ago, when they raced through these fields and played at pirates and smugglers. But every time he thought of it the pain of remembrance returned. He pictured his father so clearly, telling him precisely what his future held, and Ben could do nothing more than push the thought away.

But after that day in the pastures with Johanna, the memory of his father exacting his future no longer held the bite it once did. He wanted to examine the meaning of it, but his days did not provide the leisure of reflection, and his nights, well, his nights were filled with her.

After that first night, she'd taken to entering his rooms at the end of their long days, dressed in nightrail and robe, her hair braided over one shoulder. She'd slip into bed, propping herself against the pillows as she relayed her thoughts on the events of the day.

How she thought the use of turnips in the once fallow fields was a good idea, but should they try clover the next season? The Tanners were short a pig this year, and could they provide one from another tenant? Surely, someone had to have had a surplus of piglets that year.

The only way to get her to cease her chatter was to kiss her. And kissing led to, well, other things. Things he still couldn't quite fathom.

She wanted him. Every night. And nearly every morning.

It was so easy to push aside his misgivings, to set aside the hurt of his past when she opened her arms to him. In her arms was the only time he felt whole. Like he was young again, and he hadn't yet been forced to pay for Lawrence's sins.

The guilt over what he had done to Johanna was gradually lessening, but he knew he would never live without it. But somehow seeing Johanna's happiness—no, it was more than that. There was a drive in her now, more than he'd ever witnessed before.

She had always been determined, always vibrant and curious. It was greater now as she directed her energy toward Raeford Court. He recalled what she had said on their wedding day, and it became clearer now that he could see her love for the estate.

This land was as beloved by her as it was by him.

It settled in him with a thud, and he couldn't wrap his arms around it. He had always dreamed of Raeford Court being his, but he'd never considered that someone else might love it as much as he did.

It left him somewhat unsettled and cautious, and he knew she could tell. She treaded carefully around him, her eyes watchful as if she expected him to hurt her again.

The notion was enough to shred his heart, but at the same time, his need for self-preservation prevented him from being any different.

And so they went on like that as the days turned into weeks as they worked to get the herd settled. It would be enough this year for the tenants to survive on, but if his designs for selective breeding were to pan out, next year would see a profit in their dairy production.

He'd been kept abreast of actions in Parliament, thanks to his mother and her rigorous newspaper reading, and he felt a niggling of guilt for not being there himself. Johanna had received a letter from Andrew, indicating his intent to stop at Ravenwood Park on his way north to Scotland. Ben had hoped to stop in and see his friend to determine what news came from the ending of Parliament's session, but he wondered if he would be welcomed.

In the meantime, he struck out every morning with Johanna as they went from parcel to parcel, monitoring the progress of the herd. The tenant farmers reported the usual difficulties in settling a herd to new pasture, but there was nothing out of the ordinary.

Still, tension tightened his shoulders, and he wasn't about to let it ease. This could still fail, and if it did, he would be unable to start anew until the next season's crops turned a profit.

If they turned a profit.

Commodity farming was always a gamble. He knew that, and it was why he was reluctant to rely on the crops to support his breeding strategy. This herd had to flourish or Raeford would be in trouble once more.

They had a rare morning to themselves a week later when the herd seemed settled, the drainage project in the west parcels had been completed, and the fields were not yet ready for harvesting. They had ridden out early that morning, fog still thick on the ground as the sun had yet to rise, burning the stuff from the fields.

They went to the stream, of course. They took their time picking their way across the fields and around the lake. When they reached the forest, dawn had begun to break along the horizon, and they slipped through the shadow of the trees as if escaping before they were caught.

They let their horses to the grasses on the bank and made their way carefully down the steep slopes to the rock beds below. It hadn't rained in some days, and the waterfall was soft and languid, the pool shallow.

Johanna took a spot on the wide flat rock where they had sat—was it now months before?—and bent her knees, settling her chin on her hands on top of them.

"It's so peaceful here." She rolled her shoulders. "I still cannot fathom the physical work it takes to run such a vast estate." She turned and peered up at him. "Did you imagine it would be like this? When we were children, I mean?"

He dropped down on the rock beside her. "I had a suspicion it would not be easy, but I'm finding it rather more enjoyable having you here."

He was surprised by how much he meant the words. She

was apparently surprised as well because she turned a stricken face to him.

"You are?"

He felt that needle of guilt. "I am," he spoke with confidence, propping his arm on a bent knee as he scanned the stream. "You're not nearly as annoying as you were when we were children."

She elbowed him, and he laughed.

"I take it you find me just as annoying."

Her gaze was calculating. "I expect even more so."

They settled into silence then, the sound of morning song and the tumble of water the only noise to fill the space around them. After a time, Johanna rested her head on his shoulder, and he shifted, drawing her into his arms.

"Do you think the herd will make it?" she asked.

He nodded. "As long as we continue to monitor their health and ensure their nutrition meets our standards, then they cannot fail to improve."

She turned her chin up to face him. "You do not sound optimistic."

He kissed her nose. "I am a farmer, Johanna. Farming is tough work, and no matter what precautions are taken, sometimes things fail."

She eased back in his arms. "You were not always so pessimistic," she observed.

He shrugged. "Life has taught me to be pragmatic."

She seemed to consider this as a line popped up between her brows. "There's a fine line between pragmatism and negativity."

"Which side of the line are you on?" he asked, even though he knew the answer.

"It will pain you to know I'm on the pragmatists' side." She settled back against him, and he propped her up, holding her in front of him by her shoulders so she could see the disbelief on his face.

"You are most certainly not."

She raised an eyebrow. "I most certainly am." She poked him in the chest. "You forget that I spent the better part of my formative years in love with a man who thought me no more than a pest. What lessons do you think such a thing taught me?"

He swallowed, a new kind of guilt flooding him. "I should think it would have greatly damaged your confidence."

Her eyes widened at this. "I assure you, Your Grace, there is nothing faulty about my confidence. One would say it is far too great."

He studied her face. "How is it that you *are* so confident, Johanna?"

He'd never really thought of it, but she'd plainly just stated the truth. He hadn't ignored her, but he had thought of her as not much more than his best friend's little sister. Surely such a distinction could not have been comfortable when she found herself in love with him.

Even thinking of it sent a wave of heat through him. Heat and incredulity. Would he ever be able to accept the simple truth that she loved him?

He feared he wouldn't. Every time he faced her love he saw Minerva and what she stood for, and his ability to believe, to hope for something different crumbled.

Johanna smiled now, and he saw the freckles that had sprouted across her nose from so much time spent in the sun. Even with the aid of Smothers's hat, which she claimed as her own now, she still had taken on a warm glow from the days they spent in the fields. It was like she had come alive, and with it, the old Johanna had returned. He felt a lifting inside of himself at the sight of it.

"Your ignorance never concerned me," she said with the same confidence.

He raised an eyebrow. "Ignorance?"

She leaned toward him, tapping him on the chest with emphasis. "Sometimes the most difficult things to see are the ones right in front of us." She leaned back, spreading her arms. "Look how long it took you to see me."

He wanted to share in her confidence. He wanted to wallow in it, but his past never left him.

"I do see you, Johanna."

Her smile never wavered, and she canted her head as if enjoying the moment there on the rocks with him.

At that moment, the first of the sun broke through the tops of the trees, illuminating the rocks around them.

Johanna groaned. "I suppose this means we should return and start the day."

She made to move, but he stopped her, his hand covering the one she had braced against the rock beside her.

"I do see you, Johanna." It came out as nothing more than a whisper, but just then he felt an urgency to speak the words regardless of how they were uttered. "I do see you."

She lifted her free hand and stroked his cheek. "I know you do," she said, but her eyes lacked the conviction her words held.

There wasn't time to tarry further, and he reluctantly got to his feet, pulling her up with him. They collected their horses and struck out across the fields toward the main house, only to encounter Blanstock riding toward them.

He raised a hand to signal them, and they slowed their mounts, waiting for the man to approach.

"Gibbons is reporting one of the new cows is sick. Hasn't been eating and has some discharge around the nose and eyes. Probably something it picked up in the new fields, but it'd be best if you have a look at it." His words were directed at Ben, but his attention included Johanna, and Ben realized how much a part of this she had become.

He turned to her now. "Do you mind having a late breakfast?"

She smiled. "You know I wouldn't miss the opportunity to tag along."

* * *

THE ENTIRE HERD was dead in four days.

She stood in the stable yard, its elevation providing a view of the tenant farms down the hill, spread out before her on the rolling Yorkshire fields.

"Cattle plague," Smothers muttered beside her as they watched the plumes of smoke billow into the air from where they burned the carcasses, hoping to banish the sickness from the farms.

The air was rancid, and her lungs burned with every breath. They'd been burning the bodies since the previous day, and everything reeked of smoke and burnt flesh. She'd tried to bathe the previous night before they'd collapsed into bed, their bodies not even touching as they'd fallen into a deep slumber, but she'd awakened to the rotting scent, and she feared it was forever burned into her nostrils.

Ben was out there somewhere. He'd left at first light to continue the task of ridding the farms of the infected carcasses. She and Mrs. Owens spent the mornings preparing baskets of food for the tenants who now faced utter destruction.

"I've seen it once or twice before but never this bad," Smothers went on, shaking his head. "It can take out a herd faster than anything. Even the food stores will need to be burned."

She turned to him at this. "The food stores?"

"There's no telling if they've been contaminated. Everything will need to be burned." He shook his head again and scuffed his feet against the dirt of the stable yard. "God almighty, the poor master."

The words were spoken softly, reverently, and Johanna understood yet again how much the staff understood of the battles Ben faced. The battles he had always faced.

Something roared inside of her, so furious and so complete, angry tears instantly came to her eyes.

He had faced those battles alone, but she was here now.

But what could she do?

"How does one eradicate cattle plague?" she asked, her eyes moving from one column of smoke to another. "Is this all that can be done?"

Smothers shrugged. "It's all that must be done. Burning the carcasses and the food stores. Destroying anything that might still carry the disease. It's what's been done before and proven to work." He cast a solemn glance upon her. "As I said I've seen this before. It's quick and deadly and gone with nothing more than a good sweep." He shook his head and pulled a handkerchief from his pocket, swiped it across his brow. "There's nothing scarier. Something so lethal, so stealthy, so easily eradicated. But the damage will already have been done by the time you must act."

Was it only a handful of days ago that they had sat on the flat rock in their stream and talked of the dangers of farming? The unfair and startling swift nature of it? One day success, the next failure.

She saw it now in her husband when he returned home battered, weary, and smelling of acrid smoke. She saw it in the worried gaze of the stable master. She saw it in the scarcity of Duchess, who had taken to hiding in her cottage as the world ravaged around her. Johanna couldn't fault the woman.

Smothers made a noise of despair then and tucked his handkerchief away. Johanna studied him, waiting.

Smothers must have been nearing his seventieth year, and his jaw had taken on that perpetual beard of old age, a whisper of gray stubble he sometime let grow longer when the needs of the horses dictated the brevity of his toilet. His hands were gnarled with arthritis, and his shoulders curved from years of bending over an upturned horse hoof.

Yet she'd never seen a stronger man as he gazed out over the destruction of the estate he had been a part of for likely more than fifty years.

"The master will not have the funds to undo this."

Johanna almost missed the words as they were spoken so lightly, but the raw emotion in them was unmistakable.

"How do you know that?"

Smothers met her gaze directly. "We all know it, my girl."

In the past few weeks, Smothers had been the only one reluctant to address her by her title, and every time he spoke her childhood nickname, warmth spread through her in memory.

"All of you?"

He gestured behind him at the main house. "We all saw just what it was the last duke did to the place. Squandering his money on immoral women and gambling." Smothers sniffed and worried his lower lip. "We saw the coffers drain as if we were studying the ledgers ourselves." He pointed in the distance as if knowing where Ben was at that moment. "His Grace has worked so hard to try to save it. To think, it won't be enough."

Despair sliced through her, hot and vengeful, and directly behind it, she felt a surge of protection.

She would not let this happen.

It wasn't about money or fortune. This was personal. This was about Ben, the man she loved, and she would be damned if she'd let something as arbitrary as cattle plague ruin him.

She grabbed fistfuls of her skirts. "Please excuse me, Smothers. I must attend to an important matter."

He turned to her. "More baskets for the families then?"

"No," she said now, her eyes moving to the horizon. "It's time for something a great deal more effective than baskets."

Smothers's smile tipped up on one side. "And what would that be?"

"Money," she said. "Please have Grindel saddled for me. I must pay a call on someone." She didn't wait for a reply. She tore off across the yard into the main house.

She burst through the front door, the massive oak panel banging against the wall as she came into the foyer.

"Mrs. Owens!" Her cry rang through the marbled entrance, and the sounds of rustling skirts could be heard down the hallway.

Johanna peeked into the mirror stationed in the front hall by the door and grimaced at her reflection. She'd slept poorly since the herd began to perish, and the smell of smoke was everywhere, causing her to imagine a layer of soot coating her.

Mrs. Owens appeared looking no more flustered than a matron at church services.

"I must go to Ravenwood Park. Should His Grace return, please tell him I shall return as soon as possible."

Mrs. Owens nodded. "Yes, Your Grace. Is there anything—"

Johanna pulled the woman into a hug. She wasn't sure who was more surprised by the gesture, but suddenly Johanna very much wanted to feel connected to something, and Mrs. Owens's familiar face sent a wave of certainty through her.

By the time Johanna returned to the stable yard, Grindel

was there, stamping an impatient hoof in the dirt. Johanna caught the reins from Smothers even as she was already vaulting into the saddle. She gave the horse her head and soon they were flying across the fields of Raeford.

Johanna did not take the road. There was a much better, more familiar way to get to Ravenwood Park, and she followed it now, more out of sense than actual direction. She took Grindel over hedges and stone fences, the horse lengthening and flying as if she were meant for such sport.

Soon the wild fields turned to manicured lawn and the march of oak trees that flanked the drive leading to Ravenwood Park loomed ahead of her. She turned, directing the horse toward the main house.

She slid from the saddle even before Grindel fully stopped, and the horse shook her head, whinnying a sound of pleasure from the exercise. A footman sprang from the front door, his arms aloft as she tossed him the reins. He scrambled to catch them.

"Miss—" he began, but she was already gone, her skirts in her hands as she raced up the front steps.

The smell hit her first.

Ravenwood Park had always smelled of lemon and beeswax, and for a moment, she was struck by a nauseating sense of homesickness. There was a maid on the stairs who looked vaguely familiar, and she turned when Johanna burst through the door.

"His Grace?" Johanna all but shouted at the poor maid.

The woman raised a shaking hand in a vague direction toward the back of the house.

"Thank you," Johanna said and continued running.

She burst through the door of Andrew's study seconds later, and without greeting, declared, "I need Louisa's dowry."

Her dear brother merely looked up from the papers he was reading at his desk.

"Johanna." It was neither a question nor a greeting. It was almost as if he expected one of his sisters to invade his study at any moment.

She pushed inside, her hands still clutched in her skirts.

"Please, Andrew. I know Sebastian didn't accept Louisa's dowry, and I know Father set aside the money for our dowries before his death. Please. I need that money now. I must save Raeford."

Andrew sat back, his arms relaxing along the arms of his chair.

"I thought you'd already given of your own dowry to save Raeford."

She walked to the doors that led out to the terrace and flung them wide.

"Do you smell that?"

They were some distance from the first of the fires, but the air carried easily in Yorkshire, and she knew soon, the aroma of burning flesh would reach Andrew's study.

His nose wrinkled first before he shot out of his seat and came to stand beside her.

"What on earth is that?"

"Cattle plague."

Andrew glanced sharply at her. "No."

"Yes, and the last of my dowry was already spent to acquire the herd that is now dead. If we do not find a new healthy herd this fall, we will miss an entire calving cycle. Tenants will go without dairy and be forced to continue to barter through the winter. It will…it will…"

"Devastate Raeford," Andrew murmured, his gaze going back out the terrace door as if he could see the fires from there.

He cursed, a hand going to knead the back of his neck.

Johanna stilled. She'd never heard Andrew utter a word

more foul than the most banal of words to describe biological functions.

"Andrew, Ben is your friend too—"

"My friend?" He whirled, his eyes wide and harsh. "My friend who caught my sister to take her dowry? That is the friend you speak of?"

She took a step back, feeling the hurtful truth of Andrew's words.

"Yes, he did do that, but he did it for the right reasons."

Andrew crossed his arms over his chest. "And just what, precisely, are the right reasons to betray your best friend?"

Johanna crossed her own arms. "He betrayed me too. You do not get to be alone in your hurt, Andrew."

He blinked at this and continued to pace away from her. "And now you ask me to give the man even more money than that which he already bilked?"

She took a step forward before regaining control of herself. "He did not steal it. I gave of it freely."

"It was not yours to give."

She didn't need to speak. She saw the moment Andrew realized he had overstepped.

She rolled her shoulders back, raised her chin. "Do you know what it is like to be the only one who has no memory of our mother when you and the others share stories of her?" She paused. Andrew said nothing, his eyes sliding slowly shut as if in remorse. "Do you know what it is like to watch every one of your siblings leave the schoolroom and you behind them?" She took another step forward. "Do you know what it is like to watch the man you love marry another and leave the country?"

Andrew's eyes flew open, his gaze steady on hers.

He hadn't known. None of them knew. It was so easy for her to go unnoticed, she sometimes took advantage of it. Like then. Keeping her love for Ben all to herself.

Andrew laid a single hand atop his desk as if to steady himself.

"This is what you want."

It wasn't a question, but she answered anyway. "Yes, it is. I —" The words clogged her throat, all of them wishing to burst forth at once. But instead she simply said, "I love him."

Andrew turned away and walked behind his desk, sitting carefully in his chair. He rubbed at his forehead before once more meeting her gaze.

"You know what happened to him. What his father did. Minerva."

She nodded.

"And yet, you still..." His voice trailed off, but she stepped up to the desk, planting both hands atop it to lean over, drawing close to emphasize her point.

"I don't love him still because of the things that have been done to him. I love him because of them."

Andrew's eyes passed over her face, and finally he shook his head.

"I thought when I married the lot of you off I would be done with you, but it seems only that you've acquired entirely more complex issues I must deal with." He picked up a pen. "I'm doing this for you. Not for him."

She reached out and closed her hand over his arm. "Do this for our best friend."

CHAPTER 16

*H*e'd summoned his solicitors from London as soon as the first cow died. He'd known immediately what it was, but despite his best efforts to contain the disease, it had spread viciously and swiftly. The entire herd was gone within days.

He pulled down the cravat he had tied around his mouth and nose to stop the putrid smoke from penetrating as he stepped safely away from the fire. The last carcasses burned now across the parcels that had contained the herd, and he turned away, sucking in a breath that wasn't saturated with the stench of burning flesh.

More than a week had passed since the first cow had sickened, since he'd sent the letter to his solicitors, and he'd taken to spending his nights in the pastures with the tenants. Taking turns at snatching sleep and tending to the fires. Working through the night they'd been able to eradicate the infected carcasses and the contaminated feed stock, and from that, he drew some solace. From that, he could pretend he wasn't staying out here to avoid his wife.

Because he couldn't tell her they must sell Raeford Court.

Blanstock stood some distance from him, and he raised a hand to draw the man's attention. "I must return to the house. I'll expect a report at the end of the day."

Blanstock raised a hand to acknowledge he'd heard him and then returned to speaking with the tenant of this parcel, a Mr. Evans.

By the time Ben arrived back at the main house, the sun was dipping low in the sky. His solicitors should have arrived, and he felt the inevitability of Raeford's demise like a physical thing, hanging about his neck and sapping the last of his energy.

He went straight to his study, not bothering to wash up. The stench of burnt flesh was imprinted in his nostrils, and no amount of scrubbing would get the ash out from under his fingernails.

He wasn't surprised to find his solicitors, a Mr. Harbinger and a Mr. Charles, waiting for him, a tea cart situated between them. They stood as he entered and he bade them sit.

"Gentlemen, I thank you for coming all the way from London. I'm sure by now you've had time to process the enormity of what has occurred and can provide some insight on what would be best for the liquidation of the Raeford estate."

The men exchanged quizzical glances, and after a pause, Mr. Harbinger said, "You wish to liquidate, Your Grace?"

Ben shrugged as he discarded his ruined jacket. "I have no such wish, but I see little more that can be done. We can't guarantee the return of the crops come harvest, especially in the current climate, and I will not see Raeford fall to despair. If someone of means can save it from destruction then I see no better course of action."

It burned, hot and deep, the idea of giving up Raeford, but in the days he spent watching the future of Raeford go up in literal flames, he had had plenty of time to think. Selling it was the only option. He only hoped someone of means and a modicum of sense purchased the property.

He felt another stab of guilt that he had not discussed his plans with Johanna. He had made a promise to her, but in the extreme case of their current situation, he couldn't bring himself to honor that promise, his need to protect Raeford overwhelming him. He hated himself further, but in all, it was much the same.

His life had been a trail of disasters and disappointments. Why should he not continue the record?

Mr. Charles stepped up now. "But surely there is enough in the recent funding to repair the damage that's been done." The solicitor turned to where a small case had been opened on the low table in front of the chairs on which they'd been sitting. He ruffled through the papers, selecting one to hold aloft, adjusting his spectacles until he could read it. "Yes. Yes, I'm quite sure there's enough in the accounts to replace the herd and food stores. It can be done immediately."

Ben knew his solicitors were getting on in age, but he doubted the men could both suffer from some sort of senility.

"I believe you speak of the dowry transferred upon my marriage to Lady Johanna Darby. Those funds have been spent. If you look at the most recent—"

Mr. Charles waved the paper in front of him. "No, Your Grace. I do not speak of that at all. It's the most recent transfer of funds of which I am most concerned. Do you not think it sufficient?"

The first lick of suspicion trailed down the back of his neck. He stepped forward, reaching out a hand for the paper Mr. Charles wielded like a sword.

The solicitor gave it up easily, and Ben scanned the sheet,

his eyes passing once, twice, thrice over the words in order to ascertain their meaning.

"There's been a second transfer." He looked up. "From the Ravenwood accounts to Raeford."

Mr. Harbinger nodded. "Yes. Quite a significant sum it would seem. We received word of it by messenger when we were already en route. I'm sure—"

He didn't hear the rest of it. He stormed from the study, taking the stairs to the upper floors two at a time. He passed the door to the ducal chambers and went directly for the duchess's rooms. He didn't bother knocking, entering the room at a clip, the damning piece of paper stretched out in his hand.

She had just stepped from a bath when he entered, and he faltered, his arm with the accusatory paper dropping as he averted his gaze.

Damn, she was beautiful, and his angry words caught in his throat at the sight of her, utterly naked, water sliding down her flat stomach, her lush hips, her curved thighs.

God, he'd missed her. The days and nights he'd spent in the fields had been long, and his body rocked at the sight of her, longing flooding him with an intensity that nearly choked him.

"Ben!" she exclaimed upon seeing him, her face lit with a smile that quickly dimmed at the sight of him. "Oh, you're sore with me again. What is it I've done this time?"

He shook the paper at her, his words still jammed in his throat.

"Are you suffering from a fit of apoplexy? I cannot read that paper." She extended a hand dripping with bathwater. "Should you like me to take it?"

He'd nearly handed it to her before he regained his senses. "Ravenwood transferred funds into the Raeford account. Did you know about this?"

Her chin went up. "Your tone would suggest that you've already found me guilty, so why are you bothering to ask the question? Perhaps if you had returned to the house in the last few days you could have asked earlier. And his name is Andrew, or have you forgotten?"

There wasn't a shred of remorse in her tone, and her damnable chin remained raised.

"When were you going to tell me about the money?"

"Just as soon as I dressed." She spread her hands, indicating her nakedness. She hadn't even reached for a towel to shield herself, and he took in her every curve glistening with bathwater. His body responded even when he thought he might drown in his anger with her. "Unless you wish me to be seen by your solicitors in this state." Her words met their mark, and he swallowed, averting his gaze. "When were you going to tell me you'd sent for them, Ben?"

Her tone was a great deal softer than his, and he felt another stab of guilt at his forceful reaction to her duplicity.

"I had no other choice. The herd is dead, and I haven't the money to replace them." He shook the paper. "Not before the arrival of this."

It was only then that her expression changed at all, her eyes losing their brightness as she exhaled deeply, her shoulders deflating.

"I don't need charity, Johanna."

Her eyes flashed. "It's not charity. It's Louisa's dowry. Sebastian refused it upon their marriage, and my father had explicitly set it aside for use in marriage negotiations. Whether you choose to acknowledge it or not, this is a marriage."

Her voice wavered ever so much on the last words, and his stomach tightened, but he fortified himself with years of abuse, first at the hands of his father and then the hands of his first wife.

He stepped closer, his body nearly touching hers as he leaned in close, his lips brushing her ear.

"And what is it you're negotiating with this money?"

He'd played this game before, and Minerva had taught him well. He knew how accurately he had struck when Johanna sucked in a breath. His only mistake was in forgetting Johanna did not play games.

Her fist found its mark directly in his abdomen. He doubled over as the air shot from his lungs, and his mouth opened, attempting to suck in a breath.

"I will not stand here and allow you to imply I'm a whore, Ben." She grabbed him by the front of the shirt, hauling him up, forcing him to look her in the eye. "I'm getting tired of telling you this." Her voice had gone soft as though they were the only two people in the world. "I'm tired of reminding you that you are not your past. The things they did to you, your father and Minerva, they do not determine who you are. I will not allow you to behave as they taught you to."

He wanted to believe her, but he could only hear his father's voice over and over again in his head, hear Minerva's unending cries.

She released him, and so intent had he been on her words, he stumbled, his legs coming up against the copper tub. He was off balance enough that there was no saving him. He toppled backward, landing squarely in the tub of used bathwater. It rushed up and over him in a waterfall, soaking him and the paper he held. He sputtered and shook the water from his eyes.

Johanna loomed over him, clearly taking no pleasure in his mishap.

"That money is to be used for the rebuilding of Raeford just as my dowry was. I will expect to see the progress you've made, or I shall demand reports directly from Blanstock.

Whichever way you choose, I will see to the management of those funds."

He sat in the bathwater, hating himself for thinking her so beautiful. No, not beautiful. Strong. She was a column of strength standing before him. Her jaw hard, her eyes unflinching, her hands to her hips. God, her gorgeous hips, her firm breasts, her gorgeous thighs. So much of her spoke of a strength he'd never possessed, and he hated her for it. Then he hated himself worse for thinking it.

"I understand." The words nearly choked him.

She turned, and something ripped loose inside of him. She was walking away, and somehow he knew, she was walking away from *them*.

"Johanna." He scrambled, trying to gain purchase as he'd fallen awkwardly in the tub, his hands slipping along the metal rim.

Finally, he hauled himself out, water sloshing on the carpet. It was helplessly soaked, and it squished beneath his feet as he made his way over to her. But when he got there, he couldn't think of what to say.

He searched her face, trying to find the words that were stuck somewhere inside of him. He wanted to tell her the truth, suddenly and ferociously. He wanted to tell her everything, but there was nothing she could do. The damage had already been wrought.

A line appeared between her brows.

"Oh, Ben," she whispered.

He put everything he was feeling into his eyes, hoping she would see it there. See how much he wanted her to save him.

But instead she only shook her head. "I tried, Ben. But maybe I was too late or what they did to you was too great." She shrugged, the saddest shrug he'd ever seen, and it was in that moment that his heart gave up.

She reached up a hand, and he thought she might touch

him. Maybe then he could find the words to say something, but she didn't touch him. Her hand fell back down to her side.

When she met his gaze again, there were tears in her eyes. "I guess I was just hoping my love would be strong enough to pull you out of this darkness." She bit her lower lip as if she struggled to hold back the tears. "But it wasn't." The tears started now, her voice quivering with them. "I wasn't strong enough."

No.

He reached for her, but she'd already moved away, shutting the door of her dressing room firmly between them.

* * *

IT WAS easy to slip back into the routine she had acquired when Ben was gone. She woke early and went to the stables, spending most of the morning with Grindel and Smothers. She joined Duchess for a late breakfast when she was sure Ben had left the main house for the day.

Without speaking of it, they moved their terrace luncheons to Duchess's cottage garden where they lingered longer and longer each day. Johanna didn't know when it had started, but there wasn't anything to pull her away, not anymore, so she just let herself be.

She was once more where she had started. She belonged to nothing and nothing was hers. She whiled away hours in Duchess's gardens, helped the woman with whatever her latest passion was. Then helped Smothers exercise a new mare come afternoon.

But it wasn't enough. She was just tagging along after other people's whims. She hadn't even visited the tenants. Ben's fury at her intervention imprinted on her mind, and she couldn't work past it. She'd stayed away. It was best that way. He would have what he wanted and maybe then he'd be happy.

She didn't go to the stream. There were too many memories there. She exercised Grindel in the park surrounding the main house, lingering along the lake and the edge of the forest, but never returning to the spot that filled so many of her memories.

She even stayed away from her beloved cap-house. Not only for its intrinsic memories, but also because she didn't want to see Ben leaving the house or returning. She didn't want to see him at all.

She moved her rooms to the opposite end of the family wing, so she wasn't forced to hear him in his rooms at night. She took her supper trays there, never once giving an excuse for an absence. She simply wasn't present at dinner.

It went on like this for weeks. She knew the harvest must have started, but she didn't go down to the tenant farms to witness it. She'd heard from Smothers a new herd had begun to arrive, and she wanted nothing more than to see them brought into the pastures, but she didn't. She'd stayed in her room for days, summoning the energy for nothing more than moving from her bed to the window bench in her bedchamber.

But it wasn't like her to sulk, so she'd finally emerged to resume her half existence.

This was it. This was to be her marriage. She thought she'd finally made a decision on her own, claimed something that would be only hers, her choice to help run Raeford Court, but Ben's scars ran deeper than her need for something to claim as her own.

No, it wasn't that. She could press her claim as the money that funded Raeford Court was Ravenwood money, but it was seeing this side of Ben that she couldn't bear. She could give up her need for more if only to avoid witnessing the man her husband had become.

How could he let the actions of others rule his future?

But wasn't she doing the same by not fighting for more?

She'd visited Andrew several times, but it wasn't the same. The memories at Ravenwood Park haunted her, and she missed her sisters with a fierceness. She thought of going to London, of seeing Simon and hearing George's laughter.

But she couldn't leave Raeford.

Whatever Ben did she still belonged to the land here, and it gave her comfort.

She decided to walk to Duchess's cottage one day for their usual luncheon. The air was beginning to turn from the heat of summer to cooler temperatures of autumn, and she wanted to enjoy the walk while the sun was still warm on her shoulders.

She wasn't surprised to find the cottage garden gate open, a spilled basket of flower pots just inside on the walkway. She followed the path around to the back of the cottage where they usually took their luncheon in the circle of mismatched chairs.

She found Duchess kneeling over her rock garden. At first, it looked as though she were merely arranging the sand, but at a second glance, Duchess's movements were agitated, her brow furrowed as her hands swept through the sand in the circular base of the old fountain that formed the garden's perimeter.

"Duchess." Johanna rushed forward, picking up her skirts as she fell to her knees beside the older woman.

Johanna placed her hands on the woman's shoulders, kneading the muscles there as she attempted to calm her.

"Duchess, tell me what's wrong. What's happening?"

She didn't answer, plunging her fingers in and out of the sand.

Johanna watched the abrupt movements, so unlike the usual graceful way she meditated over the sand.

"Duchess," Johanna tried again. "Duchess, tell me what is wrong?"

Duchess only shook her head, her fingers stabbing the sand.

It was then Johanna became aware that the other woman was muttering, slowly and so softly Johanna almost missed it. She leaned closer.

"Duchess, why don't you tell me what's wrong?"

The woman sat back abruptly, her hands throwing sand in her haste.

"He won't talk to me."

Johanna felt a surge of anger.

"Ben? Ben won't speak to you?"

Was it because of Johanna? Had he taken out his anger on his mother because of her? Because of their close relationship?

Duchess's face folded in agony, her hands beating uselessly against the stone edge of the rock garden. Johanna captured her hands to prevent the woman from harm.

Duchess shook her head. "Ben, my dear boy. Ben. Dear boy. Not Ben."

She'd taken to swaying back and forth, her hands still caught in Johanna's.

"Not Ben?" Johanna looked about them.

Duchess never left Raeford Court, and as far as Johanna knew, her circle of acquaintances included her son and the servants and now Johanna. Was it a servant who wouldn't speak to her? She would relieve the man of his post immediately.

Johanna rubbed the woman's hands vigorously.

"Duchess, please tell me. Please tell me who won't speak to you."

Finally, Duchess's gaze cleared and her attention shifted to Johanna's face. She stopped moving, all at once and completely, and a smile spread over her face.

"Johanna, my darling. When did you get here? Is it time for luncheon already?" She looked down to where their hands were still connected. "What is this? Are we playing at some sort of game?" Her eyes lit at the prospect of playing a game.

Johanna shook her head. "No, it's not a game. Duchess, you seemed agitated. You were poking at your rock garden and saying he won't speak to you."

A shadow passed over Duchess's face, but she soon regained her smile. She pulled one hand free to pat both of Johanna's.

"Oh, that's nothing but the mutterings of an old woman." She pulled free of Johanna's grasp and used the edge of the rock garden to push to her feet.

Johanna studied the woman as she took several steps away, but her movements were sure and strong. Johanna stood, following her mother-in-law to the table that had been laid with luncheon.

"It appears Cook has sent over some of her leek and potato pasties." Duchess clapped her hands together in enthusiasm. "Oh, I do hope she used that cheese she got in London the last time she was down there."

Johanna pulled out her usual chair. "Cook goes to London?"

Duchess nodded. "Her daughter lives there, and Cook goes down twice a year to visit her grandchildren. She has seven of them." Duchess threw up her hands. "I cannot even think what that poor mother endures. Do you know they own a patisserie?"

Johanna sat and drew her napkin onto her lap.

"A patisserie? Like a bakery?"

Duchess shook her head. "No, nothing so mundane as that. Cook's son-in-law is French. He studied under the great pastry chefs of Paris." She made some indistinct noises of satisfaction. "His choux buns make my toes curl."

Johanna smiled at Duchess's expression of utter contentment, but she couldn't help but remember the woman's earlier agitation.

She plated some of the cold hen and salad Cook had sent with the pasties and passed the plate to Duchess who was already biting into one of the crusty delights.

"I shall keep that in mind the next time Cook leaves for a visit. Perhaps she can bring back enough treats for the entire house."

Duchess's eyes widened at the thought, and Johanna couldn't help but laugh.

Duchess's smile dimmed. "You haven't been laughing much lately, my girl. I think it's my son's fault. The arse."

Johanna choked on her first bite of pasty, reaching for the lemonade to clear her throat.

"Excuse me?"

Duchess shook her head, her gaze moving thoughtfully off into the distance.

"He came out broken, Johanna. I know that. I tried my best to fix the pieces that others broke, but he's just not like me. He takes what they said, and he holds it in his heart." She shook her head again. "He never learned to release those things that do not make him better."

Johanna set down her lemonade glass carefully, as if she might spook Duchess from her moment of clarity.

"What are the things that fail to make him better?"

Duchess's gaze sharpened, and she turned her attention back to the table. She pushed the pasty around on her plate.

"I told you of what his father did to him, but that was only the surface of it. He hurt Ben so much more, so much deeper."

Johanna had to force herself not to hold her breath. "How?"

If only she could discover what it was that tormented Ben, maybe she could help. Maybe she could bring back the man she had fallen in love with.

Duchess looked up from her plate, and for the first time in years, Johanna thought she might be seeing the real woman. Elizabeth "Betsy" Carver, the dowager Duchess of Raeford. Not the persona she had crafted to hide herself. Not the duchess she had created to protect herself from further harm.

This was the woman who had married into the Raeford title, who had born two sons to it. This was the woman who had had the strength to find a way to survive in a situation from which she could not escape.

With a jolt, Johanna realized she was looking at her future. She, too, found herself in a situation from which there was no escape, and she knew one day she must find a way to live in it. She couldn't keep hiding. She couldn't keep avoiding Ben.

Duchess had built her own world at the dowager cottage. She'd erected something that was entirely her own, and in it, she'd thrived.

A coldness so complete washed over Johanna then. Was this the life she was destined to live? One of isolation and loneliness? One of being attached to Ben in every way that mattered except the one of greatest importance?

She swallowed, bile rising in her throat as her stomach heaved.

Duchess held her gaze for a long time, but in the end, she only shook her head.

"It is not for me to tell. If Ben wanted it known, he would

have told you." She picked up another pasty, set it back down. "He won't tell you though. He won't tell you what he must." She worried her lower lip, and for a moment, Johanna saw the woman she'd found moments ago at the rock garden.

She reached out a hand and touched Duchess's arm as if to draw her back to the present.

"It's all right, love," she whispered. "Ben mustn't tell me anything. I've known all along that it was too good to be true."

Duchess looked up at this, her eyes clearing. "What was too good?"

Johanna picked up her lemonade, suddenly uninterested in her luncheon.

"Love," she said simply.

CHAPTER 17

*B*en was somehow not surprised to see Andrew Darby, the Duke of Ravenwood riding up his drive.

His chest tightened at the sight of his old friend, and an avalanche of feelings passed through him all at once. Resentment, anger, frustration, and the worst of all, guilt.

Andrew dismounted at the circular drive, handing the reins of his horse off to a footman before walking the short distance to where Ben had been meeting with Smothers in the stables.

The stable master had an idea for breeding one of the stallions, and the plan would need to be put into place should they wish to take advantage of the opportunity. Rarely did such matters pull Ben away from the everyday demands of the estate, but he found comfort in the horses. It was more than just familiarity. It was their smell and noises and gestures. It reminded him of being with Johanna.

He faced Andrew now, unsure whether to apologize or pulverize the man.

"I've come to tell you you're being an idiot," Andrew said first off.

Pulverize it was.

Ben cursed softly and rubbed the back of his neck with one hand.

"You'll excuse me if I cannot ascertain the reason why. As of late, there are a host of reasons for such a conclusion."

Andrew looked down the hill toward the tenant farms.

"You must understand I know of the cattle plague that was brought in with the last herd. Whether you believe it or not, I am sorry for the trouble. Cattle plague can be devastating to an estate."

His tone was sincere, and Ben felt the tension ease somewhat along his shoulders.

"Thank you. But as you know, we had the funds to repair the damage. The new herd seems to be settling in. I personally inspected the pastures where the bovines were kept and went with the handlers to move them into the new pastures."

Andrew was nodding as he spoke. "I wouldn't expect anything less from you."

While the words were complimentary, Ben couldn't help but feel chafed. The feeling was intense and immediate, and he hated himself for it. How was it that he couldn't bring himself to accept praise even from an old friend?

"If it's not the herd you've come to scold me about, what is?"

"My sister is in love with you."

Ben cursed, the tension coiling tenfold in his shoulders. "Did she tell you that?"

Andrew turned a bewildered eye on him. "Tell me that? Good God, man, she rode hell for leather to the park and barged into my library with more fury than Medusa, demanding Louisa's dowry. Her motives were clear enough for a blind man to see and yet I understand Johanna remains unhappy. I can only lay the blame at your feet."

Autumn was coming to Yorkshire, and the sun no longer held the warmth it once did, but standing there in the drive at Raeford Court, Ben felt heat spread through him, heat and something else. Something invincible.

And all at once, something let go.

"My father forced me to marry Minerva when my brother got her with child."

He'd never spoken the words out loud. Never in five years. There were only four people privy to the lies on which his first marriage had been built and three of them were dead.

Suddenly another knew. Another knew of how low his father had thought of him. Not worthy of Raeford Court. Worthy only to solve the issue of his worthy son's by-blow.

Andrew sucked in a breath. "And you never once thought to tell me? Your best friend? Jesus, Ben, even I thought our friendship meant more than that."

The words startled him.

"You would…wish to know?"

Ben had squirreled away his humiliation, all too happy to flee to America so no one would realize his shame, least of all his best friend.

Andrew turned a fiery glare on him. "Yes, I would wish to know. Your father was the worst kind of bastard, Ben. To have made you—" His words died off in a string of expletives then.

Ben knew his feet remained on Raeford soil, and yet he felt at sea, awash in waves that threatened to swamp him.

"You're not…you're not disgusted with me?"

Andrew's eyes widened. "Disgusted? Is that what that bastard told you? That you disgusted him?" Andrew stepped forward and seized Ben by the shoulders. "That man used your mother for fisticuffs practice. He doesn't get to determine the meaning of *disgust*." Andrew practically spat the last word and released his friend, pacing away.

Ben stood motionless, years of torment suddenly upended now that he'd spoken it aloud, now that someone else knew.

He hadn't expected this. He hadn't expected the release he would feel once someone knew the truth. He had expected shame and distaste, revulsion and loathing.

He'd never expected…acceptance.

Andrew whirled. "Ben, where is the child?"

Ben flinched. "She lost the babe in the third month."

"Hell's teeth," his friend whispered softly.

It needn't matter how the babe was brought about. The loss of a child was never easy.

"And Minerva?"

Ben dropped his gaze to the ground and when he'd gathered his thoughts, he looked directly at his friend.

"It was the last thing she had been holding on to. A piece of Lawrence all to herself. She hated me from the beginning. From the moment our father decided she wasn't good enough for Lawrence. But after the babe was lost…" He let his voice trail off. Andrew knew what came next.

Years of emotional and mental anguish and abuse. Years of torture and solitude. Years of being separated from the people who mattered most.

Johanna.

He heard a click deep within him, and his world shifted under his feet.

Johanna.

"Andrew," he said, his hands curling into fists. "I think I've been an idiot."

Andrew did not take that opportunity to mock him. His expression was one of sad understanding.

"I know, friend." He gestured to the house as if Johanna might be in there. "Can you not speak to her?"

Their last fight came back to him in a rush. The words he had flung at her as if mere speech could protect himself from her. No, protect her from him. He'd made a mire of the entire thing, and he didn't know if it could be undone.

He raked both hands through his hair, letting out a soft curse.

"I don't know." The words faltered, coming out as nothing more than a breath. "I...I..." But the words wouldn't come.

They stood like that for several seconds until Andrew moved. He pulled Ben into a solid embrace, his arms strong and unyielding, and all at once, Ben felt it.

The true meaning of friendship.

Tears burned at the backs of his eyes, and he returned Andrew's embrace before pulling away.

"I'll speak to her. I promise. I'll try anything to set it to rights." The words rushed from him as Andrew stepped back, but he stopped speaking at the smile on his friend's face.

"I know you will," Andrew said softly and turned back to his horse. "Now if you'll excuse me, I'm owed a stalking trip in Scotland."

He mounted and turned the horse toward the drive.

"You're still bent on going to Old Man MacKenzie's?"

Andrew called back over his shoulder. "At least I know there will be plenty of ale."

Ben laughed as his friend rode away, a lightness settling around him.

He must speak with Johanna. He turned to do just that when Blanstock rode up. The cows had broken through the Kendall pasture. He scrubbed a hand over his chin but mounted up. Johanna would have his head if he let anything happen to the new herd.

He wasn't sure when it was the sky began to darken, but

the wind picked up enough to make their job nigh impossible. Every time they got a panel into place the wind would blow it in. They settled for wrapping thick ropes about the parts that were still sturdy to hold a makeshift fence into place. They would need to return on the morrow, weather permitting.

Blanstock headed off for the steward's cottage while the tenant farmers took shelter in their cottages. Ben headed for the main house, spurring his horse on faster to outpace the coming storm.

It had been unusually dry the past several weeks, and he was only glad the harvest had been taken in before drought could damage it. But if the skies opened as they appeared they might, the parched ground would not take the water, and flooding would be a real danger.

Even as the wind whipped at him and battered his horse enough for the animal to falter, his thoughts remained on his encounter with Andrew that morning. He still felt unsteady, unsure of what he might say to Johanna or what it might do.

But he knew now his father had put a wedge between him and the people who truly mattered, leaving Ben trapped in a world where his father could control him completely through denigration and manipulation.

What hurt the most was the man still held power after death. Power Ben had given to him.

Not anymore.

No matter what insecurities still plagued him he would listen to Johanna first. She was nothing but truth and light. She'd been since the beginning, and yet he couldn't see her. He couldn't see for the lies his father fed him. The lies his brother and Minerva perpetuated.

No more.

He handed off his horse to Smothers and dashed into the house just as the first of the raindrops fell. He made for the stairs. Johanna was likely in the cap-house, but his mother stopped him, emerging from the back of the house like a sprite, her arms extended.

"Benedict, we must speak."

He halted, one foot on the stairs. Would he never get to speak to his wife?

He rested one arm on the banister as he leaned over to see his mother more clearly.

"What is it, Mother? I have an urgent matter to attend."

She crossed her arms over her chest. "You've had many urgent matters of late, but I fear you're misguided."

He stepped back down to the foyer. Did everyone think him an idiot then?

"Mother, you're right."

Her mouth snapped shut on what she'd been about to say, her eyes searching.

"I am? But you don't even know what I was going to say."

He walked over to her and gently laid his hands on her shoulders. "You were going to tell me Johanna loves me, and I've done nothing but get in my own way about it."

Her frown was furious. "I was not going to implicate you in any way. I was going to call your father several choice names and tell you what he had to say was utter nonsense." She grabbed the lapels of his jacket with a strength he could not have foreseen. His mother rocked him onto his toes with ferocity. "Your father condemned you because in you he saw the man he would never be."

She released him as suddenly as she had gripped him, and he rocked back on his feet. Once more his world shifted, and he was left grasping at what he thought had been reality.

She shook her head. "I should have shoved the man down the stairs when I had the chance."

She turned and began to walk away.

"Mother, what are you speaking of?"

She looked over her shoulder. "Your father. I always dreamed of shoving him down the stairs. I had hopes he'd break his neck."

She adjusted the cashmere scarf at her neck, the same scarf Johanna had helped her make, and the corridor should have been the ballroom of a grand home for the way his mother sauntered down it.

He went after her.

"Mother, did you really have designs on murdering my father?"

She turned, her eyes clear. "Of course, I did." She shrugged. "He wasn't worth it though. He enjoyed hitting me when he had nothing better to do and was lost in his cups." She wrinkled her nose. "That is a weak man and a spiteful one. He wasn't worth my attentions."

She tried to move down the corridor again, and he stopped her.

"Mother, you're saying that my father isn't...he wasn't..." He tried to find words, but he couldn't even grasp his own meaning. He gestured to her ensemble. The scarf, the beads wrapped about her ankles, her gown, embroidered flowers covering the holes in it.

She looked down at herself. "Do you have something to say for my appearance?" She cocked an eyebrow in challenge.

He dropped his hands. "No, I wouldn't dare such a thing."

"I thought not." Her smile softened then. "It's not a sadness your father created in me that I battle, dear boy. It's a sadness born of true love."

If he could have, he would have sat down as his legs seemed to give out.

"True love?"

She blinked. "Of course, it was true love. Have you heard differently?" Her expression turned quizzical with an edge of fire as if she would duel whoever contradicted her.

"I haven't heard any mention of love."

She pursed her lips and poked him squarely in the chest. "Willoughby and I loved one another, and I shall mourn him until the day we are reunited."

Ben blinked. "Willoughby? The gardener?"

His mother raised her chin. "That was a man of character, Ben. Don't ever forget it."

He let her go then, memories of his past falling on him like bricks. The apiary. Willoughby's dedication to seeing it through. The rock garden. His mother's beloved rock garden. Willoughby had built it for her.

Ben had never known.

Warmth flooded him, quick and pure, and he knew even if the damage his father had wrought still lingered inside of him, it only mattered that he'd found the most important thing of all.

Hope.

His mother was several feet away when Mrs. Owens appeared at the end of the corridor. The sight of her was so unusual, Duchess stopped completely. The housekeeper held her skirts in her hands as she rushed toward them, her chatelaine of keys bouncing at her waist.

"Your Grace!" she cried from several yards away. "It's Johanna. She hasn't returned. She went for a ride, and Smothers just sent word that her horse has returned without her."

"Oh Ben, the stream," Duchess whispered, the shock making her voice like air.

But Ben didn't hear anything more; he didn't feel anything more.

He was already running for the door.

* * *

She would forever be the one to say it was a mistake to bring along a bonnet, and that day solidified her belief.

She'd gone to the stream.

Their stream.

She'd risen that morning with a renewed sense of urgency. She couldn't live like this. It wasn't living. It was merely sustaining. She had to face the reality in which she found herself and carve out her own existence just as Duchess had done.

She'd taken her usual morning ride and spent a late breakfast with Duchess. She'd then returned to the stables to collect Grindel, planning to sit on the flat rock at the stream until she figured out what she would do.

It was hardly a plan, but at the moment, it was all she had. The day was warm and bright, and it was likely the last of the summer sun they would have. She would make the most of it and hope by the time the sun began to set, she knew what she would do.

She'd left Grindel along the bank and made her way carefully down to the flat rock. It was warm from the sun, and she removed her bonnet, tossing it aside as she spread out the blanket she had brought. She shed her pelisse, wrapping it into a makeshift pillow so she could lie back and let the sun envelope her.

That was when she'd fallen asleep.

She hadn't realized how tired she was. The stress of trying to avoid Ben, the agony of her thoughts swimming one after the other with no direction had all crashed together to leave her boneless and exhausted.

Sleep had come almost immediately. It was by no means a comfortable sleep, which only spoke to the depth of her exhaustion. She woke several times to turn and adjust, and each time the sun had moved a little farther across the sky.

But the next time she woke it was to raindrops striking her face.

She sat up immediately, her mind muddled somewhere between sleep and wake, but the raindrops that had started as a mere drizzle turned into a downpour within seconds.

The stream.

She was alert within seconds, her body tensing to flee. The rain was coming in torrents. Her eyes darted to the waterfall, noting how it had picked up volume just in the minutes since the rain started. She had to get out of the stream bed before the water rose.

She stood without watching where she put her feet, and her boot hit the silky ribbon tie of her bonnet. She lost her footing, her feet sliding out completely from underneath her, and she fell hard, white hot fire shooting through her elbow as she scraped along the rock gone slippery with rainwater.

She caught herself before she plunged into the pool below, her foot wedging between the rocks along this side of the bank. She took precious moments to catch her breath, her body shaking from the near drop into the pool below.

She glanced at the waterfall, her stomach flipping as she saw it had grown to a roar. She had to get out of there.

She turned and braced her hands on the rock behind her even as pain surged through her elbow. She pushed.

Nothing happened.

She tried again.

Nothing.

Panic gripped her, and she sucked in a breath, steadying herself. Panic would get her nowhere. She peered down, pushing her skirts out of the way. Her foot stuck between two boulders where it had caught when she slid from the flat rock. She wiggled her toes inside her boot, feeling no pain. It wasn't broken, but it was steadfastly stuck.

She bent over, planting her hands on the opposite boulder, applying all her strength, and levered herself to pull only on her stuck foot.

It didn't budge.

She tried again, and her hands simply slid off the rock she was using to brace herself. Her palms bled now, pebbles imbedded in the torn flesh.

Fear caught at her throat, and she struggled to gain a full breath. The storm pounded around her, the stream flooding, the water rising.

This was it.

After everything, she was going to drown in their stream.

But even as the thought descended upon her, the sound of galloping hoofbeats broke through the rush of rain.

Her heart thudded, hope surging through her limbs. She turned to the bank, holding a hand above her eyes as she tried to peer through the rain.

Had Smothers come to find her when the rain started? But how much help could an arthritic old man be in this storm with her foot wedged between the rocks? She felt a pang of guilt at the thought, but she couldn't help it. Despair passed through her like a ghost, and she shivered.

Cold wracked her then as she strained to see through the rain, but the hoofbeats had stopped. Had her would-be rescuer gone to search elsewhere? Had he thought it unlikely she would be down in the stream bed?

But then there he was, at the edge of the bank, and she strained to make out who he was as the rain was fierce now. He was on foot, likely having left his horse at a safe distance from the rocky bank. He took the bank with expert steps, and suddenly she knew.

Ben.

She reached out, her arms going soundlessly to him. He was there in seconds, his arms wrapping around her, his warm lips pressed to her ear.

"Are you hurt?" She knew from the vibration that he must have shouted it, but through the torrent of rain, it was as though he'd merely spoken the words.

She shook her head, turning her lips to his ear. "My foot is stuck." She pointed down to where her boot was lodged between the boulders.

He moved swiftly, climbing down until he could get both hands on her boot. He tugged, and she tried to help him by lifting her foot. He straightened, his lips once more at her ear.

"I'll tug at the same time as when you pull." He leaned back, and she nodded.

He bent again, and she felt him tap out against her leg.

One, two, three.

She pulled at the same time he tugged.

Nothing.

This couldn't happen. Not now. Ben had come to save her; it had to mean something. She couldn't die.

He straightened, his face hard, and she opened her mouth to say something, anything that might keep him from giving up.

But he wasn't giving up. He pulled a knife from his boot and bent once more to her foot. She grabbed her skirts, frantic to see what he might do.

With one swift motion he cut the ties of her boot. She felt the pressure give the slightest of degrees, and her survival instinct roared. She heaved with all her might, and her foot slipped free, faster than she'd expected. She toppled, but Ben was there, catching her against his chest with one arm.

He sheathed the knife back in his boot, keeping his arm around her. Together they scrambled up the bank as the water roared behind them. Only when they were safely up the escarpment did she look back. The water was over the flat rock now.

She swallowed down her panic, but she didn't have time to wallow in the enormity of what had just happened or almost happened. Ben pulled her toward his horse.

She looked about for Grindel, but the animal was gone. She froze, tugging back at Ben's grasp.

He turned, and must have seen the confusion on her face, because he bent his lips to her ear.

"She came back to the barn without you."

Gratitude. That was the feeling that spread through her. Gratitude for the horse that had been her companion through this and her savior when it mattered most.

She vaulted onto the saddle in front of Ben, leaning back into the shelter of his arms as he spurred the horse into a trot. The ride back to the house was torture, but the alternative was that she would be still stuck in the stream bed, the water rising around her.

She closed her eyes against the thought and nestled back into Ben's embrace, cradling her elbow as best she could as the motion jostled her.

She opened her eyes again as the horse's gait began to slow. The first thing she saw was Smothers, standing under the overhang of the stable, his hand holding his hat to his head in the biting wind. He reached for the reins Ben tossed as the horse stamped to a halt under the protection of the overhang.

Ben had already slid from the horse and reached for her before she could gather the words to ask if Grindel was all right.

And then Ben carried her away.

He never once let her feet touch the ground even as she squirmed in protest. Her bootless foot bounced in front of her, and with the ground beneath them turning to mud, she thought it was best to let him carry her.

But he didn't stop when they reached the house. He marched inside, rain following them in on a gust of wind, and he carried her right past the astonished faces of Mrs. Owens and Duchess. He took the stairs two at a time, and she became aware of the enormity of feeling that must have propelled him.

Was he angry with her? Did he think she had purposely endangered her life?

She readied herself for the moment he would release her, when she would be forced to defend herself, but it never came. He took her directly to his rooms, kicking the door shut behind them.

A fire had been laid in the hearth and a stack of clean towels rested on the chair in front of it, almost as if someone were expecting them.

Grindel had returned to the stables without her. The whole house must have been alerted to her absence. Guilt twisted inside her. She must have alarmed so many people.

Ben set her down, her feet uneven on the carpet thanks to the lack of boot, but he didn't let go of her.

Instead, he ripped her clothes off.

It wasn't as sensual as it sounded, but her husband hadn't touched her in weeks and despite the risk to her life she had just endured, it was nothing compared to feeling her husband's hands on her after so long apart.

"Ben?" His name was a question, but she didn't know what to ask.

Had he forgiven her? Did he blame her for what had happened? What did he think?

He didn't say anything though. He shed her of her wet clothes before going to work on his own. He pressed a towel into her hands and wrapped another around her soaked hair. Carefully, he plucked the pebbles from her scraped palms, wrapping them in clean linen.

He did the same for her elbow. She was thankful it wasn't broken, but an angry red scrape marred her skin.

Only then did he pull the blankets from the bed and toss them in front of the fire. When he pulled her down beside him, wrapped her against his warm body in a thick quilt, she thought her heart may never survive.

"Ben, I didn't mean to—"

He kissed her, slow and deep, and desire warred with her confusion.

He pulled back, cupping her cheek with one hand.

"Don't ever do that to me again. Promise me." His voice was fierce, his eyes wounded.

She pressed a hand to his chest, feeling the rapid beat of his heart against her palm.

"I promise," she said.

He looked past her then at the fire, and his eyes searched as though readying himself for something.

She waited. She prepared herself for the rejection. Understood he would want her to believe this meant nothing but that wasn't at all what happened.

When he looked back at her, he said, "I love you." He shook his head. "I wouldn't let myself believe it because I thought I didn't deserve such things. But I do. I deserve it, and I love you."

Her lungs squeezed as she struggled for breath, struggled for words.

But Ben went on, "There's so much I need to tell you, Johanna. So much I should have told you from the start."

She pressed her fingers to his lips. "I told you your past doesn't matter to me."

He snatched her fingers away, holding them once more against his heart.

"I know you feel that way, but my past is a part of me. It's left scars. Scars that have tried to control my life, and I won't let them, but I'm going to need your help to overcome them."

Her heart soared at his confession, but the meaning of his words soon descended upon her.

"Ben," she said, stroking the hair from his forehead. "What happened?"

He didn't speak. He captured her mouth in a kiss and turned her, coming atop her as he pressed the length of his body against hers.

He made love to her, sweetly and slowly, there before the fire. It was simple and pure, no moments spent on building the desire between them because it wasn't necessary. This was about claiming one another, nothing more and nothing less.

When they lay entwined afterward, their bodies warm now and satiated, he told her.

He told her everything.

He told her about Minerva, about the baby, and his father's manipulation. He told her of the isolation in America, of his desperation to find a new path even as he longed for the one of which he had dreamed.

She held him as he told her, pressed a kiss to his lips when the words became too difficult. They held each other like that, the past echoing around them like a ghost, no longer the demon that had once haunted him, but something with which they would both need to face in the future, but now they would face it together.

The fire had burned down, and reluctantly, she let him slip from their cocoon to build it back up.

His body was chilled when he slipped under the blankets with her again, and she wrapped her arms around him, rubbing his skin to warm it, and she felt the tension of an unasked question in his muscles.

She leaned up on one elbow to face him. "What is it?"

He didn't question how she might know. He simply asked, "Did you know my mother had an affair with Willoughby?"

She blinked. "The gardener from when we were children?"

He nodded, his brow wrinkled with questions.

She shook her head. "It can't be. She—" She shut her mouth as realization dawned.

"What is it?" he asked then, tucking her hair behind her ear.

"I caught your mother one day at her rock garden. She was very agitated, and she said he wouldn't talk to her." She felt the sting of tears at the realization of Duchess's loss. "She meant Willoughby." She reached for Ben's hand and squeezed it. "Your mother must talk to Willoughby at the rock garden he built for her."

It was one of those moments when time seemed to coalesce between them as if it were a thing they could touch, and she knew they both understood just how rare and incredible it was, the thing they shared.

She bent her head, pressing a soft kiss to his lips.

"I love you, Johanna Darby," he whispered when she lifted her head.

"I love you, Benedict Carver. I always have."

He growled as he spun her over, toppling her into the blankets. She laughed, the sound vibrating through the room as he set out to make her every dream come true.

CHAPTER 18

"Do you think this is a good idea?"

"I think anyone who might visit will request an explanation."

They stood at the side of the lake, watching the workmen as they laid the foundations for an enormous rectangular garden.

Fall had descended upon Yorkshire with a force that somehow celebrated the close of a vibrant summer season while heralding the quiet slumber of winter. The trees that lined the lake were splashed with their fall colors, sending a kaleidoscope of hues across the lake in their reflections.

There on the bank between the lake and the workmen stood Duchess, her cashmere scarf wrapped tightly about her neck. She wore a pelisse she'd beaded herself with a rainbow of glass beads, and they clinked and flashed in the autumn light as she danced about, directing the workers just where to lay the bricks.

Ben shook his head beside her. "As long as it makes her happy."

They had decided to construct the enormous rock garden after learning of Duchess's lost love. They'd chosen the spot by the lake because it received the most sun year-round, and Duchess had the best chance of being marginally warm when she went to visit and talk to Willoughby, which they both determined would be a considerable amount.

The new herd was flourishing, and the harvest had yielded a fifty percent increase in return. Johanna was hoping for sixty percent the following year while Ben wagered it would be fifty-five. They had placed money on the outcome, so she was going to pay particular attention to the sowing come spring.

Grindel was showered daily with carrots and apples and a gallop across the fields. This was in addition to the carrots she knew Ben slipped the animal when he thought she wasn't looking.

"Do you think it will be finished by Christmas?" she asked as the workers carted the bricks back and forth.

Ben scanned the construction site and his mother dancing in the background. "I certainly hope so. How much energy can that woman have?"

"A lot," Johanna said with a nod, and Ben laughed.

He turned his gaze on her. "Are you suggesting we host your family here? Is that why you ask about the garden's completion?"

She had received letters from each of her sisters indicating their desire to spend the Christmas holidays at Ravenwood Park as it had been years since they'd gathered there. She saw it for the ploy that it was, her sisters' attempt to once more intrude upon her life, and she reveled in the very suggestion of it.

She missed her sisters terribly, and she knew their mention of the park was simply their way of vying for an invitation to Raeford. Duchess would be ecstatic, and she knew Ben would enjoy spending the holidays with his old friend should Andrew ever decide to return from Scotland.

But it was more than that. For Johanna, it was a chance to show them this place, this place that was hers and theirs and always would be. It was something for Johanna, *finally*.

"Did Andrew say whether he's had any success on his stalking trip?" she asked.

While her sisters had written to her, Andrew had been keeping Ben abreast of his trip to the Highlands.

"He said he caught something, but it was not what he was expecting. He said he'd explain upon his return."

She wrinkled her nose. "Whatever does that mean?"

He shrugged. "I haven't a single idea." He peered up at the sky. "We should be getting along if we plan to visit the Stock-wells this afternoon."

Mrs. Stockwell had had a difficult birth with her latest child, and Johanna wanted to bring her a cache of foodstuffs so the poor woman must not worry about feeding the rest of her family for some time.

"I suppose you are correct. Duty calls," she said, the feeling of home and belonging filling her with excitement.

This.

This was what she had longed for. Home. A place where she was seen and heard. A place where she was whole. No matter what happened, she would always have Raeford Court. She would have Ben's love and she would have Duchess. Finally, it was enough.

She thought Ben would offer her his arm as they made the climb back to the house, but instead, he skittered a few feet away from her.

"Race you," he called back over his shoulder as he sprinted for the house.

He was too far away to hear the curse she flung at him as she picked up her skirts and ran.

But even as she raced after him, she took comfort in one thing. Through everything, Benedict Carver remained singularly annoying.

ABOUT THE AUTHOR

Jessie decided to be a writer because the job of Indiana Jones was already filled.

Taking her history degree dangerously, Jessie tells the stories of courageous heroines, the men who dared to love them, and the world that tried to defeat them.

Jessie makes her home in New Hampshire where she lives with her husband and two very opinionated Basset hounds. For more, visit her website at jessieclever.com.

Made in the USA
Las Vegas, NV
05 August 2022

52784287R00166